Table o

Table of Contents

Bad Memory

The Complete Series
Second Edition

Written by: M. A. Melby
Cover Art by: Sinmantyx & Johannes Day

To Blaine -
Yes, we all write because
winter isolation makes
us weird. lmao

Copyright © 2023 M. A. Melby
All rights reserved.
The characters and events portrayed in this book are fictitious. Any similarity to real persons, living or dead, is coincidental and not intended by the author.

Content Note:
This book contains mature themes and is most appropriate for readers ages 16+
Two of the main themes of this work are trauma related mental illness and unhealthy relationships.
Please feel free to contact the author directly if you have any questions about the content before reading this book.

Content Information:
Suicidal ideation, sexual situations, sex work, violence including gun violence, physical injury resulting in disability, police brutality, an abusive situation involving a minor, brief descriptions of sexual violence, murder, revenge porn, promiscuity, homophobia including slurs, biphobia, hospitalization, incarceration, emotional abuse and manipulation, online harassment, PTSD, death, therapy, medication, age play and pedophilia is mentioned.

Book One: Big Picture

Porn

From Nik's point of view.

I looked at the big screen TV. I looked at my tiny phone. I looked at the TV. I looked at my phone and then the door to my bedroom.

The apartment was small, and my roommate, Jaimes, worked from home so he was nearly always around.

He was always bringing strange men home, too. What a bother. Why our friend, Mandi, thought us moving in together was a good idea, I had no clue.

But today Jaimes actually had to go into work for in-person meetings, so I was alone for once.

I looked at the TV again, debating with myself. Why the heck not? I turned it on and changed the input to my casting device.

After pulling the curtains over the sliding doors that opened onto the balcony, I sat back down on the couch and turned the volume way down. Unlike some people, I realized we had neighbors.

I brought up my favorite site, found my favorite video, and started casting to the TV from my phone.

Watching porn on a large television felt naughty. Such a cute couple. His curly hair, so adorable. This isn't going to take long, I joked to myself, undoing my pants and pulling up my shirt. My goodness, how can they be so rough and sweet at the same time? So damn hot.

I held my shirt up with my teeth so that it wouldn't get dirty, watched TV, and started to rub one out. When I was close, I tensed up, closed my eyes and listened to them.

"So, want any help?" I heard a voice ask, much too close to my face.

I literally screamed. What an asshole! Why did he come home early? I pulled up my boxers and put down my shirt as quickly as I could. I fumbled with the phone to turn it off and accidentally turned up the volume. I panicked. And this jerk was laughing at me.

"'Hot porn couple birthday sex?'" Jaimes laughed. "So, what's your type, the guy with the curly hair or the one with the tattoos?"

"None of your business," I said, finally managing to turn off the TV and my phone. "You know, a gentleman would have noticed and gone for coffee or something."

"I haven't even left yet," he said, walking to his room. "I got down to my car and realized I forgot my bag. You are so uptight."

"Sorry I'm not like you, Mr. Shameless." I stood up and tried to comfortably fasten my pants. "That was really not cool."

"You're jacking off in the living room. If you want to be shy, you have a bedroom."

"I thought you were going to be gone. You could have," I paused to think of the right words while being thoroughly embarrassed, "handled that differently, you know."

"You're right, I could have *handled it* differently," Jaimes said, laughing at his own joke.

"Shut up."

He stopped to look over at me on his way out, holding his bag. "You're really upset, aren't you?" He seemed surprised.

"You think?" I said, a bit louder than I intended to.

"Fine, fine. I'm sorry," Jaimes said, a little flustered. "Whatever, I can't be late." He left, shutting the door solidly behind him.

I grabbed a pillow from the couch and screamed into it. What a jerk! Who does that? He does that. I considered spending the day looking for an apartment of my own.

"Jaimes is a rude asshole," I messaged my friend Mandi. "You suggested this. If it gets any worse, I'm sleeping on your couch."

"What happened?"

"Everything. You know how he is. Inconsiderate. Shameless."

"Just talk it out. He's not a bad guy. Anyway, Traci is visiting for the weekend so it would be inconvenient for you to stay here. If you really can't work it out, you can stay with me, but not until Monday. Stick it out for three days."

"Okay. Fine."

I threw my phone on the couch and took a deep breath. Then I looked at the TV. Then I looked at my phone. The TV. My phone. I grabbed the phone and went into my bedroom.

Where were we? I laid down on top of my bed. My room was a mess. Whatever. I turned on my phone and went back to the site. What a cute couple, I thought. I didn't even start the video. I just stared at the preview for a while.

Oddly, I didn't feel turned on at all. It made me sad. What the heck was wrong with me? Maybe I'm tired. I cleared my phone and put it on my nightstand. That jerk ruined the mood.

I took off my pants and crawled back into bed. I was now under the covers, resting there, and staring off. What was I going to do? My phone buzzed. It was a message from Jaimes.

"So, the curly haired guy or the tattoo guy?"

"You're a dick," I messaged back.

"Not as big as yours."

"Screw you."

"If you ask nice."

"Seriously, stop."

"Sorry. Just joking around. Are you really mad?"

"Would you make fun of me if I was? Quit being a jerk, okay? I'm not like you. I'm not comfortable. You make me uncomfortable." I wrote the message but erased it.

"I'll live," I sent.

I should have cleaned my room, gotten groceries, and done my laundry. Instead, I played video games. It was my day off, damn it. I tried to get my mind off Jaimes. If only I could live alone, but rents were too high.

"Would you like a trade agreement with the Reptilian Space Conglomerate?" I asked myself out loud, reading off the computer screen. "No. Eat my ass, Reptilian Space Conglomerate."

I heard a knock on the door. Who the heck could that be? I put my pants back on and walked to the door. It was Jaimes.

"Why did you knock?" I asked.

"Just in case you needed a *head's up*," he said as if he were making a pun.

"Good one," I responded sarcastically.

"Who's that?" I heard a voice from the hallway ask.

"My roommate," Jaimes answered.

I glared at Jaimes. "You're kidding. It's 4 p.m."

"He works nights."

"Is everything okay?" the guy asked, poking his head into the apartment. "Hello Jamie's roommate," he greeted me cheerfully. "Jamie, right?"

"Jaimes," Jaimes corrected.

"Sorry. Jaimes."

"Seriously!" I said, not being as polite as I probably could have been.

"Is there a problem?" the guy asked, looking at the two of us, back and forth, probably trying to gauge our expressions. "We can do this another time."

"It's fine. My bedroom is over here. You know, my own room where I do personal things," Jaimes said glaring back at me. "Don't be a cock block," he whispered through gritted teeth.

"I'll go get groceries," I said with a sigh. "You two have fun." I grabbed my keys off a hook by the door and put them in my pocket.

"You don't have to leave if you don't want to," the guy said with a wink.

"I appreciate the offer, but no thanks," I said, exasperated. "I need to get my phone and my wallet, and then I'll leave you two to do whatever. Message me if you want anything from the store."

Three days. I can deal with this for three more days.

By the time I grabbed my things, the two of them were already in Jaimes' room. I could hear their lips smacking together. How does he even do this? He must be on every goddamn app out there.

"Your roommate must have a tight ass," the guy said dismissively, seeming to say it just loud enough to be heard.

Jaimes chuckled but then they got quieter. As I walked past his door, I could hear him say, "Don't be mean. He's complicated."

"Complicated?" the guy asked, sounding genuinely concerned. "A sad story?"

"I'm not sure. But let's not talk about him, okay?"

I left the apartment quickly, shutting the door behind me and leaning up against it. This was not okay. I can't keep living with this guy. I took a deep breath to calm down and started down the hallway. I could tell they were already at it. That was the familiar sound of Jaimes appreciating a good blow job. So obnoxious. Our neighbors must hate us.

I got in my car and went to the supermarket. I hadn't even made a list, so I had to try to remember what we needed. Chips. Cereal. Apples. Pasta. Eggs. Frozen vegetables.

My phone buzzed. It was Jaimes. "Condoms," the message said.

"You fucking..." I yelled out loud at my phone without thinking.

A lady with kids gave me a look.

"Sorry," I apologized with an embarrassed smile as she walked away. "Excuse my language."

Then, I stood there staring at the text.

"Just tell him no. Just tell him no," I muttered to myself but didn't respond back. I put my phone away and kept shopping.

Frozen pizza. Yogurt. Butter. Condoms. Fine. I'll get you your goddamn condoms. Do you need lube too, you bastard? Why don't I pick you up a cock ring? Maybe a butt plug? Do they even make ones big enough for such a gigantic asshole? Whatever. Licorice. Gummy bears. You like gummy bears. Ridiculously expensive chocolate bar. That's for me. Popcorn, I forgot popcorn.

I bought the groceries, drove home, carried all the groceries up the stairs, and got to our apartment.

"He's back!" I heard the guy say.

"Hey," Jaimes called out from his room. "Could you open the door a crack and throw them in?"

"Are you kidding me?"

"Pretty please?" Jaimes asked in a cutesy voice.

I dropped the bags on the floor and fished through the groceries and found the condoms between the gummy bears, licorice and spaghetti. Three days. Three days and I could stay with Mandi.

I walked to the door of his room and swung it wide open. He and the guy he found who-knows-where were laying naked on his bed. "Here's your fucking condoms!" I threw all the stuff in my hand straight at his face and then slammed the door shut.

"Are those gummy bears?" the guy asked.

I went back into the kitchen and started putting the groceries away, throwing things in cupboards and slamming doors. When I was done, I went to my room, fell onto my bed and put my pillow over my head. Three days.

Three more days of this? I thought, maybe I could call Mandi and beg her. I had nowhere else to go.

"Sorry about that," I heard Jaimes say. "Maybe some other time."

"Jamie. Jay. Jaimes. Sorry. Jaimes. You need to sort that out," the guy said, like he was a teacher or parent or something.

"I don't know what got into him. Jesus, is he crying?"

"You don't know what's going on?" the guy asked incredulously. "Figure it out, Jaimes. Good luck."

"Thanks, I guess," Jaimes sighed. I could hear the front door open, close, and lock. A short time later, I heard a knock on my bedroom door.

"Are you okay?" Jaimes asked. "I sent him away."

"Do you even know his name?" I asked. "He got yours right on the third try."

"Don't be like that. I don't need your judgment. Could you please tell me what's gotten you this upset?" I could hear the door to my bedroom slowly open.

"I don't even know," I answered sincerely from under my pillow.

"I'm sorry if I embarrassed you this morning. You know my sense of humor. I guess I took it too far. I'm sorry, okay?" Jaimes said, sitting down at the end of the bed.

"I'm going to move out. I'm not comfortable here, living with you." Finally, I was being honest. "I've been upset for a long time. I just didn't tell you."

"Don't approve, huh?" Jaimes scoffed. "I'm not going to change, so if you have a problem with me, yeah, it's best you leave."

"Don't get me wrong." I took the pillow off my head and looked over at him. "I'm not some prude, okay? I don't think you're a bad person or anything like that. I just can't be here."

"Whatever. Give me some time to find a new roommate. I can't afford the whole rent either."

"That shouldn't be difficult for you," I said, with a hint of venom.

"What do you mean?"

"You can put yourself out there, like nothing. I don't understand how you do it. You have guys over all the time. You meet new people constantly,

7

and you never seem nervous. Even when that one guy stole your wallet, you were like, 'Oops, guess I got to cancel my cards.'"

"Being able to find hookups doesn't mean I'm going to be able to find another roommate right away. Sorry to disappoint you." He sighed and shook his head. "I admit, I was really rude to you today. I thought I was being funny, you know, alleviate the tension. I shouldn't have flirted with you like that, now everything is awkward."

"Flirted?" I sat up perplexed. "What are you talking about? You were making fun of me."

"I asked about your sexual preferences and complimented your dick." Jaimes looked at me with his head slightly to the side as if he was eying some alien creature. "You didn't realize I was flirting?"

"Both," I blurted out.

"What do you mean both? What are you talking about?"

"I like them both. Curly haired guy and tattoo guy. Don't make fun of me, okay. I know it's porn, and they're putting on a show, but they are a real couple, you know. Even if it's acting, you can see it on their faces. So, both."

"When was the last time you went on a date?" Jaimes asked.

"I told you not to make fun of me. Quit being a jerk."

"I'm not making fun of you. Do you really think I'm such a jackass that I would be making fun of you right now?"

"Sort of."

"Well, I'm not," Jaimes said defensively. "How long has it been?"

"My last date was over two months ago. Don't you remember Shawn?"

"Oh yeah, I don't think he liked me very much. What happened to him? You didn't tell me. Did he get some sun and spontaneously combust?"

"Very funny. He was really pale, wasn't he? No, he saw a picture of me and my old girlfriend on my phone and got this idea in his head that I couldn't be trusted. Maybe he thought that I would leave him for a woman anyway, so what's the point? Or that I would cheat? I'm not even completely sure, to be honest. He seemed to think that me liking women was betraying him."

"What? What an ass."

"It wouldn't have worked out anyway. He was so self-righteous. He went on for 10 minutes once about the environmental impact of Greek yogurt. I timed it. It was literally a 10-minute lecture."

Jaimes started laughing. "Ten minutes?"

I cracked a smile, too. "I mean, if he just said, 'Hey, I heard that regular yogurt is better for the environment', I may have been on board, but he went on this rant. But yeah, it didn't work out. That was my last date. I know, you get dates all the time."

"Hookups aren't dates. C'mon, you know better than that. That guy who just left. Lars? Or Larry? He's probably going to remember you because you threw gummy bears at me more than he'll remember me for, you know – something you don't want to hear about. I haven't been serious about anyone in a really long time."

"I didn't think you wanted to be. You seem pretty happy with the way things are. And look, I'm not judging you. It's just, I'm right next door. Do you understand? Even with my headphones on, it's annoying. I don't want to hear that."

"C'mon. You said you weren't a prude. You watch porn."

"But when I'm watching porn, it's not you." The moment I said it, I regretted it. I didn't want him to get the wrong idea. "I mean, those aren't people that I know. They aren't actually physically next door. And with porn I can turn down the volume, so the neighbors don't worry. Remember that one guy you brought over at like, midnight? He woke me up. Then the neighbor knocks on the door asking me who is getting murdered because the guy is screaming. I really wanted to say, 'Well, I'm sure he'll be wrecked but he'll survive, sir. He's actually having the time of his life.' I had to make up some silly excuse about playing video games with the volume too high so that he didn't call the cops."

"You're joking."

"No, I'm not. You didn't even know, did you? And what's worse, the neighbors who do realize you're having sex think we're a couple. Lynn from down the hallway keeps telling me how brave we are and grinning at me like she's having thoughts."

"I had no idea," Jaimes said, trying not to burst out laughing. "Thoughts," he wheezed. "So that's why she keeps looking at me like that. So funny."

"See. This is what I'm talking about. You can blow this stuff off, but I can't. It's awkward, it's uncomfortable, and I don't like it." Finally, I said it out loud.

Jaimes took a deep breath and looked at me seriously. "I really didn't know. I'm sincerely sorry. I'll try to be more discreet."

I nodded. "Thanks. Sorry I messed up your good time."

"Hey, are you hungry?" Jaimes asked.

"Yeah, I guess."

"Let's get out of here."

Coffee

From Jaimes' point of view.

I sat across from Mandi at Rainbow Coffee sipping my flat white.

"So, I brought someone home, and I realized we're out of condoms," I explained. "It was really inconvenient, but Nik was already at the grocery store, so I texted him to pick some up."

"You didn't," Mandi exclaimed, her eyes wide.

"Why wouldn't I? What's the big deal, right? We're all adults. He gets home, and I ask him to throw them into the room. He got really angry for whatever reason, opens the door – we're both on the bed buck naked – and he throws the condoms and a bag of gummy bears at my head and screams, 'Here's your fucking condoms.'"

"He didn't," Mandi said, licking the whipped cream off the top of her triple salted caramel Frappuccino.

"I know right? What's with the gummy bears?"

"Did he actually hit you in the face with the gummy bears?"

"Yes."

"Did it hurt?" Mandi asked.

"Nik threw it, what do you think?" I said, making a joke. Nik probably never worked out in his life.

"Oh, that's mean. You should be nicer to that boy."

"I try. I really do, but he's so sensitive. He literally started crying."

"Crying?"

I could tell Mandi was really worried.

"What was I going to do? I sent the guy home, and I went to talk to Nik. I guess he's been really pissed at me for a while and didn't bother telling me. That boy's not well." I put my coffee down and looked at Mandi with seriousness. "I don't know what to do."

"I don't know if I should tell you this, but he plans on moving out. He begged me to let him sleep on my couch. I think...you know...your lifestyle..."

"Save it." The last thing I wanted was another fucking lecture about my sex life.

"Don't get me wrong..."

"Stop. Stop, Mandi, okay. You're going to tell me you're not really judging me; you're just judging me."

"Sore spot?" I could tell she wasn't happy with me.

"As a matter of fact, Mandi, it is. Living with someone who gives me disapproving looks every goddamn day doesn't help. He even asked me if I knew the guy's name. How rude is that?"

"Well, did you?"

"That's not the point, Mandi." It was Lars. Lars. Larry or Lars. "I thought if I had a gay roommate, maybe he wouldn't be annoyed when I was gay around him."

"Bi roommate," she corrected.

"Whatever."

"You know what? I think he's lonely," Mandi said. "Have you ever considered that? He's a bit timid, you know. I don't think he's judging you. I think it upsets him because he's lonely."

"Lonely?"

"Yeah."

"I guess that would make some sense. We talked about his dating life, but he's also really concerned about what the neighbors think. He's neurotic."

"So, was he okay?" Mandi asked. "I mean, you said he was crying."

"I guess. He calmed down, and I suggested we go out to eat."

"On a date?"

"No, not on a date. Jesus Christ, Mandi. I felt bad for him."

How could it possibly work between Nik and me? Why would I go out with someone who can't stand living with me? What was Mandi thinking?

"Why don't you set him up?" Mandi suggested.

"Set him up? Like find him a date?" For fuck's sake, why was this my responsibility?

"Why not? I mean, you're his friend, right? Maybe he wouldn't be so uptight if, you know..."

"He got laid."

"I wasn't going to say it."

"But that's what you meant."

"That's totally what I meant."

"I think our neighbor Lynn would be down," I laughed. "I guess she has thoughts."

"What's she like?" Mandi asked.

Oh no, she thinks I'm serious. "She's about 50 years old, watches Korean dramas all day and when the landlord visits, she puts two of her cats in our apartment."

"Oh," Mandi said, looking at me, disappointed. "Don't knock it 'til you try it, Jaimes."

She said that while I was drinking. My flat white immediately went up my nose, and I had to put the cup down in order not to spill it. "Thanks for that."

"You deserved that."

"I totally deserved that."

Picture

From Nik's point of view.

I stared at the screen. I looked at Jaimes. "This is ridiculous."

"I'm trying to help you out," Jaimes insisted.

"Mandi put you up to this, didn't she?" I asked, knowing the answer.

"Yes."

"She's not going to leave us alone until this happens, is she?" I asked, knowing the answer.

"She is not. Anyway, how else are you going to find men?"

"People." For the 300th time Jaimes, I'm bi.

"Whatever."

Did he seriously just say that? Such an asshole. Whatever.

"Okay. Name, Nik. Birthday, enter that in the right format. Sex, male. Looking for men and women."

"You're totally going to get unicorn hunters if you do that. They usually go after women but..."

"I'm going to get what?" My goodness, this man speaks another language.

"Straight couples looking for people to play with," Jaimes explained.

"That's a thing?" I felt so naïve. "How is that straight?"

"Well, not gay."

Is he serious? I hate this man, with my entire soul. "Bisexual people exist, Jaimes."

"Whatever."

That's it. I'm going to kill him in his sleep. "I'm keeping it how it is."

"Just make two accounts," he suggested.

"Jaimes. Look. I don't want what happened with Shawn to happen again. It was awful. Anyway, look at all these questions, it shouldn't be hard for people to know that's not what I want."

"Just warning you."

"Thanks, I guess."

Unicorn hunters. Sounds like a character class for a role-playing game. Actually, that sounds kind of fun.

"Why are you grinning?" Jaimes asked.

I don't know, thinking of wearing a horn on my head and prancing around like a little horse while a married couple chases me. "I'm not grinning."

"Freak," Jaimes laughed.

Jeez, could this guy read my mind? Anyway, I needed to focus.

"Looking for, long-term dating. Monogamous. Now it wants me to upload pictures."

I went into my camera roll from my phone, linked through my PC, and looked around for something that might work.

"You really don't have many pictures of yourself," Jaimes commented.

Well, unlike some people, I don't take three selfies a day.

"I guess not," I said. "How about this one?"

I clicked to upload a picture of me smiling at the pier and making a peace sign. Damn it, that's Shawn in the background. I hate my life.

I deleted it.

"Why did you delete it?"

He had to ask, didn't he? "Shawn was in it. He's in all the pictures on my phone. I hate this."

"All of them?"

"Yeah."

"Okay. I'll take some pictures of you. I'm here to help, remember? Give me your phone," Jaimes insisted.

"Fine." I opened the camera on my phone and gave it to him.

"Okay, stand against the wall and look sexy."

I couldn't believe I was doing this. I walked in front of a clear space on the wall and tried to smile.

"You look miserable," he said.

"I am miserable."

"Act," Jaimes commanded with more than a hint of impatience.

I tried to smile again. "Cheese."

"Now you look deranged."

"I'm not good at this stuff."

"Mandi said that you needed to get laid, and I suggested you fuck Lynn," Jaimes said as he held the phone steady.

"What the...? That's not funny! She's like twice my age. Mandi said I needed to get laid?" By the time I was done talking, I noticed that Jaimes was looking through something on my phone. "What are you doing?"

"This one." Jaimes turned the phone around to show a picture of me, thoroughly pissed off, my jaw clenched and my mouth pouting. "Anyone ever tell you that you look hot when you're angry?" he asked, grinning.

"I can't believe you did that." Two more days. Two more days and I could sleep on Mandi's couch. "Wait, did Mandi actually say I needed to get laid?"

"In a manner of speaking," Jaimes said dismissively. "Anyway, admit it, this is a great picture of you. Now we have to do the ab shot."

"I'm not doing an ab shot. People will think I want hookups if I do an ab shot."

"You don't want hookups?"

"I just selected that I didn't. Long-term dating. No hookups."

"How about a Lars sandwich?" Jaimes asked, holding up my phone.

"Are you taking pictures again?" I started reaching for my phone, and he jumped on my bed to avoid my reach. "Stop it." I crawled onto the bed but lost my balance and fell. He jumped off onto the other side and ran out the door of my bedroom. "Give me back my phone."

"Give me a real smile!" Jaimes laughed as he jumped onto the coffee table.

"C'mon, Jaimes. Quit it!" I tried to grab at the phone while I was standing on the floor, and he was standing on the coffee table. I knew he was trying to cheer me up, but I was starting to get frustrated and upset. He never knew when the joke went too far. "It's my phone, seriously. Give it back."

"Fine. Fine." Jaimes stepped off the coffee table. "I must have gotten a couple good ones."

He sat down on the couch and started looking through. I sat down next to him, waiting for him to finally give me my phone back. He suddenly stopped looking through and then looked over at me. His expression was really strange, like someone died.

"This one," he said.

He handed over my phone. The picture was looking down at my face. My eyes were slightly watery and wide. My mouth was just a little bit open. My hair was a slight mess. I looked like I wanted something, badly.

"Yeah, that one's nice," I admitted.

Well, at that point, I would have done me. I was starting to think this dating site business might work.

"All right," I said, after getting back to my computer. "I uploaded the pictures. Now it's asking me to introduce myself." I started typing. "I got my Phlebotomy Technician Certificate..."

Jaimes started laughing. "This isn't a resumé. Is that how you would introduce yourself to a date?"

"I've always known everyone I've dated before we started dating. Well, except for Shawn," I explained. "What types of things should I say?"

"Move over. I'll write something," Jaimes suggested.

I got up from the chair and let him take over.

"Hello, I'm Nik," he wrote. "I'm sometimes too serious and overthink, but I'm young at heart. I'm smart and creative, so I'm really good at strategy games, which is my guilty pleasure. I chose a career where I help people. I can be shy at times so I might seem cold at first, but I truly care about others and desire meaningful relationships."

"This is what you think of me?" I looked over his shoulder. "Guilty pleasure?" I laughed. "You make it sound like I'm embarrassed."

"You don't like it?"

"Let me."

Jaimes moved and I started editing.

I ended up with, "Hello, I'm Nik. I'm a sincere person who sometimes overthinks things. I chose a career where I help people and I deal with a lot at work, so when I'm at home I like to unwind. I play video games and watch sci-fi movies. I can be shy around people I don't know well, but once I build a relationship with someone, I cherish it."

"I guess you didn't need my help."

"No, you helped a lot. I didn't know where to start. Okay, now what am I looking for in a partner?"

I stared at the screen for a while before finally starting to type.

"I want someone who is about my age and doesn't have too many cats," I wrote, bursting out laughing.

"What did you write?" Jaimes asked as he looked over to read what I wrote. "Poor Lynn."

I looked over at Jaimes, smiling. He had his phone out. "Got it," he said. "You need at least one picture where you are smiling. I'll message it to you."

He got me. I chuckled and looked back at the screen. Okay. Okay. I had to finish this up. I wrote, "I want to meet someone who can be courageous for me at times, who is curious like me and wants to experience the world. I want someone who I can be comfortable with and open with. I need someone who can accept me as I am. I want someone who will ask me how my day was and accept an honest answer."

"That's nice," Jaimes said, looking over my shoulder. "It might hint too much that you have some baggage though."

"That's probably not a bad thing," I said, getting a little more emotional than I wanted to.

"Shawn was a bit of fuckhead, huh?" Jaimes asked, cautiously.

I just nodded, and we were both quiet for a while.

"I was his first," I said, once I got the courage to admit why I was upset. "He's younger than me. Of course, I didn't push him at all. It was all really sweet actually. I don't know why he had such a hang-up about it, but he accused me of lying to him when he found out I dated women. He acted like I tricked him into sleeping with me or something. It was really terrible. He said really awful things to me." I was still torn up about it. I certainly didn't want to explain it all.

I felt Jaimes' hand on my shoulder. I grabbed it and turned my head and let myself cry. Screw it. I needed a good cry.

"I remember you stayed in your room a lot, but I didn't know you were going through that."

"I'm sorry," I said. I hated being this way. "Sorry." I wiped my eyes with my hand. "I'm being pathetic."

"Nik. You are not being pathetic. Why are you so hard on yourself?"

"I know Shawn was being unreasonable, really unreasonable, but I still feel guilty. I can't help it."

"Look. If it was a dealbreaker for him, he should have asked. In fact, on your profile, list your deal breakers. Be honest about what you want and don't want. Don't worry so much about what other people think," Jaimes said sternly and then turned my chair until I was looking right at him. "And when I ask you how your day was, you give me an honest answer, okay? We're friends. Maybe we aren't the most compatible roommates, but we're friends. You don't need to go through everything alone."

I was looking at him and wondering who this person was. Did I really live with this man for almost a year and never see this side of him?

"Thanks," I said, because I wasn't sure what else to say. "I'm going to finish the rest myself, all right? Anyway, I bet you have a date...I mean, a hookup."

He bit his bottom lip, like he was guilty.

"I saw you glancing at the time," I explained. "It's okay."

"Don't worry, I'm going over to his place."

"I appreciate that. Don't forget condoms," I laughed but then became serious. "And be safe, okay?"

"You worry too much."

Phone

From Jaimes' point of view.

"Mandi! Mandi!" I screamed into the phone once it beeped. "I need your help. I need your help now. I don't care what you are doing. Call me back right away."

Shit. I needed to tell Nik, but he was at work. Damn it. I fucked up. I really fucked up this time. I started to redial Mandi. Wait, she was with Traci. I had Traci's number.

Traci answered the phone sounding as if she had just woken up. "Hello?"

Thank God. "Traci, this is Jaimes. Please get Mandi on the phone."

"What's wrong?" Traci asked. "She's sleeping. It's 7 a.m. on a Sunday."

"Please wake her up. My phone got hacked, probably last night," I said freaking out. "I'm going to come over right now."

"Your phone got hacked?" Traci asked. "Are you sure?"

"Yes. Hacked. My phone got hacked. Someone got access to the pictures on my phone."

"We'll come to you," Traci suggested. "You seem upset. I don't think you should be driving right now. Where are you?"

"Okay. Okay. I'm at home. Nik is at work. Please hurry."

I hung up and put my phone down on my desk. I stared at it. I should tell Nik. I should call him. No, Mandi was going to help me, and we were going to deal with it. He didn't need to know. Wait, no. I had to tell him, even if he ended up hating me for the rest of his life. What kind of piece of shit would I be if I didn't tell him?

Fuck. What was I thinking?

I picked up my phone to message Nik, but I decided to wait for Mandi. She would know what to do. I turned on my phone and turned to the picture I took of Nik.

"I'm so sorry. I didn't know this would happen." I put my phone back on my desk. "Hurry up, Mandi. Please."

My phone buzzed. It was Mandi. I picked it up. "What's going on?" she asked the moment it connected. I could hear traffic noises in the background.

"I think my phone got hacked."

"Why do you think you got hacked?"

"This morning someone sent me a picture that only lives on my phone. I don't know how they could have gotten it," I explained.

"Did you disable sharing, Bluetooth, and wi-fi on all your devices?"

"What? No."

"Seriously? Do that. Do that now. Turn it all off and unplug your router. Then put your phone in tinfoil."

"Tinfoil? Are you serious?"

"Just do it. Did your phone link with your computer?"

"I don't think so."

"Good. Now get off the phone right now, and we'll be there soon."

"Okay, but there's something you need to know. Um..." I didn't want to own up to it, but I had to. "It was a picture of Nik. I took it without his permission."

"What do you mean?" Mandi asked. "What kind of picture?"

"Him...touching himself."

"What the fuck, Jaimes! You really did it this time, didn't you?"

"I feel like shit. Please help me." I started to sob. "I'm worried it will wind up all over the place."

"Get off your damn phone and turn everything off like I told you to. I'll deal with it when I get there."

"Okay. Okay."

I did all the things she told me to do. When she got to the apartment, she took over. She ran programs and apps I had never heard of and checked folders I didn't know existed. I let her take control.

Traci was there, too. She was trying to calm me down. I didn't deserve to be comforted. Nik was so shy and nervous. How could I do this to him?

"You can plug your router back in. Everything seems clean. Call your bank and card companies. Have them lock your accounts," Mandi said, handing me my phone. "Then you'll need to change the passwords to your email accounts and all your other accounts using your computer. If you are locked out of your email, we're really in trouble. We'll have to check to see if anything was sent to other people using your accounts."

I followed her instructions. "Nothing weird is in my sent folder," I said.

"Here, let me check. They could have deleted the files," Mandi said, sitting down at my computer and doing her thing. "Who do you think hacked your phone?"

"Some guy I hooked up with last night, I guess. I don't know. I took the picture on Friday morning."

"Do you know his name?" Mandi asked. "Like, his real name?"

"I'm not sure," I answered.

"Damn it, Jaimes. I'm just going to do this for you. Hope you don't mind me getting into your personal stuff. Wouldn't want to violate your privacy," she said sarcastically.

Mandi started changing everything with unnerving speed, going back and forth from my computer to my phone. "Okay, you now have a decent password manager, two-step authentication on everything, and malware protection on your computer. You're welcome."

She barely took a breath before laying into me again.

"Do you have any idea how much damage this person could have done? This is your work computer. For fuck's sake, Jaimes. They could have sent Nik's dick to your entire contact list. If they knew what they were doing, they could have bricked every device you have access to. I'm sure having your printers at work turned into nonfunctioning modern art at a graphics design business would have made you friends."

"Not everyone is as skilled as you, Mandi," Traci said flatly. "Maybe they caught Jaime's phone when it was unlocked, turned on sharing, and downloaded the pictures to their own phone. Even I could do that."

"It's better safe than sorry. We're talking about Nik's dignity. If you knew him like I do, you'd understand why I'm so upset."

Mandi had known Nik since high school. I met Mandi and Traci in college. Traci and I only knew Nik through Mandi, and we didn't know him very well, at least, not like her. We both knew that Mandi and Nik were incredibly close, though.

"You don't have to make me feel worse," I said, taking a deep breath. I didn't think I could feel worse. "I need to tell Nik, don't I?"

"He's at work. They don't allow cell phones in that area of the hospital. The only way to get a hold of him would be to call the main line," Mandi explained. "Let's see how bad it is first, before we worry him. I need the picture."

She handed me my phone.

I found the picture and handed the phone back to Mandi. I was sitting on the floor, using my bed as a backrest. I put my knees up to my head and wrapped my arms around my legs.

"How did you even get the picture?" Traci asked.

"He had the day off, and I had to go to meetings. I left, but then realized I forgot something and came back. He didn't notice when I opened the door. I had a weak moment. I knew it was wrong, but I didn't think anything like this would happen. I planned on deleting it. I just ... didn't get around to it. I must have left my phone unlocked at that guy's place when I went to the bathroom or something. I'm so fucking stupid."

"You need to write down as much information about him as you can think of. You need to do that right now," Mandi said, with a renewed sense of urgency.

"How bad is it?" I asked, looking up at the computer screen. "Oh Jesus Christ." The screen was full of image search results. I crumpled into Traci's lap. I wanted to scream and cry but kept it together. "What have I done?"

"Why did you take a fucking picture like that in the first place?" Mandi asked, infuriated.

"Why do you think? Don't make me say it out loud," I answered, starting to break. "Please, Mandi. I'm beating myself up enough."

"Beating yourself up? More like beating off to a picture of my best friend, you fuck. No wonder he wants to move out. I hope you can live with yourself."

"Mandi," Traci said. "Calm down. We all care about Nik. We're all upset."

"Sorry. I'm so fucking pissed right now. I could seriously hurt you right now, Jaimes. I really could."

I'd never seen Mandi this angry in my life. We had been friends since my freshmen year. I wondered if she would ever speak to me again after this.

"Jaimes," Mandi continued after taking a moment. "Start writing down what you know. The photo is obviously on his hard drive. Even if I get all these scrubbed, he'll still have it. We need to deal with him. Okay?"

"Okay," I said, sitting up.

"I'm going to appeal to admins' better nature," Mandi said, starting to click on links. "Since you took the picture, you are the copyright owner. If they don't take the picture down voluntarily, we're going to have to start sending legal threats based on the fact that it's your intellectual property."

"What? The picture legally belongs to me?"

"That's how this works. I know it makes no sense, but you're the photographer so it's your picture. If they pull some bullshit like claiming their version is a derivative work, we might need to lawyer up."

"The hell?" I was so confused.

"Let's hope it doesn't come to that. Usually, admins are willing to take this sort of thing down without too much of an issue unless the cruelty is the point."

"What do you mean?"

"Do you have any enemies?" Mandi asked.

"What?" I was distraught. Her words stopped making any sense.

Traci took a piece of paper out of my printer, put it on a clipboard, and found a pencil.

"Why don't we focus on finding this guy?" Traci suggested. "First, who sent you the picture in the first place?"

"It was a random account on a dating app. It was basically blank. He messaged me and asked if the picture was my roommate. I'll show you."

I tried to open the dating app on my phone, but it didn't work. I realized Mandi changed all my passwords, so she had to give it to me. After entering the new ridiculously complicated password, I opened the profile that sent me the picture. It wasn't the same.

"They changed the account. It's all filled in."

"Well, what does it say now?" Traci asked.

"Document it right away," Mandi said. "Take screen shots."

"Okay." I started taking screen shots and skimming through it. Holy mother of God. What the fuck was this person's problem?

"What does it say?" Traci asked.

I held up my phone so Traci could read it.

"Mandi," Traci said soberly. "The cruelty is the point. That's the motivation. Someone is angry at Nik. Really, really angry."

"There's a link in the account," I said. I didn't dare click on it. "Here."

I gave Mandi my phone.

She did a few odd things first - I suspect she was checking it for viruses or whatever - and then she got really quiet and stared blankly at the screen for a long time. Traci and I were afraid to say anything.

Finally, Mandi looked over at us, shaking with rage. "Whoever did this, I'm going to end them. I'm going to destroy their world until there is nothing left. I'm serious. I'm going to make them bleed."

"What is it?" I finally asked.

"A video. It's a video of Nik and some guy." Mandi paused it near the beginning and then pointed the phone at me. "Do you recognize him?"

"Lars. It's Nik and Lars."

Breathe

From Nik's point of view.

I was a little worried about Jaimes. Still, he deserved it. He was so thoughtless. He needed to learn. One of these days something bad was going to happen. Oh well, his choice, not mine. His life.

Why couldn't I stop thinking about him? He spent so much time in my head. I was at work. I needed to focus. Why did I have to be the one so good at my job? Sometimes, I wished they would stop calling me in for the hard cases, or at least, stop blowing all the good sites before I got there.

I played with my food in the cafeteria, poking at some weird rice bowl thing Nutritional Services was trying out. I couldn't help but be nervous. I kept looking at my phone.

There it was! A text from Jaimes. "I screwed up. Mandi and I are working to fix it."

Oh no. He got Mandi involved?

I texted back, "I'm on lunch, what's going on?"

"It's probably best to talk about it after you are done with work. Come straight home."

Come straight home? He must have freaked out.

"Fine," I texted back. I decided to let him suffer a few hours longer. He absolutely deserved it. "Don't worry so much," I added for humor.

Oh hey, the icon for the dating app had a notification. Oh neat. A message.

"Hello. I saw your profile. What video games do you play? I've been playing a lot of Star Imperium lately." Oh cool. That's the game I played. "My wife and I would love to have coffee with you sometime."

Oh, for goodness' sake. I looked at his profile out of curiosity. There were pictures of him and his wife at a sci-fi convention in cosplay. They looked like nice, fun people, but no buddy, not my deal. But that beard. I laughed at my own joke. And your facial hair, too. Oh gosh, be nice.

The rest of my day wasn't so bad. Just routine blood draws. Some mother threatened me with death if I woke up her son, that was interesting. She was usually so easygoing. I guess stress does what stress does.

I clocked out and started out the door. I had gotten used to it, but it always sounded so strange when our shift ended. When we got through the double doors, everyone turned on their phones at once and there was this buzzing all around as everyone's notifications flooded in. I turned on my phone and it started pinging like mad.

What the heck? I looked around me and many of my co-workers had stopped walking and were staring at me. What was going on? I opened my phone to see where all the notifications were coming from.

It was my work email.

I started opening my messages: "What the hell, Nik, I don't need to see your dick." "Did you get hacked?" "Quit replying-all everyone! Learn how to use email." "Someone put a ticket into IT." "Nik, is this you? What's going on? Why would you send this?" "I'm not gay like you, Nik. Keep your perverted crap to yourself." "This is sexual harassment. I'm contacting HR."

I felt my breath changing. I knew what was happening, but I couldn't stop it. "It wasn't me," I muttered, as all eyes were on me. "I didn't send it. It wasn't me."

I stopped being able to talk because my breathing took over. I started hyperventilating.

I couldn't see well all of a sudden, but I heard a voice following the protocol for an anxiety attack. "Everyone, give him some space. Nik, can you hear me? You're here at the hospital. You're safe. You'll feel better soon. Is there someone we can call?"

"It wasn't me," I said, once my breathing slowed down enough and my chest stopped hurting. "What's going to happen to me?"

Why did he do this? How did this happen? How did he get into my account? He ruined my life. Why?

"You're going to be all right. We know you didn't do this. Okay. Who should I call?"

I realized the person talking was Haydan. She was a friend.

"Mandi," I answered, giving her my phone. "Please call Mandi."

Joke

From Jaimes' point of view.

Mandi was doing all sorts of things using my computer that I didn't understand. She talked to herself every once in a while, about VPNs and ISPs. I didn't understand any of it.

Mandi's phone rang. She picked it up and looked at it.

"It's Nik," she said. "You talk to him."

She handed the phone to me.

"Hello."

"Is this Mandi?" someone who wasn't Nik asked.

"No, this is Nik's friend Jaimes, but Mandi is with me. Who is this? Is Nik all right?" I asked, anxiety creeping in. Why would some stranger have his phone?

"He's fine. Don't worry. I'm his friend Haydan, from work. Something a bit shocking happened and he's upset. He asked me to call his friend Mandi. Can you put her on the phone please?"

"Who are you talking to?" I heard Nik ask in the background.

"Jaimes," I said.

"It's Jaimes," Haydan relayed to Nik.

"Give me the phone," Nik told her. "Jaimes," he said, his voice at full volume now. "I really screwed up. Someone hacked my work account. Just know, it wasn't your fault. It wasn't your picture."

"You know about the picture?" I was confused. "I was going to tell you, I just..."

"Look," Nik interrupted. "Look at the two pictures closely. They aren't the same. I was playing a joke on you. I wanted to teach you a lesson. I should have just talked to you. I'm sorry. I guess the joke's on me. Jaimes, he sent it to the entire clinic. How can I keep working here?" Nik's voice was breaking. He was crying. "What am I going to do?"

"Who sent it?" I asked flatly, somehow keeping my cool.

"Lars. It was Lars."

It was hard to believe that Lars would do such a thing. What was his motivation? It didn't make sense.

"Why?" I asked.

"I don't know why, but it's him."

I could barely understand what he was saying. Nik was completely losing it. I knew he wouldn't be able to explain anything very well right now.

"Hand the phone back to Haydan," I told him.

"Okay."

"Yes," Haydan said.

"Can you get him home safely?" I asked.

Nik usually took the train. We chose our place because it was close to the right line for him to get to work.

"Of course," Haydan told me, and then asked Nik, "Can I give you a ride home?"

"Please," Nik said. "Thank you."

"Thanks," I said, relieved. "Thanks, Haydan."

"No problem."

I ended the call to realize that Mandi was staring at me.

"Well? What happened?" she asked.

"Lars hacked his work email and sent the picture to the clinic." At this point, I was numb. Mandi looked like she was about to start breaking things. "Nik was really upset and not making a lot of sense. He said something about there being two pictures. That the pictures weren't the same and it wasn't my fault."

"How did he get access to Nik's accounts? I checked everything. I mean, none of your accounts seem compromised at all. Who is this guy? I mean, even on your phone, there were no traces at all that it was broken into. It's almost as if..." Mandi stopped midsentence. "Show me the picture on your phone again."

I gave it to her. She held the phone up to the screen next to the pictures she had found through the image search.

It wasn't the same picture. It was Nik. He was wearing the same clothes. He had his shirt in his teeth, and he was doing what he was doing, but it wasn't the same picture. He wasn't quite sitting in the same place. His shirt wasn't draping quite the same way. His hand wasn't in the exact same position. The angle wasn't exactly the same.

"That's not my picture," I said incredulously. "It's not my picture."

"That's a problem," Mandi said. "I sent false legal statements to about a dozen sites. If they bother to fight it, we're fucked."

"How does he know it was Lars?" I asked, thinking out loud. "Wait. Nik said he was the one who screwed up, that he was trying to teach me a lesson."

"Maybe Lars took the second picture," Traci suggested. "I mean, someone had to, right?"

"But how did they know about the original picture in the first place?"

I tried to remember everything that happened when Lars was over. We were waiting for the condoms, and it took a long time. We were bored so I got out my phone.

"Oh God. Lars saw Nik's photo on my phone."

"So, Lars could have told Nik about the photo," Traci said.

"I wish I could get into Nik's computer," Mandi said, as she got up and went into Nik's room. "We should probably unplug the router again."

"I'm on it," I said.

"So, Jaimes wasn't hacked, but Nik was," Traci said. "Poor Nik. Why would that guy be so angry with him?"

"Nik was why I called off, you know, having sex with Lars. Nik was upset, so I sent Lars away," I explained, as we walked into Nik's room to see Mandi staring at Nik's computer lock-screen, "but he didn't seem bothered at all. And who would go this far over something that petty? It doesn't make sense."

"Well, I solved one mystery," Mandi said, pointing at Nik's web cam and then following the line-of-sight to the bed. "Why didn't I think of something so obvious? Devious little shit made it look like he used a phone. Damn it!" She flicked off the camera. "I'll fuck you up!" She clumsily unplugged it from the computer and threw it across the room.

"Um, Mandi?" Traci said, concerned.

Mandi sat back down in Nik's chair. "All we would have had to do is tell him to change the passwords on his accounts when he checked in with us during lunch and this wouldn't have happened. Once I saw the video, I should have figured it the fuck out. How could I be so stupid? This is what I do and he's my best friend." She took a deep breath. "It seems so obvious now. Why didn't I do that?"

Traci squeezed Mandi's hand. "Be kind to yourself."

After a while, we heard the door open. It was Nik. At this point, I was exhausted. But I knew that I had to do everything I could to help him. He said it wasn't my fault, but at the end of the day, it sure as hell was.

Sorry

From Nik's point of view.

When I walked into the apartment, I could see the couch right away. If I'd just gone to my damn bedroom, none of this would have happened. I guess other people get to take risks and have fun. The moment I do anything at all, my whole life breaks apart. That was the story of my life.

I walked toward the hallway, and Jaimes was standing there. His face was puffy. His eyes were red. He looked like hell. A sound came out of his mouth, and I wasn't even sure what it was. He said it again, "I'm sorry."

"Jaimes, please, let me explain. Sit down. You're going to need to sit down," I said. "I'm going to need to sit down, too. I almost passed out at work, so..."

Mandi and Traci came out of my room. Why were they in there?

"I need you to unlock your computer, and I need to get into your email accounts," Mandi said. "Unlock your phone and give it to me."

"Okay." I wasn't sure why she needed all of that, but she looked very intense. I was starting to think that there was even more going on than I knew. It hurt me to think that Jaimes thought this was all his fault. It was all my fault. All of it. I went into my room and logged onto my computer. I unlocked my phone and gave it to Mandi.

"I'm so sorry," I told her. "Thanks for your help. I really appreciate it. I do."

"This Lars guy, he's going to regret it."

Mandi seemed angry beyond words. It scared me. What was she planning to do? I had to get back to Jaimes, though. I left and let Mandi work.

I sat down in the living room with Jaimes. We looked at each other for a moment, like two kids that had gotten into a fistfight and were too beaten up to continue.

"Lars found my account on the dating app right away," I explained once I found the courage. "He invited me out for coffee yesterday while you were gone. He actually seemed really nice, you know, easy to talk to. He had this idea that we were crushing on each other. I said he was wrong, and he asked me, if we weren't crushing on each other, why would you have a dirty picture of me on your phone?"

Jaimes looked like he was going to say something.

"Just wait. Let me explain. Okay, so I was angry. I was really pissed off. It was so over-the-line, you know. I said, what if it got leaked somehow? And he and I thought of a prank. We'd take an identical picture and then have a sock account send it to you to freak you out. It was supposed to be a joke, nothing serious. So, I brought him back to the apartment, and he took the picture with my phone."

Jaimes looked at me blankly.

"I had no idea this would happen," I continued. "I have no idea how he got access to the picture or my account, but he's the only one who knew about it, so I don't think it could be anyone else. I don't know why he would do such a thing. He seemed so nice. Why would he do this?"

"You slept with him," Jaimes said. "Maybe he got weird about it."

"What? How do you even know that?" I got this sinking feeling that the second shoe was about to drop.

"I'm so sorry. Nik. There's a video. He put a link to it on the sock account you made."

It was like I didn't really hear what he said. My brain made it into gibberish. "What did you say?"

"He made a video when you two were together, using your webcam. Mandi has been finding the picture and the video around the internet and getting it taken down," Jaimes said.

I started to shake. I buried my face in my hands. Why would Lars do this? Why? Did he get off on it? The one damn time I think, I'll open up to someone, this happens. How could he? I started weeping uncontrollably. I didn't want to be this way in front of Jaimes. I didn't want to worry Mandi and Traci. But I couldn't help it.

"We're your friends," Jaimes said. "We'll help you through this."

"The Lars in your phone contacts is him, right?" Mandi asked me from the other room.

I just nodded. I couldn't speak.

"It is," Jaimes answered on my behalf. "It's him."

"Who wants to come with me to commit a felony?" Mandi asked.

"Mandi, please," I answered back after composing myself as best I could. "I don't want you to do anything that will get you in trouble."

"Trouble?" Mandi said coming out of the room with a weird shit-eating grin on her face. "People who commit crimes don't report crimes. You have no idea how much I've wanted to do this. This might be the only chance I get."

"Is this fun for you?" I asked Mandi much too loudly and before I could think better of it.

"Sorry," Mandi said. "Look. I want to help. This whole situation is awful."

"Please, please tell me you didn't watch it," I said, hanging my head. "Please, tell me that none of you watched it. Please, tell me you didn't watch it."

"Just enough to know what it was," Mandi said. "Without the sound."

I felt violated. I wanted to hide. I didn't want to go on some revenge mission. I wanted to scream. I was surprised how much of my anger was directed toward Jaimes and not Lars. I kept it in check, because it didn't make sense. He took a picture. So what? Jaimes seemed genuinely broken up about it. All my friends were coming together to support me even though it was me who screwed up. What was wrong with me? I was seething. I didn't even want to look at Jaimes.

"I'm going to stay here. I want to be alone," I finally said.

"Are you..." Jaimes paused. "Are you sure that's for the best?"

"Yes, I'm sure!" I yelled at him, losing control of my good sense. I tried desperately to keep my cool, but I couldn't. I needed to hide. I got up, ran to my room, slammed the door and screamed into my pillow.

Mandi came into my room a short time later. "I'm sorry. I need to work on your computer. Okay?"

I heard her sit down. I could hear her typing. She would swear under her breath occasionally. At a few points she asked herself, "Who is this guy?" as if she was impressed by his skills. She said things like, "I wouldn't have found it if I didn't know it was there. Holy fuck. Devious little shit." At some point, she got up and left, finally giving me some peace.

I could hear the three of them talking in the other room in hushed tones. Eventually, Traci came into the room to talk to me.

"Nik. We're going to go. Mandi put all your accounts in a password manager. She cleared your computer of the remote access and did some tracing. Your phone and computer should be safe to use. She left a note telling you how to access the password manager so you can get back into your accounts. The work email seems to be the only one he used to send anything. Mandi sent a message to your work IT folks explaining that you were hacked and showing metadata that proves it wasn't you who sent the messages, but obviously you should call your HR at some point. She deleted the sock account on the dating app. Your other social media accounts didn't seem to be vandalized, but, when you're up to it you should look through to make sure. I'm so sorry this is happening to you."

"Thank her for me. She's amazing, really. Tell her I'm sorry for getting angry. This is just a lot to deal with."

"I'll tell her."

"Are you going after him?" I asked, staring at the opposite wall.

"We are. He likely has a copy on his hard drive. So, we're going to deal with it."

"Thank you. But please, don't get in trouble because of me, please."

"Don't worry," she assured me. "Mandi has a plan. We'll be fine."

Don't worry. What a joke. "All right. I trust you."

"We're more worried about you."

"I'll be fine. I just need time to calm down."

What did they think I was going to do? Jump in the car and never come back? Get drunk and wake up in a ditch? Jump off a bridge? Overdose? What were they worried about? I was too much of a coward to do anything like that.

"Call me if you need anything, okay?" Traci said, putting my phone down on my desk. "You'll get through this."

"Thanks," I said, because that's what you are supposed to say. "Be careful."

Wrong

From Jaimes' point of view.

"I know he works evenings. So, he might still be home when we get there," I told Mandi. "He probably had the day off yesterday, since he was with Nik."

"Well, this isn't going to work if he isn't home. If we can catch him right before he goes to work, that's perfect."

"I'm really worried about Nik," I said.

"Let's focus on dealing with the problem so he can put this behind him," Traci suggested.

"Is this what you expected our weekend together to be like?" Mandi asked Traci.

"Yes, this is completely what I expected," Traci said with a straight face.

Mandi started laughing. Then Traci laughed. I chuckled. We needed a laugh.

"You probably had plans, didn't you?" I asked.

"It's okay," Traci said. "This is at least a bit more exciting."

"More exciting than going to the aquarium at the mall?" Mandi asked. "Not possible."

"Well, I hope it's not too exciting," Traci clarified.

"You have bail money, right, Jaimes?" Mandi asked.

I laughed.

"No seriously."

"Jesus, Mandi. Um. Yeah. I do. I have a little savings set away if it really comes to that."

"Good to know," Traci said.

The whole operation was surreal. My job was to observe Lars from across the street. After finding his address somehow, Mandi learned that he lived in a newer apartment building. She brought up the plans from the city records and found which unit was his. She figured out where I would need to be to have a good view and stationed me there. I ended up on a nearby parking ramp. Traci got into the building by waiting for someone to leave and grabbing the door as they left. Mandi was sitting on the ground with her laptop open right underneath his apartment, which was on the second floor.

We were in luck. Lars was there, sitting in front of his computer. I could see him through the open window. I used my phone's zoom function to look as closely as I could. All of us were on a three-way call.

"I think it's an all-in-one. I don't see a tower," I said. "It looks like the same operating system as mine, whatever that is."

I could feel Mandi judging my lack of knowledge, but since Lars could recognize me, this was the only job I could do.

"The keyboard is wireless. It's pink and has round keys. Right now, he's flipping through his social media accounts and making some comments on cat pictures...I think those are cats."

How could he be this chill after doing something so horrible?

"Okay. I think I have it. Now, tell me when he's typing," Mandi said.

"He's clicking around. Now, typing. Still typing. He paused. Typing."

It felt weird doing this. I thought it would feel exciting like I was in a movie, but I was incredibly nervous about getting caught.

"Wrong one. Give me a minute," she said. "Okay, now."

"Typing. Still typing. Stopped. Typing. Stopped. Clicking around. Typed something in his search bar. He clicked on a link."

"Got it," Mandi said. "Okay Traci, now."

Every light in the building went off when Traci turned off the breaker. She was in the utility room. Lars' computer, of course, also went dark. He raised both hands up in frustration and looked around. He looked like he was about to make a call, when the lights came back on, and his computer started to reboot. The lock screen came up and he entered his PIN to open his computer.

"Yes!" Mandi said. "Now we wait."

"Not for long, it looks like he's leaving," I said.

"All right," Traci whispered.

Then, I heard stairsteps. She must have been running up to the second floor. A little while later, I saw Lars leave the building. Thank God.

"He's gone," I said quietly.

That meant that, hopefully, Traci had stopped his door from closing without being noticed and was in his apartment.

"You're going to be mad," Traci said in a quiet voice.

I got anxious and quickly looked back at Lars' room and saw Traci sitting in front of his computer.

"It didn't even close," Traci giggled.

"Son of a bitch."

I guess Mandi wanted to do a keyboard hack for ages, and we didn't even need the numbers she got. Hilarious.

Traci buzzed Mandi into the building. After a short while, Mandi was at Lars' computer doing her thing.

I stayed at my position and kept a look out. I thought that all I cared about at this point was fixing the problem, but I was wrong. When I saw that Lars was coming back, I had an excuse.

I put my phone in my pocket and flew down the stairs of the parking ramp. He was still about half a block from his complex, carrying a coffee. Apparently, he had left to buy it.

I crossed the street in a barely safe way, and I called out, "Hey, is that you? Lars? Right?"

"Oh hi! Yeah. What's up?" Lars asked, slightly nervous and looking around.

I considered making stupid small talk and pretending like neither of us knew what was going on. That would probably be the smart thing. Fuck, I could probably ask him for a quickie right now. Wouldn't that be funny? But that's not what happened. Instead, I lost it.

"What's up? Huh? You know damn well what's up, sorry piece of shit," I yelled at him.

"Jaimes. Jaimes it was a joke. Nik was really upset about you taking that picture. You two work it out. Leave me out of it."

He was obviously scared of me. I was almost a foot taller than that old scrawny twink. He knew the score. He kept looking forward to the door of his apartment.

"What? You upset you got caught? Sick fuck!" I shouted. "How could you do that to Nik? Huh? What's your fucking problem?"

He tried to make a run for the door, but I got in front of him and squared up.

Lars stepped back like he was about to run. I grabbed his shirt with both hands.

"He told me you weren't a couple," Lars insisted. "I'll stay away from him. Let me go."

"Don't play stupid! Nik was so upset he passed out at work. He's going to lose his job. What the fuck is wrong with you? Why would you do this?"

"Wait, what?" Lars looked terrified and confused. "What are you talking about? What happened? Is he okay?"

It took every ounce of my self-control not to beat his fucking head in.

"How could you do this to Nik? What did he ever do to deserve this? Huh? Tell me why!" I screamed, inches from his face. "Tell me why you're still breathing."

"Jaimes! Jaimes!" I came to my senses long enough to realize that Mandi was yelling at me. "Jaimes!" I quickly looked behind me and saw a crowd recording us with their phones. Mandi was desperately screaming at me, trying to get my attention. "He didn't do it! It wasn't him!"

Traci was trying to get the people who had stopped to gawk at us to move on. "Show's over. It was a really bad misunderstanding. Please don't post it. Please. It was a misunderstanding. Everything is fine, now. Show's over. Please don't post it. Please. Seriously, don't post it."

I slowly let go of Lars' shirt. "Jesus Christ. Lars. I'm...It's...I'm so sorry." I turned around, walked a few paces away and tried like hell to calm down. My heart was beating out of my chest.

"What on God's green earth is going on?" Lars asked, straightening his shirt. His voice was shaking. His coffee was on the ground, spilling out onto the grass.

"Lars, someone did something really terrible to Nik, and they framed you for it." Mandi said. "Let me help you."

"Help me? Jaimes looked like he was going to kill me!" Lars shouted, pointing. "You're crazy!" He looked over at Mandi and Traci. "And you two. Why were you in my apartment building? What is going on? Someone better start talking."

"I understand that you are really angry right now. We will explain. Please hear us out," Traci said calmly. "We'll try to make it right. You wanted coffee.

I'll buy you a coffee, and we'll tell you everything. This is all a really bad misunderstanding."

"First things first. Is Nik all right?" Lars asked.

"He's not physically hurt," Traci explained. "But it's bad. He's not okay."

"Let's go get coffee," Lars agreed.

Kitty

From Nik's point of view.

I had laid there, in my bed, for some time, letting my brain rest and convincing myself that what had happened had actually happened. When I was calm enough, I called HR at work.

It was a horribly awkward call but much better than I thought it would be. They told me that IT had confirmed that I was likely the victim of a crime, but they were still investigating. They acknowledged that continuing to work at the clinic might be difficult, even after issuing a statement to the people who were sent the e-mail. They gave me a week of paid leave, starting immediately and said they would work on a transfer to one of their other affiliated sites. I kept my composure while on the phone but had another good cry as soon as the call ended. Slowly, the whole bizarre situation was becoming more real.

I texted Mandi, "Let me know what you find out."

A little while later, Traci called me. "Please let me know what's going on," I blurted out immediately.

"All right," Traci said. The background sounded like she was in a restaurant or something. "First thing, it wasn't Lars. We looked at his computer and there was no sign of any remote access or the files."

"What? Oh no." I was the one who sent them after Lars. I felt awful. "I was wrong?"

"Not just you. Whoever actually did this is skilled enough to plant evidence. I don't understand it all, but I guess they were basically using Lars' router information like a VPN does or something?"

"No. Not at all." I heard Mandi say. "But whatever."

"Anyway, good news, it doesn't look like Lars is going to call the cops on us," Traci continued.

"I haven't completely decided," I heard Lars say in the background. It was hard to tell if he was joking or not.

"We're negotiating right now," Traci explained. "Jaimes and Lars almost got into a fistfight."

"A fistfight?"

"I am very sorry about that," I heard Jaimes say loudly.

"So, we have no idea who did this," I said, matter-of-factly.

"Whoever it is, they want to hurt you," Traci said. "Lars is pretty upset about the video as well. We need to find out who it is. You need to think, is there anyone who is angry at you or might have complicated feelings about you?"

"I'm not sure. Nobody recently," I responded, but that was a lie.

"We're basically out of clues. Whoever did this said some pretty awful things on that sock account that you made. Jaimes documented it. Maybe if you read it, it might help you figure out who might have some kind of motive. Nobody has watched the entire video either. There might be some clues there. I'm so sorry. We did our best."

"Were the pictures and videos taken down?" I asked.

"Some of them. The internet is a big place. If they still have access to the picture and the video, even if we got everything taken down, they could re-upload it," Traci explained.

I started to breathe funny again.

"Nik. Nik. Shh. Shh. It'll be okay."

I could tell that the table of people, wherever they were, had gotten quiet when she started to comfort me. I hated this so much.

"The moment...the moment I do anything. The moment I do anything at all, this happens," I complained, feeling sorry for myself. "I never do these things. It's not my style. The moment...the very goddamn day..."

"Shh. Shh. Nik. I think we should come back. You shouldn't be alone. It's not right."

"Am I cursed?" I kept ranting. I needed to say it out loud and Traci was willing to listen. "It's like the universe was waiting around for me to take a risk, to do something wrong, so it could punish me."

"Maybe it wasn't the universe who was waiting around," Traci suggested after pausing to think. "Mandi, could you tell when the computer was taken over?"

"The remote access started on Saturday afternoon, a short time before the video. My original idea was that Lars decided to target Nik on Friday, so he set everything up beforehand. Then when he came to visit on Saturday, Nik gave him his unlocked phone to take the picture and so he was able to gain access and train his own phone to link with Nik's computer. Then, when I was tracking the uploads, they appeared to be coming from Lars' apartment complex. I mean, it all made sense. It all pointed to Lars."

"If it makes you feel better, we were all really surprised that you'd do something like that," Jaimes said.

"Cold comfort. Cold comfort," Lars replied.

"But if it wasn't Lars, how could the person know what was happening in order to start using the webcam right beforehand? How would they know about the photo? How would they know anything?" Traci asked. "Are they a fly on the wall?"

Everyone was quiet for a moment, contemplating the answer.

Once it dawned on me, I immediately left my room. Apparently, somehow, someone knew what was going on in my apartment. Somehow, someone was spying on me.

"Where are you? I'm coming to you," I said. "I need to get out of here."

"I'll text you the address. Drive carefully, all right?" Traci said. "Be safe. See you when you get here."

I grabbed my wallet, phone and keys and went out into the hallway. Lynn was there holding a laundry basket. I wasn't in the mood for small talk. I raised my hand briefly to acknowledge her and kept walking.

"Nik, are you okay?" Lynn asked.

Oh no. "I'm fine. Thanks for asking," I said quickly, trying to leave.

"Did you and that other boy have a fight?"

"We're fine."

Just then a cat jumped out of Lynn's laundry basket. She was raining cats! She put down her laundry basket quickly to pick up her cat, but it decided to come over to me and rub against my leg. I picked it up and it rubbed its face against my head.

"I'm so sorry," Lynn said.

"It's okay," I assured her, getting a little weepy however hard I tried not to.

The kitty was so sweet. It started purring.

"I think she likes you," Lynn said. "Thanks again for taking my cats that one day that the maintenance people came over. I really appreciate it. I'm sorry to pry, but you seem like you're having a bad day. Let me know if there's anything I can do to help. You two seem like such nice boys. So brave."

So brave? For goodness sakes, Lynn.

"Thanks," I said, chuckling a little bit as the cat started licking my face. Unconditional cat love. Kitty doesn't care who I sleep with. Kitty doesn't care about my past, do you kitty? Cute kitty.

Suddenly, something occurred to me.

"Hey, Lynn. About a month or so ago, the building did a lighting inspection, but you didn't ask us to take your cats. Did someone else take them or did you just not worry about it?"

"Lighting inspection?"

"Yeah. They were thinking of retrofitting the lights for some sort of energy rebate."

"No. I don't remember that happening," she said. "Oh gosh, I hope they didn't go into my apartment without telling me. That's against the law, you know."

"Maybe they only inspected a few of the apartments. You know, just one of every floor plan or something." I didn't want her to worry. "I was just curious."

She started to take the cat away from me, but it didn't want to go. It tried to hang on for a moment with its claws and scratched my neck.

"Oh no. I'm so sorry. I'll get some ointment."

"It's okay. Really. It's not a big deal. I guess the kitty likes me too much," I said with a smile. "I'll see you around, Lynn. You're good people."

"Thanks. I try. So are you. You're good people."

Am I? Or did she not know me very well?

Watch

From Jaimes' point of view.

By the time Nik finally made it to the coffee shop, we were done with our drinks, and we were chatting. Lars was taking everything very well, considering. If he decided to be awful about it, he could make life difficult for us. He was a good guy. He didn't deserve to get caught up in all this drama.

When Nik came over to us, carrying his coffee, we all got quiet. He was a wreck.

"Please don't look at me like that," Nik said, sitting down at our table and staring into his coffee.

He always ordered some sort of mocha latte with weird flavors. He once tried orange and the whole thing curdled. He was so disappointed.

"We care about you," Traci said. "We're all worried about you."

"I know," Nik said. "I appreciate it, but it makes me uncomfortable."

"We're all friends here," I said.

The moment I started speaking, he glared at me.

He said he was upset about how we looked at him, but the way he looked at me was unbearable. I couldn't imagine what he was going through. The last thing he needed was me getting oversensitive. He had every right to be angry at me. I tried to ignore it, but it bothered me.

Mandi extended her hand to Nik. He took it and squeezed.

"Mandi. Thank you for helping me. I called HR, and they seemed convinced that I didn't do it. That's because of you. Thank you so much."

"Anytime Nik," Mandi said. "You know me. I like to show off."

"I'm going to have to watch it, aren't I?" Nik asked. "I'm going to have to watch that video."

"Yeah," Mandi answered. "We need more clues."

"I need to know what's out there," Lars said. "So, we should both watch it. Mandi says I can help get those pictures taken down too. I'll do what I can. You don't deserve this."

"Thank you," Nik said, letting go of Mandi's hand and sipping his coffee.

Nik looked mortified, and Lars looked uncomfortable in a really weird way. What the hell did those two do? I hadn't watched any of the video.

Mandi simply told us that it showed Nik and Lars in bed together. She stopped watching it the moment she realized what it was. Mandi was able to find it and get it taken down immediately from the larger upload sites. We were lucky that she knew what she was doing.

"I think someone got access to our apartment by pretending to be an inspector," Nik explained. "I talked to our neighbor Lynn, and the inspector didn't come to her place. The inspector was a white woman, maybe in her late 20s or early 30s, maybe? I think she was blonde, if I remember right. She didn't have a uniform, but she had an ID badge and a clipboard. She was already in the building and knocked on the door. That's all I remember."

"It might not be her," Mandi said. "She could have been hired."

"Obviously, you didn't recognize her," Traci said. "I mean, this has to be somebody you know."

"How do you know that?" Nik asked, sounding defensive. "I mean, couldn't it be someone who's doing it just because they can? You know, my bad luck? Maybe someone I don't know who doesn't like queer people or something."

"Whoever is doing this to you, hates you, personally," Mandi said pointedly. "Really hates you."

"How do you know?" Nik asked, looking annoyed at Mandi.

"We know this because of what they said on that sock account," Traci explained.

I had read some of it while I was documenting. At the time, I thought maybe it was just basic homophobic bullshit, using slurs, using rude language to describe sex, all those things. However, when Mandi said we needed more clues, I started to read it more carefully.

"I think it has something to do with Shawn," I said.

"Shawn?" Nik asked, tensing up immediately. "Why?"

Of course, he knew why. He probably didn't want to think about it. I didn't want to say anything in front of the whole crew. It was much too personal. So, I showed Nik my phone and pointed at a phrase under the heading of "What I am looking for in a partner?" It read, "Some young virgin boy to fuck – bonus if I make him cry." I took the phone away before he could keep reading. It got worse.

Nik got quiet. I could see his hands start trembling. Shit, did I make a horrible mistake? Maybe this wasn't a good place to show him that. Damn it. I was really fucking up.

"I'm sorry," I said.

He glared at me with such disdain that I immediately looked away. I thought that our relationship was different. I thought that we joked around, and he got mad about stuff, but in the end, we were friends. Good friends. I was wrong. He hated me. He really hated me. It hurt. It really hurt.

"Let's go to my place," Lars said. "It's close. We can talk more openly there."

"Thanks. We appreciate that," Traci said, starting to stand up.

Nik kept sitting there. He was shaking so bad that he had to set down his coffee and put his hands in his lap.

"I'll have them put it in a paper cup," I told him.

I took his coffee to the counter. I noticed that Traci stayed behind with Nik as the rest of us started leaving. He eventually got up, but she was practically leading him. It was like he couldn't even function anymore. I realized that he probably hadn't eaten much. I got him an apple turnover. I was pretty sure he liked those.

Eventually we found ourselves in Lars' apartment. It looked like he hired an interior designer – from a decade ago. Pastel colors and flower arrangements, centerpieces and framed art were all placed just so. I put Nik's coffee and pastry on the kitchen table.

Lars was usually a live-out-loud type of guy. That was my first impression anyway. This situation was fucked up, so he wasn't being his usual effervescent self. I felt awful. He was probably still a little shaken up from before.

"Welcome to my home," Lars said with a hint of sarcasm. "I know at least a couple of you have already been here."

Nik looked a little confused.

"I broke in," Traci said.

"We had a whole covert operation going," I explained.

"You broke into Lars' apartment?"

"We committed crimes," Mandi said. "Very cool crimes."

47

Lars didn't seem impressed. He ignored Mandi and directed his attention to Nik. "I know it will be difficult, but we need to watch the video. How do you want to do this?"

"Privately," Nik answered, his eyes firmly fixed on the floor.

Nik couldn't look any of us in the eye. The only time he looked at me was when he was giving me the look of death. I had to set that aside though. I needed to.

"We can watch it in my room," Lars suggested. "I have earbuds. Mandi sent me a copy."

"You're being really good about this," Nik said. "I mean, how do you know we aren't lying?"

"I don't think Jaimes is that good of an actor," Lars explained solemnly. "I don't think anyone can fake that."

"Fake what?" Nik asked, walking toward Lars' bedroom. I knew exactly what Lars was implying. I think Nik knew, too.

"You three adorable master criminals, make yourself at home," Lars said, seeming to purposefully change the subject. "The punch in the fridge is spiked. Just warning you."

Nik and Lars went into his bedroom, leaving the rest of us standing around, not quite knowing what to do. We ended up sitting in the living room trying to think of something to talk about that wasn't our friend being a victim of revenge porn.

"I know this is painful," we heard Lars say. "If you want, you can go back to your friends, and I'll watch the rest."

"No, I need to watch it. I need to know," Nik said. "I need to remember."

We could tell that Nik was on the verge of sobbing. It was so uncomfortable.

"That's it," I said. "Just a second."

I got up from my seat, walked the short distance to Lars' bedroom door in his tiny apartment and knocked.

"What?" Nik asked, annoyed.

I opened the door a crack to talk to them. I could see out of the corner of my eye, Lars and Nik holding hands. It surprised me. I didn't like it. They are going through something together. It doesn't mean anything, I told myself. It doesn't mean anything.

"The walls are thin," I finally said. "We can hear you talking. Lars, is it okay if we watch TV?"

"Yes. That sounds like a good idea," Lars said. "Thanks for letting us know."

The moment Lars answered me, Mandi turned on the TV. Mandi found some silly distracting animated show. It had something to do with a flying horse. I wasn't going to complain.

I had to admit, to myself, that I had a burning desire to know what was in that video. It was absolutely none of my business, but I couldn't get over how strange they were acting. I mean, I understood. It's sex, right? It's embarrassing to have something like that made public, but there had to be more to it. Did they do something kinky? Did they have a really private conversation? They were acting like some dark secret was involved.

I tried to focus on the flying horse show. I wondered what was more unrealistic, the fact that it talked or the fact that it flew. Suddenly, the picture changed. It took me a moment to realize it was the video. It was Lars and Nik lying in bed together.

"You don't need to feel bad about it." It was Lars' voice through the television. The video was being cast to the TV.

"Stop casting. What are you doing?" I called out, confused.

Mandi was trying to turn off the TV with the remote.

"Clever piece of shit!" she yelled. "Reprogrammed the goddamn remote after we turned on the TV!"

"What's going on?" I heard Nik shout from Lars' bedroom.

Traci started yelling, "La La La La La La La La La La La La La," really loud.

"Don't just stand there," Mandi told me. "Help me move this stupid fake fireplace so I can unplug the damn thing."

I tried to come to my senses, but I could hear Nik in the video. "But I wanted him so much. I wanted to be the person he would never forget. Knowing that he hadn't been with anyone else, made me want him more."

I ran over to the fireplace and helped Mandi who was on the other side.

"We can't control how we feel. We can only control how we act." It was Lars' voice this time.

We moved the fireplace out barely enough to reach the outlet.

"But I wasn't honest. I'm an awful person. I lied to get what I wanted," we heard Nik from the video say right before Mandi pulled the plug.

"They must be in the building or right outside," Mandi said. "You can't do that from far away."

Traci ran out onto the balcony. "I don't see anyone."

Mandi and I ran out the door. Mandi went in one direction, and I went the other. I could hear someone running down the stairs. I was determined to catch the bastard.

I ran down the hallway as fast as I could and opened the door to the stairwell. Looking up at me from the landing was a woman with a blonde ponytail wearing a half-open backpack with a laptop in it.

"She's here!" I yelled, flying down the stairs to catch up to her.

I was finally able to reach her once we got to the first floor. I grabbed her backpack. She tried to slip out of it, but I was able to pull her back and get in front of her.

"Who the fuck are you and why are you doing this?" I yelled.

I looked into her eyes. I was much bigger than her, she was scared. I didn't care. I was angry. She ruined my friend's life.

She tried to get around me, but I moved to get in her way.

"What are you going to do?" she asked. "Now that you know your friend's a monster. What are you going to do?"

Mandi ran up behind her and lifted the laptop out of her backpack.

"Hey, look, evidence," Mandi said.

"People who commit crimes don't report crimes," the woman said. "Isn't that what you said, Mandi?"

Eat

From Nik's point of view.

When I got down the stairs, I saw Mandi with a laptop in her hand and Jaimes standing in front of a woman. I recognized her as the fake lighting inspector. She was the woman who had been violating my privacy for months. She likely planted a camera in my bedroom. She could have easily found out my passwords by watching me type on my computer. I had a pretty good idea who she was. Who else could she be?

"Nice to meet you," I said. "You're Ava, right? Shawn's sister. He told me about you, but we never met. I know you hate me, but Lars didn't do anything wrong. Please stop this."

She turned around to face me.

"Don't worry. I'm done. The truth came out," Ava told me. "You confessed and now the world knows."

"How could you do this?" Jaimes asked. "Don't you think this was extreme?"

I wish he hadn't said anything. I knew the answer.

"How could I? Extreme? Did you watch the video? Did you watch the whole thing?" Ava responded. "What? Nik got quiet for a couple weeks. So sad. What a joke! Shawn. Shawn is not okay. Nik doesn't get to be okay, either. Nik doesn't get to forget my brother, either. Isn't that fair?"

"What do you mean, he's not okay?" I asked.

Please don't tell me he did something terrible. Please don't tell me he did something terrible.

"Do you care now?" Ava asked me. "Too late."

"Unlock it," Mandi demanded, presenting Ava with the laptop. "Unlock it or this will not end well for you."

"Not end well?" Ava scoffed. "What are you going to do?"

"Try me."

"Fine," Ava said, unlocking the laptop and giving it to Mandi. "I know what you're capable of. I know what you've done. Do they?"

A short, but noticeable wave of shock and fear moved across Mandi's face before she buried her head into Ava's laptop.

"Will you be able to take down all the uploads?" Lars asked Mandi as he slowly walked down the stairs.

"I doubt it," Ava said smugly. "I guess you two are a big hit. 'Fun-sized daddy plays pup, gets fucked rough.'"

I wasn't even listening. I had taken out my phone and was looking desperately for evidence that Shawn was alive and well. I didn't have the new passwords! Damn it. I was blocked anyway, but there must be some mention of him somewhere. C'mon. I needed to find something. I needed to know. I needed to find him.

Lars, Ava, and Mandi were talking. I wasn't sure what they were saying. Maybe they were making deals or whatever. I didn't know. I didn't care.

"Tell me he's alive!" I blurted out. "Please, tell me that he's all right. Please, Ava. Please! I can't find him." I held up my phone. "I can't find him. Help me find him."

"Are you going to cry?" Ava asked. "Maybe you should have thought more about how my brother felt. Maybe you shouldn't have made promises you couldn't keep."

"Please, tell me he didn't hurt himself. I don't care about anything else. Tell me he's all right. What do you want me to say? That I'm sorry? I'm sorry! Okay?"

"You still don't understand, do you? You think it's my brother who's unreasonable."

"No. I don't understand," I said, being honest. "I don't understand why he got that upset. I really don't. I don't know how he went from loving me to hating me. I don't. He found out I wasn't gay. He screamed at me. He said terrible things to me. Then he shut me out completely. I don't understand. I don't understand why any of this is happening. I don't understand why he hates me so much! Why? I don't understand."

"He's fine," Mandi said. "Shawn's fine. He posted a picture of a puppy he adopted two days ago."

I felt like I could breathe again. Mandi turned the screen around. There he was, with his red hair and his cheesy smile. He was holding some pit bull looking mutt. He always thought pit bulls got a bad rap. He seemed happy.

"Ava, you're sadistic. You know that? Do you feel better now?" I asked. "Do you?"

"Yes, I do. You know why he's all right? Because I stopped him. I talked him down. Do you have any idea what that was like? Do you? He's my little brother. He's had a hard life. Growing up, I tried to protect him, but I failed. He fell for you so hard that he lost his mind, and you took advantage of him. He'll remember you. You got your wish. I was worried, for a while, that things had gone too far. Then, I found out that you are worse than I ever imagined. You deserved everything you got. You deserve worse. Monster! Predator!"

I took in every word she said. I wanted to tell her that she was wrong. I wanted to tell her that she was being unfair. But what good would that do? Shawn was alive and well, that's all that mattered.

"Let's leave. I'm going to take you home," Jaimes told me. "It's over."

I looked back at Jaimes, the man who wanted to save me from all this. He was extending his hand to me.

He cared about me. He was my friend. I hated him. It finally dawned on me why I felt that way. It finally made sense. Of course, it wasn't actually hatred, but it felt very much like hate.

"Okay," I said. "Let's go home." I gave him my keys. "You drive."

I sat in the passenger seat of my own car. It was sort of funny. Jaimes had to put his seat back. I had to put my seat forward. He's a bit taller than me.

"We should go through a drive thru or something," Jaimes said. "You like Burger Hut, right?"

"Yeah."

"I never thanked you for the gummy bears," Jaimes said.

I could tell he was trying to be funny.

I looked over at him and smiled. "You're welcome."

"I'm sure Mandi, Traci, and Lars will deal with everything. Try to calm down so you can sleep tonight," Jaimes suggested.

"I'll try."

We got burgers. Jaimes was hungry too, so he parked the car, and we ate. He knew what I usually got. I guess we'd been living together for a long time, so he knew these things. I realized that my coffee and apple turnover were still in Lars' apartment. Oh well.

"I need to know you aren't going to do anything rash," Jaimes said. "Please tell me."

"I'm upset, but you don't have to worry. That's not where my head's at."

"Good. I would not handle it well if something like that happened."

"You'd miss me," I joked. "Nobody to pay half the rent."

"That's not funny. I'd be devastated."

"Why do you like me so much?" I thought perhaps, at this point we were beyond pretending.

"I just do."

"You shouldn't. I'm not a good person."

"Don't let what Ava said get to you. She's not rational. You did not deserve what she did to you."

"How do you know? Shawn is only 19 years old. You know that? Nineteen. I lied to him to get laid. I did. I did that."

"I don't believe it. You'd never do that."

"Never?" I said annoyed that he wouldn't believe me. "I did. He made the assumption, and I rolled with it. Even when he was talking about things that I couldn't understand, I acted like I knew. He talked to me about how when he was a kid, he thought he was supposed to like girls so he would try to like them. I mean, he would stare at pictures of girls and attempt to like them and fail. I nodded like I could understand.

"It got to the point where I knew that he would have a problem if I came out to him. I kept it a secret. Even when our relationship got serious, I didn't tell him. If I really thought that it wasn't a big deal, why didn't I tell him? Huh? I didn't tell him because I knew he would be upset. I didn't tell him because I was worried that he might leave me, and I wanted him so much."

"He never loved you."

"What did you just say?" Why was he crossing the line like this?

"You heard me," Jaimes said, taking a bite of his hamburger.

"You aren't allowed to say something like that. That's not okay."

"But it's true. He was obsessed with you, for whatever reason. But he didn't love you. If you love someone, you're willing to work things out - or at least try."

"No. I violated his trust. I lied. That's what happened."

"The sister of your ex-boyfriend secretly monitors your bedroom, sends a picture of you masturbating to your entire workplace, and uploads a sex video of you to porn sites, and you're angrier at yourself than you are at her. You realize she's a nut job, right?"

"She isn't," I said. "She's actually a lot like Mandi."

"How can you say that?"

"She's trying to protect her brother."

"From you? That's ridiculous."

"Yes, from me. I'm the nut job. I'm the crazy one."

"She blames you for her brother's serious emotional problems. She's wrong to do that. You're wrong to agree with her. You are still punishing yourself because you feel bad. Because you care. You aren't the problem. Shawn may be young, but he's an adult. Your only crime was keeping your sexuality secret. That's it. That's all you did wrong, and we've all done that. If he couldn't handle it, it's his fault. There is something wrong with him, not you. Don't you think you've suffered enough? Huh?"

"I guess," I said weakly.

I wondered if he would say the same thing if he actually watched the video. If he did, he would understand why Ava blamed me. He would understand why she said the things she said.

We kept eating our food, but I could tell there was something he wanted to say to me. I was so exhausted. I was spent. I sipped my soda and ate my hamburger. Sitting in the car with him in silence was pleasant.

Mandi said that I could sleep on her couch tomorrow. I wondered if the offer was still open. I couldn't keep living with Jaimes. I couldn't stand it anymore. I couldn't move until I found out where I would be transferred. I felt like I didn't have a home.

"So, are you and Lars a thing now?" Jaimes asked out of the blue.

"No," I laughed a bit. "He's a good guy though. He really is. I don't think of him that way though."

"Why not?" Jaimes asked, starting up the car and backing out of the parking spot.

"He's too short."

"Short?" Jaimes laughed. "I didn't think you were that shallow."

"I'm joking. I feel like a kid around him. I think he's the type of guy who likes to take younger people under his wing, you know. I don't want to be his project. At least not forever."

"You like him though."

"He's easy to talk to."

"Lars sandwich?" Jaimes joked.

"Maybe in a million years."

"But it's on the table."

"I don't think his table would hold all three of us."

Jaimes burst out laughing. "I knew you could tell a joke."

That's the Jaimes I knew. I knew he was trying to make me laugh. I knew that he cared about me. I did. Even when he was being an inconsiderate asshole, I had a feeling I could count on him if things got bad. I wasn't wrong.

"Sorry I pulled a prank on you," I said.

"What?"

He said that as if he'd forgotten.

"I'm sorry I made you think that you leaked the photo. That was a mean thing to do."

"Taking the picture in the first place crossed the line. Even if it wasn't leaked, that's not something you do to someone else. It was disrespectful. I'm sorry."

Eventually, we were home. He parked the car and we both got out.

"After everything that happened this weekend, I think perhaps we should forgive each other," I said sincerely as we walked up to our apartment. "I don't have enough energy to even worry about it."

"Fair enough."

Once we got inside, I immediately stepped up on my bed to reach the light fixture. Jaimes looked around in his room and other places as well. We found three cameras. Thinking about all the things we had said and done in sight of those cameras in the last several weeks made me wonder if we really should have let Ava get away with it. Drawing things out would make life more difficult, though. I didn't want to stress out Shawn either. It wasn't worth it. Best to leave Shawn and his sister alone.

"Mandi might want these," Jaimes said. "I think they're expensive."

"We should put them in tin foil," I suggested. "It stops signals, I guess."

Jaimes threw them in the freezer and shut the door. "There."

I laughed. "That'll work."

"Are you leaving tomorrow?" Jaimes asked, getting serious all of a sudden.

"Yes."

Sleep

"Stay," Jaimes said.

"No," Nik answered him. "I can't."

"I said I'd be more discreet."

"That won't fix the problem. I'm sorry. Don't take it personally."

"Don't take it personally? I know you've been to hell and back during the last few days, but please explain it to me. I need to know what's going on. The looks you give me. I'm not imagining it. I don't understand. It hurts. Okay? I thought we were friends. Even when we're joking around, you get this look on your face like you're angry that I even exist. It's like you hate me."

"Hate you? I don't hate you. I want to *be* you. I want to be like you, but I can't. Do you know what it's like for me to hear you almost every night fooling around and having fun? Even if you are somewhere else, I know that's what's going on. You're just having fun. You're enjoying your life."

"What? Be me?"

"I hate being alone. I hate it. Then, I get to listen to you and your hookups, messing around like it's no big deal. You can take someone home and not worry. You don't worry. You pick random people up at the bar, and the worst thing that's happened is someone stole your wallet. Hell, you've taken virgins home and both of you are giggling. You show him how to do things and everything is fine and fun. Nobody is ashamed. Nobody gets upset. I've only been with a handful of people my whole life, and it is always awkward. I'm always nervous. In the end, they always reject me. Every time.

"I messed things up with Shawn so bad. I hurt him so bad. Is there something wrong with me? Am I broken? Am I weird? It never feels right. I get so jealous. I'm such a goddamn coward. And finally, I worked up the courage to take a risk and everything went to hell.

"Lars was nice. I was comfortable with him. I could talk to him. I shared things with him that I've never told anyone else. I guess, I'm not allowed to feel that way. I can't take it. I can't deal with it, especially after all this crap. I'm sorry. I know you like me, and you want to be friends, but I just can't. I can't keep watching you live your life when I'm so miserable."

"I thought...I thought it bothered you because you thought it was distasteful or wrong," Jaimes told him. "I mean, you keep saying things like, 'You know me, that's not my scene,' stuff like that. All the times I teased you, I thought you were judging me."

"I told you I wasn't judging you."

"I didn't believe you. You'd glare at me and make comments. What was I supposed to think?"

"Well, now you know. I was being pathetic. Sorry, I know that you don't need to hear me complain about my life. I was so angry at you through this whole thing, and I couldn't even figure out why. I'm so sick of needing to be saved. I couldn't stand that you have this carefree life and I'm just...pitiful."

"Stop worrying so much. It's fucking annoying. Okay? Is that what you need to hear? Nik, listen to me. It's okay to complain. It's okay to get things off your chest. It's okay to be sad. That doesn't make you pathetic or pitiful. When I ask you how you're doing, I can handle an honest answer. I told you that. I meant it. You think my life is perfect? It's not. And it's okay to be honest if I piss you off. If I ask you to pick up condoms at the grocery store and you don't want to, you can tell me to fuck myself."

"I should have thrown you the gummy bears and told you, 'Here! Improvise!'"

"You don't want to know what's going through my head right now. Gummy peach rings might work better though."

Nik laughed. "Look, I'm exhausted. I need to sleep."

"Okay. Me, too."

Nik went to the bathroom, brushed his teeth, combed his hair, and washed his face. He took off his clothes, except for his boxers, and crawled into his bed.

Jaimes used the bathroom after Nik was done, then went to bed as well.

After a while, Jaimes got up and put on a T-shirt. He walked across the hall and knocked on the door. "Can I be courageous for you?" he asked.

"What?" Nik responded, half asleep.

Jaimes opened the door. It wasn't locked. "You said in your profile that you wanted someone who would be courageous for you."

"I did."

"Do you want to be alone tonight?"

"No."

Jaimes crawled into the bed behind Nik and put an arm around him. Nik clasped Jaimes' hand. "Are you comfortable?" Jaimes asked.

"Yes."

"Good."

"Good night, Jaimes."

"Good night, Nik."

"Jaimes?"

"Yes."

"Buy your own damn condoms next time."

"Okay."

Book Two: Good Friends

Bed

From Nik's point of view.

"So, then he crawled into bed with me," I explained.

"Jaimes crawled into bed with you?" Mandi asked, after nearly spraying her ridiculously expensive and unreasonably sweet coffee out of her mouth. "So, are you dating now."

"No."

"No?"

"No."

"Once he crawled into bed with you, what happened?" she asked.

"He held me, and we slept."

"You slept?"

"That's generally what happens in bed," I said, getting annoyed. "It was only that night. I think he felt sorry for me."

"Oh, Nik," Mandi said, giving me that look of concern that I'd learned to cherish and hate at the same time. "He really does like you."

"I know, but I'm worried. I'm still torn up. I'm stressed out. We just started getting along as friends. I don't want to screw that up. But now we're sharing a hotel room. Even though there are two beds, it's awkward."

"Awkward?"

"Sharing a hotel room is different than sharing an apartment. I don't want him to get the wrong idea. We're living together. If things get weird, it's going to be awful."

"Or awesome," Mandi said.

I wished that Mandi would stop trying to get us together. Was that her plan all along? Was she trying to play Cupid?

"It would never work out," I insisted. "I know it would never work out."

"You're making yourself miserable," she said after drinking more of her fancy coffee. "We're at con. You need to have fun for once. Let loose a little bit. Jaimes has never been to one of these before, you can show him around and relax."

"I guess." I took a drink of my raspberry mocha latte. "But Mandi, I'm still scared. I am. I can't help it. I have the worst luck. The video is still out there. I can't stop thinking about it. Every time someone looks at me the least bit funny, I panic. I think, do they recognize me? What must they think of me?"

"Did you talk to Jaimes? I mean, does he know what's going on?"

"No."

Did she really think that Jaimes and I were like that? Did she think I was comfortable telling him everything?

"You might want to," Mandi suggested. "So, he can help you if things get bad."

"You've always been there for me. I love you like a sister. I do. But once, just once, I want to be the one who does the saving. I don't want to worry him, and I want to get through this on my own. Don't tell him, okay?"

"I won't, but, Nik, you don't need to deal with this on your own. We're here for you."

Mandi was always looking out for me. We met because she was looking out for me. When I was outed in high school, she heard about it and came to my rescue. It seemed like I was always the one in trouble.

"I'm getting to the point where I'm fantasizing about changing my name and moving out of the country. I'm not joking." Running away kept sounding better and better. "Everyone needs phlebotomists, right?"

"Maybe you can leave with Traci," Mandi said, getting quiet all of a sudden.

"So, she's definitely going? Did she get in?"

"She did. She's leaving. I can't hold her back. She leaves in a few weeks. She got into one of the best musicology programs in the world. I'm happy for her."

The look on Mandi's face was unmistakable. She was heartbroken.

"You're breaking up?" I asked.

I knew that Traci applied to a grad school far away, but I assumed they would have a long-distance relationship or that Mandi would leave too.

"Yeah."

"Oh no, Mandi. I'm so sorry."

They were together for two years. How? Why? How could they not work this out?

"I'll be fine," she said with a forced smile. "It's for the best."

"So, we're both going to try to forget about our troubles?" I tried to smile.

"Definitely."

"Are you ready for your panel?"

I knew that would cheer her up. She was glowing.

"I have three panels. One on white-hat hacking, one on the future of cybersecurity, and the hackers in fiction one we do every year."

"I'll be there and ask stupid questions."

My efforts only helped for a moment.

"I'm going to miss Traci so much," Mandi said, trembling a bit.

I offered her my hand. She grabbed it. How could they let this happen? I didn't understand. They seemed so wonderful together.

Move

From Jaimes' point of view.

Everyone around me was crazy. This is what Nik did for fun? I felt like a toddler. There were literally life-sized stuffed animals walking around. There was a certain funk in the air already, and it was only day one. What on earth was I going to do for three days? I guess they had a bar and there was ... anime karaoke? What was that?

Nik woke up much earlier than me and drove straight here. We hadn't even checked into our hotel room. He was used to being up at the crack of dawn because of his job. He'd transferred to a new facility, so he needed to get up even earlier than before because he had to commute. At least it seemed like things were getting back to normal.

"I'm at the Coffee Corner with Mandi," Nik had texted two hours ago.

"Where are you now?" I texted back.

"In the Star Imperium Room C."

Where the fuck was that? Maybe Mandi was around.

"Mandi, where are you?" I texted.

"Just made a grown man cry because I destroyed his Tetris high score."

Whatever.

I went through registration. Now I had this lanyard on, and I was carrying around this plastic bag full of papers and a huge schedule book. Nik talked me into this and then he decided to leave without me. I'd never felt this out of place in my life.

I decided to go check into our hotel room.

I kept getting looks from girls in cat outfits. Christ, I think I got meowed at.

Three days. I could endure this for three days.

Eventually, I found the hotel check-in desk. I guess they had the entire place booked. The desk clerk offered me a discount if I moved to a single king-size bed. Brilliant. Why did he get us a room with two beds anyway? It's just the two of us. Mandi was staying with some other friends of hers.

I wondered if Traci was around.

"Where you at?" I texted Traci.

"Getting ready to move, by myself," she texted back.

"You aren't at the convention?"

"No."

"Are you coming?"

"No. I'm leaving and never coming back."

"What's going on?" I texted.

"Ask Mandi."

"Do you want me to call you?"

"No. I'm fine. I can't talk about it anyway, so what's the point?"

What in the world was that about? I got the impression that I stepped in something I shouldn't have. I wasn't sure what to say.

"I'm sorry to hear that," I texted back.

I brought my luggage up to the room, sat on the bed, and looked through the schedule. Mandi was a member of three panels. Her picture was even in the book. I had no idea she was this popular.

They had an art show and silent auction, that might be fun.

"Are you in the room?" Nik texted me.

"Yes. Room 318."

"Stay there, I'll bring my luggage up and get my key."

"How was Space Empire?" I texted.

"Star Imperium"

"Whatever," I texted back to annoy him.

"I hate you."

So predictable. I kept looking through the schedule book. Eventually, I heard a knock at the door. I opened it up to see Nik. He was carrying a suitcase and a coffee.

"I got you a flat white," Nik said. "That's what you drink, right?"

"Thanks," I said, taking the coffee. He was so sweet sometimes.

He walked in and his expression changed. "Why is there one bed?"

"I got a discount."

"Okay..."

"Is something wrong?"

"No, of course not," he said in a way that actually said of course there was something wrong, and he wasn't going to tell me what it was. So, I had to guess, like always.

"It's not like we haven't shared a bed before," I said, trying to press his buttons.

"It's fine," Nik responded without cracking a smile.

He set his suitcase down and looked over at me, with his head slightly down so that he had to look up at me to make eye contact. His mouth was slightly open, and I swear, to the fucking heavenly father, he licked his lips. Then he sheepishly told me, "I'll live."

If he was anyone else, anyone at all, who looked at me like that, they would have had my dick in their mouth in under five minutes. But this was Nik, neurotic, repressed, clueless Nik.

Two nights. Two nights. I can get through two nights.

Two beds. Two beds would have been nice. What was I thinking?

Troll

From Nik's point of view.

Part of me enjoyed seeing Jaimes be the nervous one for once, but I wanted him to have fun. We were looking through all the pieces that had been submitted for the art contest so far.

"You should enter something," I suggested.

"What would I enter? The perfect copy?" Jaimes joked. "I haven't done anything like this in a long time."

"Why not?"

"Doesn't pay the bills. But really, I'm not into it anymore."

"Maybe you need a muse," I said with a smile. My goodness, was I flirting?

"I enjoy what I do," Jaimes responded, somewhat defensively. "Everyone thinks that fine art is the only path to fulfillment, but if they ever sized and placed a Venn diagram perfectly to make the paragraph breaks look amazing, they might change their minds."

Jaimes was staring off into space like he was having a moment.

I started laughing. "That's what I love about you. You always make me smile."

What did I just say? Love? Maybe he didn't notice. Of course, he noticed. I was worried that I was leading him on. This was bad. So bad.

"Mandi's panel is soon. We should get going," Jaimes suggested.

"Okay."

We sat through the panel even though we didn't understand anything. Every once in a while, Mandi looked over at me. I could tell that whatever she was saying was reminding her of what happened to me, what was still happening to me.

It had been a couple months now. We had scrubbed all the popular hosting sites of the picture and the video, but we were unable to get a discussion about it taken off a troll site.

Mandi assured me that it would be difficult for them to figure out who I was. I ended up having to watch the whole video again to reassure myself that we hadn't said our names out loud. Still, images of Lars and me from the video were there. A couple of them were made into memes. The horrible things they said about us were there. At least they weren't focused on Lars. They were focused on me. I was their target. They tried to find out who I was, but they couldn't find me.

Mandi had a long-standing account that she used to spy on them over the years. Why? I had no idea. They were so awful, but I guess in a way, these were her people. Eventually, she convinced them that I wasn't someone worth pursuing. She pretended to be like them. She referred to me with slurs. She put on quite a show. They agreed. I wasn't worth it. So, they gave up and moved on to someone else, I guess.

I didn't want to tell Jaimes about it, because I didn't want him to know. I didn't want him to ask questions. I didn't want him to see what they were saying about me.

"People sometimes forget," Mandi explained to the audience, "that servers are physical objects that exist in a physical place and are subject to local law. So, troll sites will shop around when they lose their hosting. However clever you might think you are, in the end, sometimes the best solution would be to jump onto a plane, break in, and take an axe to it. Maybe start the place on fire."

The crowd gasped a little bit. Jeez, Mandi, might not want to tell everyone you're a master criminal.

"Hypothetically, of course," Mandi clarified, with a smile. The crowd laughed. "Would not recommend it. But hey, if you hear about it on the news. It was me."

They kept laughing.

I was the only one who knew that wasn't really a joke. She wanted to protect me, but it was also a matter of pride. She didn't like to lose.

"Why isn't Traci here?" Jaimes asked me, somewhat quietly. "I texted her and she said she was moving."

"You texted her?" I asked.

"I thought she would be here. I was trying to meet up."

"Traci got into that grad school program in Australia. Mandi and Traci are breaking up."

"What?" he said a little too loud. "The fuck?" he followed up, much more quietly.

"I was surprised too. Mandi is really upset."

"That's terrible. I mean, I'm happy that Traci got in, but..."

"Yeah," I said, understanding how he felt. "I thought I would be in their wedding party one day. I really did."

"Well, we'll have to try to cheer her up."

"Let's buy her something," I suggested. "We haven't hit the dealer room yet."

After the panel, Mandi was talking to a swarm of people who had walked up to ask her questions.

"Let's buy her something and then meet up for dinner. She's sort of a big deal around here."

I knew I was beaming. I was very proud of her.

"What is it with you and Mandi anyway? Are you sweet on her?"

"What?"

I was a bit shocked. He'd known Mandi and I for years, and he never asked me that. Also, Jaimes was actually acknowledging that I liked girls. That was different.

"No, nothing like that. We had each other's backs in high school," I explained. "I owe her a lot. Anyway, she doesn't like boys."

"What if she did?"

I got really uncomfortable, and Jaimes started laughing at me.

"So, you want to buy her something, huh?" He was still smiling. "What would Mandi want?"

Wings

From Jaimes' point of view.

Nik held up a stuffed animal in front of me, smiling ear to ear.

"This," he said, seeming very sure of himself. "This is what Mandi wants."

"It's a stuffed animal," I said flatly. "Why is it the same price as my phone?"

"It's not just any stuffed animal. It's imported. It's a limited run. Look at these." He pointed at the feathers on the stuffed flying horse. "They are blue and purple instead of teal."

"I don't know why that's significant," I said, trying to keep a straight face.

"The original Flying Horse Warrior had blue and purple feathers, but in the English-language remake, the feathers were teal."

Nik picked up a different stuffed animal, with teal feathers, that looked almost exactly the same and was a third the price.

"That's why this one," he said holding up the one he wanted to buy, "is so much cooler than this one," he said holding up the one that was cheaper.

"Are you sure that she'll love it?" I asked, because I sure as hell wasn't spending that much money on a stuffed animal unless it would literally make Mandi orgasm.

"I'm sure."

"Okay. I'll pay for half, and you pay for half."

"Deal."

We bought the overpriced thing, then walked around for a while.

I found myself getting strange about seeing unfortunate book cover choices. I wanted to redo them all and make them perfect. Nik was having a blast. It was a nice change. He tried on a headband with a unicorn horn on it.

"Hunt me. Hunt me," he laughed, putting his arms in front of his face and curling his hands up like hooves. "Hunt me."

I gave some money to the lady selling the unicorn horns.

"It suits you," I told Nik.

"Wait. Did you buy it?"

"I did."

Nik was acting so adorable, so of course I bought it.

"Anyway, we should figure out what we're doing for dinner." I brought up a map on my phone to see what was close. "Chinese buffet? Burgers? Sushi? Pancakes?"

"Sushi," Nik said as he started to rub up against my arm with his face, pretending to be a unicorn.

It was nice to see him so happy. He always seemed stressed out.

"Where you at?" I texted Mandi. "We're going for dinner. Is sushi good?"

"I can be done destroying high scores and other people's dreams long enough to eat," she responded. "Sushi is great."

"Meet at the lobby," I texted.

The lobby was a trip. It was full of people. It was like an airport, but with costumes.

At some point this guy from across the room looked at me funny for a moment, squinted at me, then looked around attempting to avoid eye contact.

Yes, yes you did sleep with me. Funny. That's why you thought you recognized me, but you aren't sure from where. Your face was in the pillow most of the time, so it makes sense that you're not sure.

He looked at me again.

I smiled back.

Wait for it. There was the look. Finally dawned on you, huh?

I gave him a little salute. He waved briefly and went on his way.

"Slept with him, didn't you?" Nik asked.

"Good guess."

"Oh, there's Mandi!" Nik said, waving over to her. "Let's go see if you had sex with any of the wait staff at the sushi place."

"How's Lars?" I asked bluntly, to get back at him. I knew they were still hooking up. "Did he ever find out if you have a tight ass?"

Nik shot me a look. "Dick."

Mandi caught up with us, and we walked to the sushi place. I had not, as far as I recall, slept with any of the staff.

After we ordered our food, Nik gave Mandi the bag with her present in it.

"We got you something," he said with a huge grin.

"You got me something?"

"Yeah, Jaimes and I pitched in and got you something. I hope you like it."

The anticipation on Nik's face was amazing. He was like a 12-year-old at a birthday party or something. She took the stuffed toy out of the bag and smiled ear-to-ear. Then she saw the wings and her jaw dropped. She discarded the bag onto an empty seat and hugged the imported limited-run original series winged stuffed animal horse-like thing close to her chest.

Mandi started to cry. "Thank you," Mandi said through her tears, "I love it."

I didn't know what to do. I suspected she was crying because she was thinking about Traci. I didn't want to consider the implications of a grown woman becoming that emotional over the color of wings on a stuffed animal. That was too weird.

"We wanted to cheer you up," Nik said. "Totally failed."

She looked the horse in the eyes. "You did cheer me up. I'm just trying to convince myself that I'm making the right decisions."

Mandi was rarely like this. She was usually so brash and fearless. Something was going on, something she wasn't telling us. I considered asking Mandi what decisions she was talking about, but she quickly changed the subject.

"Have you taken Jaimes to the fairy room yet?"

"Not yet."

"What's the fairy room?"

They both chuckled.

"You know, the *fairy* room," Nik explained. "You'll like it."

"It's full of fairies," Mandi added.

"Are you serious?" I asked, realizing it was the gay hangout. I wasn't sure if my bisexual friend and my lesbian friend really understood how "fairy" hits, but I kept my cool. "They really call it that?"

"Yep," Mandi confirmed.

"Wings are optional," Nik assured me.

Two days. I can make it for two more days.

Hunt

From Nik's point of view.

I couldn't believe it. I was stunned. We were in the fairy room for five seconds. Not five minutes. Literally, five seconds. The moment Jaimes walked in, he made eye contact with the one other guy who looked as uncomfortable as he did, he knocked his head back slightly in the direction of the door, and they left together. That was it. That was all he did. How? How did that happen?

It took me a moment to realize that I was drunk and saying these things out loud. "I don't understand. They didn't say anything. He didn't even walk up to him. He looked at him and moved his head like one inch. It's like they have telepathy. Do gay guys have telepathy?" I looked over at the femboy to my right, wearing his cute little fairy wings and ridiculous abs that screamed "out of my league."

He shrugged.

"You keep talking about your friend," cat-eared strap-on girl whispered, pouting. "I think you like him."

She was playing with my ear, using her tongue or her nose or something. Oh god, she was purring. Oh no. I had stayed too long. The fairy room got really weird after midnight. I had this weird panic, worried that I would end up in the ER with a crocheted cock cozy stuck somewhere embarrassing, and I would have to be transferred again.

"I'm drunk!"

"Too drunk," I heard a voice say. "Too drunk to play."

"Hunt me," I said with a big smile, looking into Jaimes' eyes.

Jaimes!

"Jaimes! Save yourself. The fairy room turns into a kinky drunken orgy after midnight. I've heard stories."

Suddenly, my head was on a pillow, and someone was taking off my shoes. Once the blankets were on top of me, I fell asleep only to wake up to Jaimes' voice.

"Wow, I woke up before you for once," Jaimes said, handing me a small green bottle. "Here, it'll help your hangover."

"I got plastered, didn't I?" I asked. My voice barely worked. I sat up so that I could drink what he handed me.

"You really shouldn't get drunk like that."

"You're lecturing me on being careful? Huh? You?"

"If I knew you were going to get drunk, I wouldn't have left. Your kink-buddies are good people, though. They wouldn't even let me take you away without me proving that we were friends. I thought you were going to go to your computer game thing."

"I guess I decided to get shitfaced instead."

I was embarrassed. My friends were always saving me, it seemed.

"Did you have a good time with that guy?" I asked, trying to sound sincere instead of jealous.

"Yes. Yes, I did," Jaimes answered with a chuckle. "I guess his friends talked him into coming here, too. We bonded."

"You found the one other normie in the whole place."

"I'm talented."

He could say that again. Good grief. Gay telepathy. Where could I get some of that?

"You and Mandi go to these things all the time, don't you?" Jaimes asked.

"Yeah. We have since we were kids. You probably think we're being immature."

"No," Jaimes answered. "Of course not."

He was such a liar.

"Mandi has a competition in about an hour. Do you want to get breakfast and then go?" Jaimes asked. "You should probably take a shower first though."

I reeked of booze and coconut oil. I was also completely covered in glitter.

"Yeah. Good idea. What competition?"

"In her words..." Jaimes looked at his phone. "At 9 a.m. come to E-Game Room B to watch the will to live be sucked out of all those who oppose me. Then I will play Pong."

"Yes!" I cheered. "We can't miss this. Epic! She does this every year and every year, there is at least one person who doesn't believe the legend, and they are proved wrong."

"I am so confused."
"You'll see. You will see!" I said as I disappeared into the bathroom.

Game

From Jaimes' point of view.

I wasn't quite sure how much more I could take. It was interesting at first, but there were only so many times I could watch Mandi pull out someone's spine without getting nauseated.

Mandi was playing an old fighting arcade game. People were lined up to fight against her, and she always won. Someone came close to beating her and everyone gasped, but in the end, she impaled him on the end of some sort of pointy weapon.

"We're getting close. We're getting close," Nik cheered excitedly.

"Bullshit. It's not going to happen. You're all full of crap." I heard someone in the crowd say.

Suddenly the entire place erupted.

"Told you so!" a few shouted nearly in unison, pointing excitedly at the game.

A bunch of people got their phones out to record what was on the screen.

"You can tell your grandchildren you were witness!" some guy yelled.

"Pong! Pong! Pong!" The crowd started chanting.

I looked over at the arcade game and instead of warriors ripping each other's guts out, it was a black screen with green lines and a dot bouncing around. What the hell?

"Mandi! Mandi! Mandi!" Nik shouted and others started in too.

After a short time with the entire crowd fixated on the screen chanting, they gave out a collective "Aw!" when Mandi yelled "Damn it!" and the screen went back to the fighting game.

The crowd began to disperse.

"Thanks for coming guys," Mandi said, walking up to us. "I think I'm going to go get some sleep and take a shower." She gave her armpit a sniff and recoiled.

"Did you sleep at all last night?" I asked.

"It's con," she replied, grinning at me.

"We'll see you at your next panel then."

"I should probably be awake for that," she laughed. "Don't feel obligated to go. I know neither of you are that interested."

"It's okay," Nik said. "I missed the first round of Star Imperium anyhow. So, I'm free."

"Oh no, why?"

"He decided to get drunk off his ass instead," I answered. "I had to drag him back to the room."

"Nik!" Mandi exclaimed. I wasn't sure if she was angry or impressed. "What has gotten into you?"

She messed up his hair, like he was a little kid. Then she got really serious.

"Be careful, okay? Please, be careful."

"Okay," Nik said. He put his head down like he was ashamed and was apologizing. "You don't have to tell me."

Nik and Mandi gave each other a hug. Nik seemed weirdly upset and grasped onto her, like he was a scared child.

What the hell? Mandi was only about a year and a half older than Nik, but they didn't act like it. Sometimes the way they interacted was creepy.

Nik let go of Mandi, and then she left.

"Is everything all right?" I asked.

"Everything is fine," Nik said, putting on a smile and wiping his eyes with his sleeve.

"If you say so."

We started walking toward the art room when I saw the cat girl and fairy boy walk by, stop, look over at us and point.

"Nik." I stopped and pulled his shirt. "Nik."

"What?"

"Go over and thank them for taking care of you last night," I suggested.

"Who?"

I pointed. "They want you."

"What?"

"They. Want. To. Do. You. It's written all over their faces." I waved them over.

"They do not," Nik insisted. "What would they want with me?"

"How are you this dense?" Seriously. This boy had no intuition at all. "They want to have sex with you."

"How do you know these things?"

"Hey, Nik!" I said too loudly. "I'm going to go to that panel about self-publishing you aren't interested in. Sorry, I know you have nothing to do for the next two hours. I'm sure you will entertain yourself somehow."

"What are you doing?"

"Leaving the rest up to you."

Then, I walked away. I could hear Nik and the couple talking behind me.

"I remember you," the cat-girl said. "Hunt me!"

"You were a little drunk last night," the guy said. "Can we buy you a coffee?"

"Sure."

If that boy didn't get laid, there was no hope for him. I remembered him grinning when I mentioned unicorn hunters. So transparent. So far in denial.

"Go have fun for once, neurotic wannabe toyboy," I said under my breath.

Hunt me! Jesus Christ. I hope I didn't throw him to the wolves. Oh wait, the *wolves* were literally over there. I laughed at my own joke as three people in wolf outfits walked by. This place was wild.

I entertained myself for a few hours, hoping Nik was making the best of it. When the time came, I found a place to sit at Mandi's panel and watched the door for Nik. The other two panelists were already seated up front. I was wondering if maybe Mandi overslept.

Nik came swooping in before the panel started and sat next to me. I looked over at him. He was glowing. He totally got fucked.

"I almost texted you to ask for condoms as a joke," he said. "But they had an assortment."

I burst out laughing. "You totally should have. Did you...um, enjoy yourself?" I asked, trying to stop laughing because the panel was about to start.

"Jaimes. Jaimes," Nik said, trying to sound posh. "Gentlemen do not discuss such things."

"Very funny."

"Gosh. Where's Mandi?" Nik asked, looking around.

"I think they are going to start without her. They tried to call her, but she didn't pick up."

"We should find her. It's really not like her to blow these sorts of things off."

We left quietly and started walking toward Mandi's room.

"Well, were you their little unicorn?" I asked.

He giggled and blushed. So goddamn adorable.

We got to Mandi's door, and I knocked.

"Who the fuck is it?" Mandi yelled.

"Mandi?" Nik asked, startled by her response. "What's going on? Open up."

We could hear her stomp over to the door and open it just a crack so that it was unlocked, and stomp back into the room.

Nik flew past me and ran into her room. "What's wrong? What happened?"

I walked in behind him and closed the door.

Mandi was sitting on her bed, staring at her laptop. She turned it around, showing us a bulletin board type website.

Holy shit. There was a picture of Nik and me from this morning in the gaming room. What the fuck was going on?

"They found you," Mandi said to Nik. Her voice was weak and trembling. "One of those fucking assholes is at the con."

Monster

From Nik's point of view.

I thought I would scream and cry if this happened, but I didn't. I stood there in shock looking at the screen that Mandi was holding up.

"What...what do we do now?" I muttered.

Obviously, Jaimes could tell something was very wrong. He led me over to one of the beds and helped me sit down.

We were finally, finally having fun. We were finally, finally acting like friends. I was enjoying myself. I was joking around. I was allowing myself to be comfortable for once. For fucking once. I had just been with two beautiful, amazing people without feeling awkward or ashamed. I was happy. For fucking once. I was happy.

Suddenly, all of it was a dream. It didn't happen. Jaimes and I didn't actually look at art or buy gifts or cheer on Mandi. I certainly didn't have sex and cuddle with a cute cosplay couple. That wasn't real life. That was a fantasy. It was all a dream. It was all gone once I woke up to reality.

"Please, Mandi, clue me in," Jaimes said, sitting beside me on the bed. "Is Ava back?"

"It's not Ava. It was never Ava."

"What? How do you know?" he asked. "What do you mean?"

"I know. It's not her. Trust me. She's not involved," Mandi said. "Nik is on the radar of a troll site. They were trying to dox him a while ago..."

"Dox him?"

"Find out his name, address, employer, that sort of thing," she explained. "Someone from the site recognized him at con, took a picture, and posted it. They know where he is. They know his nickname is Nik. I'm trying to figure out who took the picture. The only way to stop this is to get the post deleted and tell them they got it wrong."

"Why would they care?" Jaimes asked. "Why are they doing this?"

I desperately didn't want Jaimes to know, but I realized I wasn't going to be able to keep it a secret. This was hell.

"They think that..." Mandi began to explain. I could tell she was trying to choose her words carefully. "They think that Nik is a bad person because of the video."

"Why? I'm sorry. I'm sick of being in the dark about this," Jaimes said, raising his voice slightly. "I mean, I don't need to watch it, obviously. I don't need to know everything but tell me something."

Mandi looked down, but then lifted her head slightly to look me straight in the eye. She looked guilty. Why did she look like she did something wrong?

"You watched it, didn't you, Mandi? You aren't just going off what they said on the site about me. You watched it, didn't you?"

My jaw clenched. I balled up my hands until my knuckles were white.

"Yeah," Mandi answered under her breath. "I did."

"You watched it!" I shouted, staring her down.

"Holy shit." There was a hint of fear in Jaimes voice. He was not accustomed to seeing me this angry. "Nik, calm down."

I ignored him.

"How could you!" I stood up and pointed at Mandi as I screamed. "How could you? You're my best friend. I told you not to!"

Jaimes moved in front of me. He held my arms down and tried to make eye contact. "Nik. Nik. Please. Take a breath. You can't be like this. You're scaring Mandi."

"I begged her not to. I begged her. She did it anyway."

Mandi started to make excuses. "I'm so sorry Nik. I had to."

"Had to? No, you didn't fucking have to! Bitch!"

I tried to get past Jaimes as I was yelling at Mandi. It was like I was someone else. I wasn't in control at all. I was starting to scare myself.

I kept yelling and screaming, "I hate you. I hate you! I'll never forgive you."

What was I going to do now? How could Mandi still stand to even be around me? How could Jaimes still like me? It was all over. I was found out.

Jaimes was still holding my arms. I tried to focus on the feeling of his hands. Breathe. I knew what to do, I worked at a hospital. Of course, I knew what to do. Breathe. Deeply. Slowly.

Once Jaimes saw that I had calmed down, he let me go.

I slid down to the floor in a sobbing mess. "Sorry," I said, getting myself under control. "I'm so sorry. I'm so sorry."

"Please, let me explain," Mandi begged me. "Please."

I nodded. I had given up.

"I was confused. I didn't know why Ava was saying that you were some sort of monster. I was worried that she wouldn't actually stop. I needed to know why. So, I watched the video and all the pieces fell into place. I contacted her and explained that she was wrong about what was on the video. She believed me. Okay? Now, I have to find out who posted your picture on the site. That's what needs to happen right now."

Mandi started to type on her computer.

"How's Shawn?" I asked after a long silence.

"He's fine. Don't worry about him. Worry about yourself," Mandi said. "Ava had a lot of really strange ideas about you and Shawn, but now she knows the truth. She's been helping me get everything scrubbed."

"You're working together now?" I asked. "You and Ava?"

"Yes," Mandi answered flatly.

"What did you tell Ava?" Jaimes asked Mandi. "What did you tell Ava about Nik that could change her mind like that?"

"I don't want you to know, Jaimes. It's private," I said, looking up at him. "Please, quit asking questions."

"You don't want me to ask questions? How about, why did you get so angry at Mandi that I felt the need to protect her from you? Do you realize how messed up that was? What the hell is going on? Why do you always keep me in the dark? That's my picture on the site, too. Don't you think I have a right to know what's going on?"

"Go ahead, tell him," I told Mandi. "What does it matter anyway?"

"I explained to Ava that Nik wasn't describing his relationship with Shawn in the video," Mandi answered. "Nik was describing things that happened to him in high school as well, not just things that happened when he was with Shawn."

"In high school?" Jaimes asked.

"When Nik was in high school, he was invited to a party on a boat and some older men...they um..."

"Stop. Stop," Jaimes interrupted. "He doesn't want me to know. Sorry I pressed."

Jaimes figured that out pretty quickly. Once he knew, I felt lighter somehow. The only thing I couldn't handle was the pity in Jaimes' voice, the distress. I was so sick of being the boy on the boat. I never wanted him to see me that way.

"I'm sorry Nik. I have to find this guy," Mandi said, turning back to her laptop. "I have to stop them before this gets out of hand. They might be a bunch of wannabe punks, but it could get bad if they actually find you. You know what they think."

I could hear Mandi typing while I sat on the floor. Jaimes was sitting on the bed now with his legs beside me. I wrapped my arms around his leg and rested my head on his knee.

Mandi was missing her panel. Instead of talking to a room full of people and giving out autographs, she was trying to track down some random guy that wanted to hurt me.

I was so, so sick of feeling helpless. I looked up at Jaimes. I was wedged between the two beds. "Can you help me up?" I asked.

"Of course," Jaimes said. "Maybe you should lay down for a little bit? I'll get you something to drink."

"There're sodas in the mini fridge," Mandi said.

Jaimes helped me up. I positioned myself on the bed with pillows behind me and my legs over the covers.

Jaimes handed me a soda and sat with me on the bed.

"I'm okay. Really. I'm not a kid anymore," I said as I took the soda. I didn't want him to worry.

"You don't have to tell me anything unless you want to. I'm sorry I asked. I didn't realize."

"Jaimes...the video...some of the things I said, some of the things we did...the way it was edited. It makes me look like I'm a dangerous person. I'm scared. I'm angry. I feel violated," I confessed. "I can't believe I said those things to Mandi. I can't believe I acted that way. I'm losing my mind."

He didn't say anything. He just extended his hand to me.

We both drank our sodas and stared at the wall, in silence, holding hands, for a long time.

After a while, I turned my head toward Jaimes. His eyes were red. I thought I saw his lips tremble. I guess he was still angry at me. He quickly turned his head and wiped his eyes with the back of his wrist the moment he noticed that I was looking.

I didn't understand.

"Got him!" Mandi shouted, raising her head after being buried in her laptop. "You little bastard!"

"How?" I asked.

"Crimes. Very cool crimes, hotel wi-fi, location data! Nah, the little shit posted a screen shot of his entire phone face once – might have wanted to crop out all your phone info, dipshit! And he took the picture when tons of people were taking video – so I found his fucking phone. Damn, troll, you done fucked up!"

"Remind me to never piss off Mandi," Jaimes said.

"Never, ever piss off Mandi."

Child

From Jaimes' point of view.

So much made more sense now. My mind slowly recontextualized what Nik had told me in the past, about being nervous and uncomfortable. I felt like shit. I was so unprepared for what he told me. I tried as hard as I could to keep calm. The last thing he needed was for me to overreact.

Mandi turned her laptop around to show the profile of a social media account. "We need to confirm it's him before we do anything drastic. However, everything points to this guy."

I guess Mandi was being more cautious after I almost beat up Lars. I still felt terrible about that.

I looked closely at the profile that Mandi was holding up. Christ, how old was this kid? His selfies were all of him in T-shirts with cartoon characters on them. What was he doing on sites like that? I mean, I vaguely knew what Mandi was talking about. I knew those places existed.

"He's a child." I finally said out loud.

Nik looked like he was going to vomit. He got up and went to the bathroom. I could hear him splashing water on his face.

"What are we going to do? Talk to his parents?" I asked.

"We need to talk to him directly. He's 14. He lives with his aunt," Mandi said, as she scrolled through his profile. "He plays a lot of Block Builder."

"How is that relevant?" I asked.

"If we know what he plays, we can find him. If we need to, we can put the fear of God into him," Mandi explained. "He's the type of kid that's going to think that I can do things I can't and can't do things I can."

"You are going to threaten him?" I asked, incredulously.

"I hope it doesn't come to that." Mandi sighed deeply. "Look. This kid is going to panic the moment he realizes that we know his username, okay? What I'm worried about is that he really thinks he's doing the right thing. He thinks these pieces of shit online are his friends, and he wants to impress them. I'm worried that if I show my hand, it's going to start a war. I can't let anyone from that site know that I'm involved, if I can help it. So, I'm counting on you."

"Counting on me?" I did not like where this was going.

"Nik is going to be recognized right away," Mandi explained. "So, you need to be the one to talk to him."

"Me?" I was not comfortable with this at all.

"Don't worry," Mandi said. "I have a plan."

"What plan?" I asked, getting a bit raw. "The plan where I go intimidate some messed-up kid? Mandi, that's not a good plan. People make assumptions. Do you understand what I'm saying?"

"Well, I'd ask Traci to do it, but she's not here. Okay? You are our only option."

Mandi was getting upset, but I wasn't going to let her put me on a guilt trip. There had to be a better way to deal with this.

"Why don't we send him a message instead of confronting him in person?" I suggested.

"I need to get ahold of his phone," Mandi insisted. "You're in the picture. For all he knows, you are just a clueless bystander who doesn't want their picture up on the site."

"Look. I'm not doing it. Find another way."

"Don't you think I've already tried everything to get the posts down in the first place? This is serious, Jaimes. Nik could be in danger. Real danger. Ava could be reasoned with. These guys can't. They think he's a danger to kids. Do you get what I'm saying? There is no actual evidence of that, but do you think that's going to stop them?"

"Let's find his aunt. Maybe she's at the con."

"What do you think she's going to think?" Mandi countered. "You think she's going to tell her nephew to quit harassing the poor innocent adult man?"

"You don't think I understand, Mandi? Me? You think I don't understand?"

As we were talking, I slowly realized that I didn't hear Nik. He hadn't come back.

"Shit!" I ran into the bathroom. "He's gone. Nik's gone."

"Fuck!" Mandi shouted. "Damn it. Damn it."

Mandi threw her laptop into her backpack, grabbed her phone, and flew out the door.

I had no idea how Mandi knew where to go. I just followed her. Mandi was trying to run through hallways full of people in weird outfits. I was barely keeping up. It was like an obstacle course of foam weapons, feathers, and puppy-dog tails.

"Hey, Mandi, you're missing your panel," someone shouted.

"She'll be late!" I yelled back.

We finally got to E-Game Room A. Mandi was frantically looking around. We looked through E-Game Room B as well. We didn't find either Nik or the kid.

"We have to find him." Mandi was frantic.

"Where are you?" I texted Nik. "We're worried."

Surrender

From Nik's point of view.

He wasn't hard to find. He played a lot of Block Builder after all. It wasn't difficult to confirm it was him, because he reacted the moment that he saw me walk into the room. I was a bit worried he would run before I got a chance to talk, but instead, he pretended like he didn't notice me. I was a monster, after all.

"Here," I said, holding out a piece of paper I stole from the sign-up desk, and wrote on with a complimentary hotel pen. "Is this what you want?"

He turned around from his monitor, shocked that I was actually talking to him. I wasn't supposed to know who he was. Heck, I wasn't supposed to be a real person.

"Take it," I insisted.

His curiosity must have gotten the better of him. He took the paper out of my hand.

"What's this?" he asked, reading it, but acting like the words didn't make sense.

"That's my name, my phone number, and my address. That's where I work. I'm a phlebotomist. That's a fancy word for the guy that sticks needles in people at the hospital."

"What the hell?"

"It's an act of good faith," I explained. "Please, can we talk?"

"I'm not going anywhere with you."

This could all go so wrong. I had to choose my words very carefully. "I only want to talk. A public place, of course. How about the hotel restaurant or the lobby?"

He took out his phone and took a picture of the paper.

"The lobby," he said.

He held up his phone so I could see it. He had placed the picture of my information within an unsent post on the thread that was targeting me. "You try anything, and I'll send this and then you're fucked. Got it?"

"Got it."

I could tell he liked bossing me around. I gave him the information so he would feel in control.

We found a place to sit in the lobby that was out of the way, but easily visible to the larger room full of people. We seated ourselves opposite each other. There was a coffee table between us.

"Are you going to try to bribe me?" the kid asked. "What's your life worth to you?" He picked up his phone and shook it in front of me, like he was brandishing a weapon. He was having a blast. "You going to start to beg now?"

"Yes," I said matter-of-factly. "Aren't you going to check the information?"

"Huh?" he asked.

"Aren't you going to make sure that I'm not lying to you?"

He used his phone for a minute until turning it around to show it to me. "That's you, huh?" He pointed at a picture of me on a social media account.

"Yes, that's me. Nicholas."

"How did you find me?" he asked.

"I noticed when you took the picture," I lied. "So, when I saw it online, I knew it was you."

He didn't seem convinced, but it was more believable than me having an elite hacker friend who looked through various posted videos of her playing Pong in order to find someone with a particular brand of phone in the same room where the picture was taken.

"Anyway, start begging," he said.

"I want you to take a picture of me. Just me. I want you to take down the old picture and replace it with a picture of only me, with no one else. Could you do that for me please?"

"What?" he seemed surprised.

My phone rang.

"Who's that?" he asked.

"Probably someone asking about the extended warranty on my car," I said, putting the phone back in my pocket. "All I want you to do is replace the picture you put up with a picture of only me, without my friend in it. I know we are in the lobby, but make sure nobody else is in it. Make sure nobody is in the picture except for me. Please."

"Why? Why should I?"

"You're after me, right? Just me. Leave my friend out of it. You do that, and I'll surrender."

"Surrender?"

"I'll give up. You just leave my friend out of it," I repeated.

The blank stare he gave me was precious. I was no fun now, was I?

"What did you want to happen to me? Lose my job? Get beat up? Public humiliation?" I asked. "Give it some thought. Take your time."

"You're fucked in the head."

"Yes, I am. Just not in the way you think."

"What?"

"Nothing."

"Are you around kids at the hospital?" he asked.

"Yes," I answered. "Working with kids, especially small children, is more difficult. I'm really good at my job, so they always put me in the children's area of the hospital. Their veins are smaller, so it's harder to get a good stick. Sometimes they bring me in after someone else has already messed up all the easier sites and I have to try to use a more difficult site when the kid is already distressed. If I fail, they have to put in a different kind of access point that has a higher risk of complications. So, it's important that I don't fail."

"I didn't ask for your life story. You shouldn't be around kids. You'll give them a disease."

"I'm not any more likely to have a disease than anyone else," I said.

"Sure, pervert."

"I follow strict hygiene protocols. I wear gloves, and everything I work with is sterilized."

"Ever cop a feel?"

"No. Of course not."

"Ever want to?"

"No. I'm not like that," I said, raising my voice slightly despite my best efforts. "You're wrong about me."

"I don't believe you. Quit your job."

"Fine. Just keep my friend out of this."

"So, all I have to do, is delete my post, take a new picture, and you'll quit your job?"

"Yes, and you know where I work, so you can make sure I do it."

"This is too easy," he said, picking up his phone, unlocking it, and holding it up toward me to take a picture.

I took his phone and ran as fast as I could.

"You, fucking lying piece of shit..." he yelled and ran after me. Fortunately, the lobby was crowded enough that he had a hard time following me.

I had to find Mandi. I knew she would come if I opened up a phone line and told her where I was. It took her long enough to try to call me. She and Jaimes texted me like 20 times.

I frantically looked for Mandi in the crowd while making sure the phone didn't lock back up.

"Give me back my phone!" the kid shouted as he ran after me. "I know everything about you. I will destroy you! You asshole pervert! That guy took my phone!"

The crowd started noticing us. I became very aware that the crowd was likely to turn against me. I needed to find Mandi before that happened.

"Give it to me!" I heard Mandi whisper-shout before I even realized she was right beside me.

I handed the phone off as quickly as I could. Mandi took it and disappeared right before the crowd surrounded us.

I turned around and the kid was immediately in my face. I was standing there, trapped, with this kid screaming at me.

"He took my phone!" the kid yelled. "This pervert took my phone!"

What was I supposed to do? What was I supposed to say? I had to take whatever he threw at me. I got to see people at their worst at work. In a way, this was nothing.

Some larger guys decided to separate us by putting their arms between us. The crowd was also making sure I couldn't leave.

I stayed cool.

The kid kept coming at me. "Just wait! Just wait! I'll get you fired. I'll get you arrested. I'll plaster your face everywhere. I'll get you killed. You piece of shit faggot!"

The whole place got really quiet the moment he said 'faggot'. Jaimes pulled me back and got in front of me, so that he was squarely between me and the kid. He started to stare down anyone who looked like they were going to be the hero that saved some kid from a phone-stealing pervert.

It was incredibly tense until Mandi, the local celebrity, calmly walked up to the kid and handed him his phone back. "Hey, kid, here's your phone."

"Mandi?" The kid's eyes got wide. He obviously knew who she was. "Why are you here? Why did you have my phone?"

"You should have done your homework," Mandi said. "Do better."

The kid was frantic. He scrambled to open his phone and check it. He quickly went from being surprised that Mandi had his phone to being enraged. "Bitch! Dyke bitch!"

"Mandi, what did you do?" I asked.

"I started a war," she answered.

War

From Jaimes' point of view.

I was pissed. I was scared to death. We couldn't find Nik anywhere and he wasn't answering our texts. My imagination was going wild. What if the kid had friends and beat the shit out of Nik? Hell, what if they kidnapped him? Who knows what these hypothetically completely unreasonable people were capable of?

Mandi finally, actually called him, and what was he doing? He was offering to quit his job so that I wasn't in the fucking picture. Why couldn't he have stuck around so that we could make a plan?

He figured out a way to tell us that he was in the lobby. We got down there just in time for Mandi to grab the kid's phone away from Nik. The thing was unlocked, so Mandi disappeared in the crowd and went to work.

This kid was getting in Nik's face and threatening him and calling him a pervert. I'm thinking, holy shit, the crowd was going to think Nik did something to this kid. This was bad.

Then I heard that word.

I wasn't going to let Nik take that shit from anyone. I got between the two of them. If the kid was older, I would have laid him out, but he wasn't. He was a child.

So, I found myself staring down this kid and all these people who were thinking Nik needed a beating. I hated it. This was exactly what I wanted to avoid. I was so angry that it came to this, but what else was I going to do?

Mandi kept saying she couldn't be the one to talk to the kid, and then she walked up to him and gave him back his phone like it was no big deal. What the fucking hell?

But then I realized that the moment she showed up, we were no longer in trouble. Everyone knew her. The crowd knew her. They trusted her to pick the right side. She was doing what she needed to do to protect us.

"I can't get into my account! You bitch!" the kid yelled.

When the convention staff arrived, one of them immediately took Mandi aside to ask her what was going on. I heard murmurs of other people giving testimony about what happened as well.

The entire time, some big guys were keeping the kid from attacking us by holding up their arms.

"Sorry about this," I heard Mandi say. "He took a picture of my friend without asking. He was verbally abusive. He was saying all sorts of weird things. My friend took the phone to delete the picture and then I took the phone to teach the kid a lesson. I'm sorry I put you in a difficult position."

One of the staff came up to us. Nik seemed nervous and distracted.

"Why did he take a picture of you?" the woman asked.

Nik froze up.

"Obviously, that kid has a problem with gay people," I said. "He took the picture to harass us."

Eventually, they decided to kick the kid out of the convention. He was still shouting as he was being escorted out the door. "Fuck you, dyke bitch! Fuck you, pervert! Fuck you, faggot!"

If I heard right, he was banned for life. Play stupid games, win stupid prizes, I guess.

Once the staff walked away from the area, I took Nik's hand and led him back to our room. He was so quiet. He walked into the room, took off his shoes, and sat down on the bed without saying a word.

"Why? Why did you do that?" I asked, still standing near the door. "You should have waited until we had a plan. You should have told us what you were doing."

"Would you have let me do what I did?" Nik asked.

"I wasn't thrilled about you giving yourself up like that."

"So you know, he never got my real information. I wasn't going to quit my job. I gave him a fake name that brought up a sock account with a picture of me. Mandi helped me set up some fake accounts to confuse them."

"That's not the point," I said.

"Then, what's the point?"

"We should have discussed it. I was worried about you. I was worried about myself. What do you think would have happened if fists started flying, huh? Mandi had to show up and smooth it all over. We should have worked as a team."

"I didn't ask for your help!" Nik suddenly shouted at me.

"But you obviously needed it. What? You opened up a phone line and told us where you were for shits and giggles? You didn't ask for our help? Bullshit."

He knew I was right.

"Do you know what it's like to constantly need saving? Do you?" he asked.

"What? What are you talking about?"

"I heard what Mandi was asking you to do. You didn't want to do it, so I did. I wanted to save myself for once. And I knew, I knew you two would try to talk me out of it. And why? Because you both see me as the one who needs to be protected. I hate it. I'm tired of it."

"You don't want to be protected? Too bad. Try and stop me."

"Dick."

"Please, Nik, get your head out of your own ass. If I needed help, you would help me, right?"

"Of course."

"Okay then. What's the fucking problem? Stop saying you don't want pity and then throwing a goddamn pity party. Okay?"

"A what?"

"You heard me."

I wasn't in the mood to deal with his crap. "Asshole! I just...I mean..."

Nik was obviously upset. I took a deep breath. I sat down next to him on the bed but kept my distance.

"Just say it, for Christ's sake," I said calmly.

He was still quiet for a while, but he seemed to be collecting his thoughts. I wondered if I was pushing too hard.

"You know that this mess is dragging up all sorts of crap that I don't want to think about, right? I didn't want you to find out what was going on at all. You think of me differently now. Of course, you do. I didn't want you to think of me the same way Mandi does. Now, it's too late."

I almost told him that he was wrong, and that I didn't think of him differently at all. I stayed quiet because I knew he would accuse me of lying. I wasn't even sure if it would be a lie or not.

"She tried to warn me, you know. Why would some college kids invite a high schooler to a party on a yacht? Right? I told her not to worry so much.

I went anyway. I don't have a clear memory of what happened. I blacked out and when I woke up, I was hurt. Mandi assumed that horrible things happened to me.

"She thought I was in denial. Now she knows that I didn't tell her everything I remembered. I told Lars stuff that I never told anyone before, even Mandi. I didn't tell her because she was already beating herself up. She blamed herself for not stopping me from going.

"She's never forgiven herself for that. Like what? Does she think that she should have locked me up or something? It was my decision, not hers. Then, she does the one thing I told her not to do and invades my privacy. I would rather the entire world know and not her. Does what I want mean nothing to her at all?"

I kept quiet. He needed to vent. Maybe saying nothing was the right thing to do.

"Listening to you two talking and trying to come up with a plan to deal with something that had everything to do with me, I didn't like it. I needed to be the one to deal with my own fucking problems for once, you know. So, I left, and I did something on my own. But I screwed it up for you two anyway, didn't I?"

"I didn't say that."

"But it's the truth."

"Who knows? Our well-thought-out plan could have sucked ass. Maybe we'd all be in jail right now," I said as straight-faced as I could.

Nik looked at me funny, like he was trying to figure out if I was being sarcastic or not. Then he caught on.

"It's possible," he said, his eye's lighting up slightly. "If it wasn't for me, we would have all been arrested."

"Good thing you saved us all."

He smiled. I was really glad to get a smile out of him.

Then, he shifted his body and put his head in my lap. I was confused. It was sudden. He wrapped his arms around my waist. Since when was that something we did? That was not something friends did.

What was going on?

My instinct was to run my hand through his hair. I wanted to kiss him on the top of his head. I knew that I shouldn't. I couldn't. I knew he didn't think of me that way. I tried not to think about it too much.

"I envy you and Mandi," I said. "You are such close friends. I don't have any friends from high school."

"You don't?" Nik asked. "I thought that you'd be popular."

"I was, but I wasn't myself." It was only fair that Nik knew more about me. I knew all these personal things about him. It was about time he realized my life wasn't perfect. "I was someone else."

"In the closet?" Nik asked.

"Deeply in the closet. I was so worried about being found out that I put up a front. I was into sports. I was sort of an asshole. I dated girls. I wasn't even open about my art. I kept all my drawing books under my bed."

"Sounds terrible. My first girlfriend outed me. She walked in on me...um.... you know...to pictures of boys in a magazine."

"She reacted poorly huh?" I knew the answer to that question.

"Yes, she did. She told everyone I was gay and was using her. It was great," he explained sarcastically.

"Well, that's what I was actually doing. I knew it too. I never did anything really terrible, but I would act like a jerk to my girlfriends in front of the guys, you know. I wanted to prove how manly I was."

"That sounds miserable," Nik said. "For everyone."

"It was. I was a bully. Pure and simple. I have a lot to feel guilty about," I admitted. "That's why I didn't want to be the one to confront that kid."

"You changed when you got out of the house, didn't you?"

"I'd like to think so."

"Was it your parents?" Nik asked.

"In a way." Christ, was it that obvious? "I could blame it on my dad, but I did the things I did. It's on me."

"I'm glad you were able to get out and be on your own."

"Me too. In high school I wasn't myself at all. So..." I paused. I wondered if I should really say it. "I never had close friends. Not really."

"Well, you do now," Nik said, moving his hand along my waist and pressing against me while his head was still on my lap.

He knew I liked him. Part of me wanted to tell him to get off me and cuss him out. Part of me wanted to comfort him. Part of me wanted to rub my crotch against his face.

This was hell. This was pure hell.

One more night. I can make it one more night. Then we'll be back to our apartment, back to our separate rooms, and back to normal. Hopefully, Nik could finally put this all behind him and Mandi could continue to do whatever the hell she was doing.

Homework

From Nik's point of view.

I wasn't even really thinking. I wanted to be close to him, so I rested my head on his lap. It felt wonderful. We were talking, in the room, all alone. It was nice. It made me feel safe.

I wondered what it would have been like if we met during high school. Would we have hated one another? Would we have had a fling? Was he really the type of guy who would make out with me in the bathroom and then bash me in front of his friends? Would he dare?

I was the scary kid. He was the jock. I wondered how that would have gone down. Mandi and the crew probably would have kicked his ass. Purple and Blue Brigade forever.

It was difficult to accept that he was ever like that. That's not the way he was now. Not at all. I wasn't the same, either. Could someone like him and someone like me be something other than friends?

Being close to him felt so good. I held him closer.

He tensed up like he was uncomfortable. Was I annoying him? What was I thinking? He was Jaimes, and I was Nik. He was the person he was, and I was me.

I woke up to reality again and sat up.

"I'm really worried about that kid," I said. "He strikes me as someone who isn't going to let it go. I'm actually a bit more worried now than I was before."

I was lying. I was terrified, not just worried. That kid is going to want to hurt us. Really hurt us. He's going to blame us for getting him kicked out of the con. He's going to feel humiliated and angry. Kids like that...they are dangerous. I should know.

I checked my phone. I couldn't help but be curious about what was happening on the troll site.

"Oh, my goodness, she really did start a war," I said.

"What do you mean?" Jaimes asked.

"She deleted the picture from the site and then posted a message using his account. It looks like she took it over." I started reading, "FHW hacked your ass. Purple and Blue Brigade. Do your homework bitches. FBI in the house. NPC rebellion."

"What the hell does that mean?"

"FHW stands for flying horse warrior. NPC means nonplayer character. I think they use 'NPC' to refer to their targets."

I kept looking through the site.

"It looks like that kid made a new account and posted the information I gave him. They figured out it was fake. I think..." I read a few more posts. "They are imploding."

"That sounds awesome."

"It sounds scary."

"Take the win," Jaimes insisted.

"That dox is bullshit, casual dickhead," I read. "Suck your own cock for wasting my time. Put a spoon over your left nut, so I know it's you. Pics or it didn't happen. Do it or I'll brick your ass."

Just then, Jaimes got a notification.

"Mandi wants to go eat with us," he said after reading her text.

I smiled and put my phone down.

"Let's have a nice meal," I suggested. "It'll make me feel better. I'll pay."

"You'll pay? Steak and lobster for me."

Walking through the hotel was nerve-racking. I was nervous before, knowing that people were out there who had seen the video or seen the picture of me on the couch. Now, my skin crawled. I wasn't sure if I was being paranoid, but it felt like everyone was giving us looks. I wasn't sure if I imagined it, but I thought I could hear voices from all around me talking about us.

Jaimes didn't seem to notice, so maybe it was all in my head.

"Nik, are you okay?" Jaimes asked.

I almost shook my head, but instead I nodded. "I'll be fine."

I noticed then that Jaimes was scanning the crowd. He was walking very close to me. I looked around again. Everyone was minding their own business. I kept telling myself that. I never thought that convincing myself that the world didn't care about me would be so comforting.

Time

From Jaimes' point of view.

"Seriously, you're going to get the lobster?" Nik asked me.

"You thought I was joking?"

"Yes, I thought you were joking," Nik said. "But get it anyway."

"Yes! I'll have the surf and turf."

"Really? Get anything we want?" Mandi asked.

"Yes, my treat," Nik said, smiling. He seemed so happy. I was worried that he was putting on a show, but I also knew he was a shitty actor. Every smile on that man's face was genuine. I think he simply really enjoyed doing something nice for us.

"Is there any news about that kid?" I asked Mandi after we all ordered.

"He got kicked out for life. A few of his friends in the game room got on my case, blaming me for everything. I smoothed things over. I encouraged them to go check on him. You know, calm him down. Try not to worry too much."

"Thanks for dealing with all of that," Nik said. "I'm still a little shaken up."

"I'm still mad at you for not cluing us in on your plan," Mandi said.

"Jaimes got on my case enough," Nik complained. "You don't have to scold me, too."

"Why didn't you tell us what was going on?" she pressed.

"Just because," Nik said with his head down.

"It wasn't a bad plan," Mandi said. "I just wish you told us."

"My bad," Nik said.

"You got another panel tomorrow?" I asked Mandi, changing the subject.

"Oh yeah. It's about hackers in fiction. That's always fun. The moderators find movie and TV clips of hackers and we live-react to them."

"Sounds like fun," I said, sincerely.

"It's always a blast. The other two on the panel are hilarious, too. They are always saying that if it were realistic, it would be boring. I tell them that if things were realistic that it would be a comedy. One of the biggest security breaches in history happened because someone wrote their government password on a whiteboard, and they had a press interview in the same room," Mandi burst out laughing. "Funniest shit."

"Seriously?" I asked, laughing and wondering if she was pulling my leg.

Eventually, they brought our food out. It looked amazing, and the bill was going to be ridiculous. Nik's good mood didn't last long. He started poking at his beef tips and mashed potatoes and kept looking over at Mandi.

"Mandi," Nik finally said. "Why aren't you moving with Traci?"

Her face went pale. "Nik. Please."

"I'm sorry. I'm worried that you might be staying because of me. I mean, it's not like I think I'm that important. But, even if it factored in just a little bit, I don't want to be the reason. I can take care of myself, you know."

"Nik. Of course, you factored in, but that's not the reason. We'd been avoiding having the talk for a long time," Mandi said, as if we were supposed to know what she was referring to. "When staying together means changing your life, you have the talk."

"The talk?" Nik asked.

"About the future. About family. About kids. Those things. And about risk. After grad school, she wants to get a job. She wants to settle down. She wants to start a family. She started asking me questions that I wish she never asked. I told her the truth."

"What are you talking about?" Nik asked.

Mandi looked around, and she lowered her voice. "She asked me if I ever did anything that could result in serious time. I have."

"Serious time...in prison?" I asked, lowering my voice as well.

"Yeah. I've also angered dangerous people. After talking to Traci, I made a decision to deal with what I've done. But that's why I'm not going with her. She didn't want that type of thing in her life."

I was speechless. Mandi was a security specialist. I always thought of her hacker persona as a lark, just some tricks and pranks she knew how to pull. You know, for fun. I thought her hack of Lars' keyboard was the most serious crime she had committed, and the internet trolls were the scariest people she had ever pissed off. What the hell was she into?

"Was that the reason you didn't want to be the one to talk to that kid?" I asked.

"Yes, in a way. But don't worry about me. I'm finally taking credit. It actually feels good."

"Are you," Nik lowered his voice even more, "going to prison?"

"No," Mandi said. "Don't be silly. I'm too smart for that." She got out her phone, flipped around to find something, and turned the phone around for us to see. "But nobody is going to be bothering you again."

There was a picture of the stuffed animal we bought her. It was posted on the troll site. "You have angered FHW. Do your homework," was written above it.

She scrolled down a bit to show a different post. "I know who FHW is. We're fucked. Abort. Abort."

Mandi grinned. "Told you he was the kind of kid that would think I could do things I couldn't do."

"I'll try not to worry," Nik said. "I just don't want them to go after you."

"I know what I'm doing," Mandi assured him. "Trust me."

"Okay."

Mandi was such a liar. She was trying not to look nervous, but she was. Nik didn't seem to pick up on it. She was being way too serious for this to boil down to using her clout as Mandi the Pong Queen to intimidate some trolls.

The rest of the meal was pleasant. We got expensive desserts as well. We were determined to bankrupt poor Nik. I think this was his way of apologizing to us for some of the things he said. I wasn't complaining.

Nik and I went back to our room afterward. He told me that normally he would hang out in the game room or the fairy room, but he wanted to rest.

I stayed with him. Frankly, I didn't think he should be alone.

When he told me about what happened to him in high school, I did my best to listen and not react too much. But to be honest, I wanted a good cry. It was too awful to think about.

Fuck.

Fuck life.

I wanted to go back in time and start busting heads. What really got to me, what I knew was going to haunt me, is that Mandi told him not to go. She knew something was wrong.

Some college boys invited him to a party on a boat, Mandi knew that sounded like a bad scene. He didn't listen. He told her not to worry so much. Nik told Mandi not to worry so much. That wasn't the Nik I knew. There's a special place in hell for those guys. They took a trusting boy and turned him into a nervous wreck.

I hope they burn. I hope they burn in hell forever.

"I'm going to take a shower and go to bed," Nik said. "Or maybe go to one of the suites. Some of them are showing movies and stuff. I might be up for that, if you are."

"That actually sounds nice," I said. "Or we could watch a movie in the room."

"But we could do that any time," Nik said, taking off his shirt. "We're at con."

"Didn't you take a shower this morning?" I asked.

"This is a therapeutic shower," Nik said. "I also didn't have a chance to shower after, you know."

"Fun with femboy and kitty," I laughed.

"If only the rest of my day were that enjoyable," Nik said. "I'll be out in a little bit." He took off his pants and shirt and headed into the bathroom.

I got on my phone and looked up the troll site. I wanted to know how the whole meltdown was progressing.

"Who is FHW?" I started reading.

So, this was the ass-end of the internet? Holy shit they sure tried hard to be offensive. Okay, a bunch of talk about whether they should out FHW.

"This is war, everything is on the table."

"No dox no frocks."

What the hell did that mean?

"FHW. Purple and Blue Brigade. Operation ShittyBoat. FBI in the house. Real Estate Capitalist gets caught stealing. Pays the price in the end. No mercy if you don't do your homework."

Was that Mandi?

I kept reading the other posts.

"Found it. Grade my homework teacher. Fuck my ass. Taking your dick would be an honor."

Good lord, these guys needed to get laid.

"Confirmed. Operation ShittyBoat."

There was a picture of some guy getting arrested and a screen shot from a news article. He was under investigation for embezzlement. His computers were seized. Illegal pornographic images were found on his hard drive. He claimed he was the victim of a hacker that locked him out of his computer and demanded money to gain access.

The news article got a huge response.

"Ransomware? OG Ransomware? Shit. We're fucked. Who is this guy?"

"Whoever they are. They are a legend."

"I told you. I know who FHW is. She's some dyke bitch named Mandi. I keep telling you, her faggot age-play pervert boyfriend took my phone."

"Shut up noob. I don't give a shit about your phone. FHW is the real deal. Snitches get stitches."

Holy shit, Mandi. Cool crimes. Seriously cool crimes.

Nik came out of the bathroom wearing a towel and drying his hair. "What's up?" he asked, picking up on my surprised face.

"I hate to bring it up, but did you ever find out what happened to the guy who owned the boat?" I asked.

"What happened to him? I assume he's still living it up with a bunch of kept boys. Hopefully sober adults who actually want to be there," Nik said. "Rich guys like him get away with murder."

"He's in prison," I said. "Embezzlement. Mandi put him there. Mandi helped get him arrested."

The look on Nik's face was priceless. Shock. Joy. Concern. Confusion.

"How?" he asked.

"I guess she locked his computers so that he couldn't get rid of evidence. She even claims to have extorted money from him. That's what she must have meant when she said she was going to take credit. She posted the information on the troll site. They seem really impressed."

"How long ago did this happen?"

I looked back at the news article clip. "Seven years ago."

"Seven years ago! She was doing stuff like that back then?" Nik looked guilty, like he had done something horribly wrong. "For me."

"It looks like it," I confirmed.

Nik was blinking like something was in his eye. He'd been through enough shit today, maybe I should have kept my mouth shut.

"Did you want to go watch movies in one of the suites?" I asked.

"What? Movies?" Nik thought for a moment and then, suddenly, he had a huge smile on his face and his eyes were bright. "Yes. Let's watch movies."

Nik quickly got his clothes on.

"He's in prison," Nik muttered under his breath. "He's in prison."

Escape

From Nik's point of view.

We found some old cartoons to watch in a room full of pillows and stuffed animals. Thankfully, it didn't seem like anyone recognized me as the supposed pervert who took that kid's phone.

"This is so ridiculous," Jaimes said.

I hit him with a pillow.

"Pillow fight!" some girl dressed as one of the characters yelled. About five pillows descended on Jaimes and me.

"Ridiculous," Jaimes said with a smile as he threw the pillows off of us.

I tried to focus on the TV screen. I had watched this show before when I was a kid, but it was new to Jaimes. I was sure he was completely confused.

"The three main characters are in a love triangle," I tried to explain. "But the protagonist is so focused on martial arts that he doesn't even realize it. His good friend becomes his enemy because he's obsessed with power and wanting to impress the girl."

"They're all 12," Jaimes said.

"And they're 12."

"You'd think that the adults would be doing the fighting," Jaimes said. "Where are these kids' parents?"

"It's just a cartoon," I said soberly.

That was a really good question, Jaimes. That was a question I didn't want to think about. Why did Mandi have to protect me? When did she get to be a kid? Who was protecting her? Where were these kids' parents?

"Are you okay, Nik?" Jaimes asked.

"It's been a really long day."

I tried to get comfortable and watch the show. I sank into a sea of pillows.

"Hey sleepy head," Jaimes said. "Nik." He sang out like he was calling for me. "Nik."

I woke up. "Oh gosh, did I fall asleep?"

"Yeah. They're shutting down the suite for the night," Jaimes explained. "I had to stop them from drawing on your face."

"Vultures!" I gave the eye to all the guilty potential face drawers.

I got up from the field of pillows and we left.

"Sorry I fell asleep," I told Jaimes.

"It's fine."

I looked at my phone. It was almost midnight.

"The fairy room is about to turn into an orgy. I'll see you in the morning," I laughed.

"Wait, you're going to the fairy room?" Jaimes asked, surprised. "Going to find cat-girl and winged boy?"

"No. I assumed you'd go and pick someone up," I said, heading for our hotel room. "I'll be sleeping. You can use the shower if you need to use our room. I don't mind."

I thought I was being polite. I mean, that was his deal. I didn't want to get in his way. I didn't want to be a bother.

"Is that what you think of me?" Jaimes asked pointedly, getting in front of me and staring me in the face.

"Why are you mad?" I asked, confused to the point of shock. "I mean, you used to get upset that I got annoyed about it. Now, you are upset that I'm not annoyed about it. Make up your mind."

"Are you trying to tell me you want to be alone? Just tell me. I'll give you space," Jaimes said.

Why was he being weird now? I didn't know what to say.

"Do you want to be alone?" he asked again.

I remembered the night when he asked me the same question. It was the night he crawled into my bed and held me while I slept. What was I going to say?

"Nik?" Jaimes asked, waving his hand in front of my face to see if I was listening. "Why are you ignoring me?"

I started to walk past him toward our room. What was I doing? I was such a coward.

"Nik?" He turned around, calling after me. "I guess I'll take that as a yes. You want to be alone. See you around."

He was angry.

I kept walking. I wanted to scream. I wanted to turn around. I wanted to run to him. That's what I wanted. That's not what I did. I walked away.

When I got to our room, I took off my shoes and pants and crawled into bed wearing my boxers and T-shirt.

Sleep. Sleep was escape. I laid there staring at the ceiling.

Oh gosh, I had to get up in time for Mandi's panel. I took my phone from the nightstand and set an alarm. I considered calling Jaimes to apologize, but I didn't. I put my phone back on the nightstand and closed my eyes.

I could not fall asleep. I tried. I wanted to fall asleep badly, but I couldn't.

Damn it. "Fine, I guess my body won't rest." I got up and put on my pants and shoes. I put my phone in my pocket and I left the room.

It was the last night of the con. All the really big events were done. The table-toppers and the e-gamers were slowing down their epic marathon sessions, except for the hardcore crew running on energy drinks and potato chips. Even the suites were slowing down, except for the partiers.

I walked around randomly, until I heard Jaimes.

"They are totally fucking! There is no way those two men are just friends. Fucking censors not letting men fuck. That, that right there was a blow job reference. He wants the other guy's dick in his mouth. Very subtle!"

He was drunk. How long was I lying in bed? I looked at my phone. It was almost two in the morning.

I walked toward his voice. Oh no, he was in the Boy Love room, which was, of course, usually full of straight girls. I found him sitting on the couch all alone watching some costume drama on their TV. He had a drink in his hand. The room hosts were cleaning up.

"We're closing up," one of them said. "Is there someone we can call?"

"I want to see what happens," Jaimes said. "How much is left?"

"There are 60 episodes," she answered.

"Fuck!" Jaimes exclaimed. "Sixty!? Sixty episodes of being best friends!"

"I'll write down the name of it for you, you can find it yourself, okay?" she suggested.

"Jaimes, time to go back to our room," I told him.

The hosts looked relieved that someone had come to collect him.

"Leave a big tip and then let's go."

"Here," Jaimes threw me his wallet without taking his eyes off the screen. I had to pick it off the floor. I took out a large bill and stuffed it in their tip cup. I put his wallet in my pocket.

"We need to go, Jaimes. Jaimes, you're drunk and you're being rude."

I tried to take his hand to lead him away.

"I'm being rude?"

"They are trying to close up," I said. "Come back to our room with me."

"Why are you here?"

"I couldn't sleep. Now, come on. This isn't like you. I don't know how to deal with you when you're drunk."

I took the drink out of his hand and set it on a table.

"Hey, that's mine," Jaimes said, reaching after it.

How damn drunk was he? If he passed out, what the heck was I going to do?

"Jaimes," I said louder. "Get up and follow me. We're going to our room, and you're going to sleep."

"But you don't want me there," he said, starting to cry. "You don't want me."

Drunk asshole. "Get up!" I yelled, losing my patience.

He complied. It's not like I hadn't dealt with a few drunks at work. Tell them what to do, and sometimes they just do it.

I led him out. The hosts thanked me.

He was so heavy. He was so loud. I hated this so much. I struggled to move us down the hallway. He was so much bigger than me.

To get into our room I had to prop him up against the wall while I opened the door. I somehow got him into the room and dropped him on the bed. I took off his shoes.

He was on top of the covers. Damn it. What a bother. I tried to pull the covers out from under him. It was awkward and ridiculous. He was barely conscious and thought this was funny.

I somehow got him in bed properly.

I took off my shoes and crawled into bed as well, staying as far away from him as I could.

"You better not touch me. I'll punch you in the face," I whispered under my breath. "I swear, if you touch me, I'll hurt you."

I had to calm down. I had to sleep.

Sleep was escape.

Fire

From Jaimes' point of view.

I woke up to Nik's alarm going off. I opened my eyes just in time to see him grab his phone and throw it across the room. The alarm didn't actually stop. It was just coming from the other side of the room now.

"Shut up!" Nik yelled. "Let me sleep."

I had a hangover and Nik was yelling. I got up and found his phone. I turned the alarm off.

"Why did you set an alarm?" I asked.

"So, I could go see Mandi's panel," he answered me, not moving from his spot. "I might just sleep. I feel awful."

"Did you get drunk last night, too?" I asked. I didn't think he did. I vaguely remembered him getting me out of the Boy Love room. False advertising if you asked me.

"No," he answered tersely.

"Are you sick?" I asked.

"No."

Dear God. Did I say something terrible I didn't remember? Nik seemed pissed.

"Are you mad at me?"

"Yes."

Jesus Christ. I didn't get handsy or something, did I? Holy shit.

"What did I do?"

"I don't know," he said sarcastically. "After scolding me for getting drunk and saying you were worried about me, you went and did the same damn thing. What? Are you invincible? You get to do those things and I don't?"

"Please, tell me what I did that upset you. I don't remember."

"As far as I know, all you did was watch some show while very loudly shipping the main characters."

Shipping? Whatever. Could he tell me already? I was trying very hard not to lose my temper.

"Tell me why you're so angry."

"No reason. I just had to drag your sorry ass up to the room and all you could say was, 'I love you, man. Did I ever tell you how much I love you, man? I love you.' You know, like every drunk bastard talks."

Why? Why was he so upset? This whole weekend was a fucking nightmare.

"Calm down. Okay? I'm sorry. You didn't seem to want me around, so I went somewhere else. Their drinks were sweet. I guess I didn't realize how strong they were. I mean, thanks for taking me back to the room, but what is up with you?"

"Figure it out, dipshit!" Nik yelled at me as he got up, went into the bathroom, and slammed the door.

Jesus fucking Christ. Oversensitive little diva. I threw my duffle bag on the bed and started packing my stuff. I knew he was going through some serious shit, but I didn't have to take that crap. I was losing my patience. We had to get out of the room anyway. This was the last day.

Once Mandi's panel was over, I was going to go home. Just a few more hours, and we'd be back in the apartment, and we could put this behind us. Right?

Who was I kidding? Things wouldn't go back to normal, would they?

This was bullshit.

Fucking bullshit.

Nik came out of the bathroom with a toothbrush in his mouth. He probably heard me throwing stuff around.

"You don't get to do that, you know," I said the moment I saw him show his face. "You don't get to call me names and be angry and not explain to me why. I know you've had a really shitty stressful couple of days, but you don't get to do that to me."

He took the toothbrush out of his mouth. He put his finger up like he was telling me to wait a second and went back into the bathroom to rinse and spit the toothpaste out. He came back and wouldn't even look up at me.

"You're right. You didn't deserve that. I shouldn't be taking things out on you. I'm sorry. Please forgive me."

"When you walked away from me last night, that was bullshit, too."

I needed to clear the air.

"I know. Please forgive me."

I could tell he was emotionally spent. He kept telling me he didn't want my pity or to be treated like a kid. I didn't know how to help him. It was awful. I left my bag sitting on the bed and walked over to him.

We looked each other in the eye.

I could see his sincerity.

"Of course, I forgive you."

He practically grabbed me. He wrapped his arms around me, and he held me tight. I guess he just needed a goddamn hug. Jesus Christ.

We held each other for a long time, way past that unspoken socially acceptable time limit for good friends. I put my hand through his hair and pressed his head against my chest.

"Are you going to be alright?" I asked.

"No," he said. "Not today."

"I'll buy you another bag of those purple jelly things you like. Then will you be alright?"

He laughed and let me go.

"It wouldn't hurt," he said. "I guess we need to pack and check out, huh?"

"Yes, we do," I said. "I also really have to pee, and you're standing in front of the bathroom."

He laughed again and stepped aside with his hand out like a gentleman letting a lady through the door first.

When I made him smile and laugh, it made me so happy. Seeing him upset and angry took a lot out of me. I was glad the weekend was almost over.

We packed up and checked out.

We bought some coffee and went to Mandi's panel. We sat up front. Mandi sat at a table with two guys, a bear and a seal.

A bear and a seal? Where was my head at?

The three of them were introduced. The bear was a technology podcaster, the seal was a science fiction author. Mandi was introduced as the one and only "Pong Queen" and a cybersecurity specialist.

They showed a clip of a show where the hacker character was surrounded by a dozen computer screens, typing away as if fighting a firewall in real time.

Mandi was in tears laughing. She asked for the clip to be paused and pointed at the picture.

"There is no computer." Mandi said, in stitches. "Fourteen monitors and no computer."

The whole audience had a laugh.

The seal talked about how the screens and real-time feel made the scene more interesting.

Mandi explained what hackers actually do to get around firewalls, which I didn't understand at all.

"Let's have a show where the hacker sits around drinking soda and eating popcorn waiting for that one intern to be naïve enough to open the attachment you told him to read before the end of the day," the bear suggested, "surrounded by his two monitors and, you know, a computer."

There was another round of laughs.

At some point a skinny guy wearing a mask from some cartoon series walked in late. He briefly stopped in front of the panel, facing the audience. That's when I heard the loud bang and then another bang and then screaming. My ears were ringing, and I was suddenly looking at the ceiling out of focus.

I heard someone barking orders.

It was Nik. Nik was telling people what to do. Nik was pushing me down. Why? I couldn't think straight. I couldn't move. I didn't know what was happening. It was all noise.

My body was wet and on fire. Nothing made sense. The whole world was nothing but noise. Something was tight around my arm like a big rubber band. It hurt. I felt sick. My chest felt strange and heavy.

"Listen to my voice," Nik said. "Focus on me. The ambulance is on the way. Please, look at me. Look at me!"

The ceiling turned white like it was an overexposed picture. Why was the ceiling white?

"Jaimes!" Mandi screamed. "Jaimes!"

Friends

From Nik's point of view.

I guess that was what happens when you do something many times a day. I swear an entire half of my brain was busy figuring out what site on Jaimes was best for an IV, as well as second and third choices.

I was aware of my panic. It was this tiny little ball, ready to explode. It was small and insignificant. It didn't matter right now.

Everything was calm now. Everything was moving slowly. I went through all the motions. I said all the correct things. This was a normal day.

He needed blood, badly. The carpet was saturated by the time I got the tourniquet tightened.

His lips were blue. I knew what that meant.

Good thing Jaimes had a smooth chest. You need hairless skin to create good contact sites for the defibrillator pads.

If he didn't wax his chest, I would have had to rip off his chest hair with duct tape. They have duct tape in these kits for that purpose.

Damn he was pale.

Panic, you need to shut up. I can't deal with you right now. You'll get your day. Don't worry. I'm sure you'll take over the moment emergency medical takes over.

When the team arrived, I gave them a rundown of what had happened and got out of their way. Despite my better judgment, I suggested which site was best for the IV. That was professionally obnoxious.

Mandi wanted answers from me. She wanted to be reassured that Jaimes would be all right. They had asked if I wanted to ride in the ambulance. I said no. I knew I would be a bother. I hated dealing with medical people.

Medical people make the worst patients. They make even worse next-of-kin.

I felt my work mode start wearing off as Mandi kept trying to get my attention and talk to me. The thing holding my panic in check was slowly melting away. I looked over at Mandi, she was sobbing uncontrollably.

"He might die again and stay dead, for all I know," I finally admitted.

Neither of us were good to drive. One of the convention staff offered us a ride to the hospital, but I still had to wash Jaimes' blood off me. I didn't want to get her car dirty.

I threw the T-shirt I was wearing into the bathroom garbage.

As I stood in front of one of the sinks and looked in the mirror, I convinced myself that we did all the things we were supposed to do. It was true. Everyone did great.

That kid only got two shots off before he was tackled to the floor. Everyone gave me everything I needed quickly. People got out of the way who weren't immediately helping. Con staff kept the area clear. I was proud of us. We did all the right things.

I looked in the mirror, at my face. I wasn't crying yet. That was actually a really bad sign. I knew what was happening, but there was nothing I could do, except clean myself.

I washed Jaimes' blood off my arms and hands like a pro.

Acute stress disorder. Great. Maybe I should call into work now. I might as well. The more notice they have, the better.

I got out my phone and called HR, still staring at my reflection in the mirror. "Hey, yeah. My friend just got shot. I won't be in on Monday."

"You need to call 911. This is the wrong number. Hang up immediately and call 911."

"I'm calling in because I can't go to work. My friend is probably in the ER by now. I'll be in no condition to work. In fact, I would like a week off. My friend was shot by someone trying to kill me. The guy missed me and hit my friend. I need to use my benefits to pay for therapy. How does that work?"

I wasn't sure she believed me.

"What's your employee number?" she asked.

I gave it to her.

"I'm not sure what this situation falls under," she said. I could tell she was sitting in front of a screen full of boxes to check. "This is just a friend, not a relative, right?"

"Just a friend! Are you fucking kidding me?" I screamed at the phone. "Pretend I have the goddamn flu! I can't go to work. I can't work right now. If my friend dies, it might be a while. Okay? Bitch!" I smashed my phone against the water facet until the screen was in a million pieces. I threw it against the wall.

I started screaming and crying.

My legs gave out, so I laid down on the floor of the bathroom, grabbing at my hair and kicking my feet. This was a good sign. This was the healthy reaction. This was the appropriate reaction.

Eventually, Mandi came in and helped me. Of course, she didn't care that it was the men's bathroom.

"Here, I got you a new one." She handed me a t-shirt with the convention logo on it. "Put it on. We should go now," she said. "I'll pick up your phone. Don't worry about it."

"I made a mess," I said.

"I'll tell the staff. They'll clean it up. Okay? I said, don't worry about it. Let's go."

Candy

From Jaimes' point of view.

Being in the hospital was so boring. At least that bigot fucked up my left arm instead of my right. That would have made various things more difficult. Nik was visiting me. That was always nice. He still felt bad about the whole thing. Christ. He literally saved my life, and he feels guilty.

"Okay, I got it all set up," Nik said. "You can cast to the television now."

How Nik? With my phone? I wasn't used to doing stuff one-handed yet. One bullet went through my shoulder and the other one shattered a bone in my arm. They told me I was going to have several surgeries. I felt like I was being held together with duct tape and nails.

It itched.

I needed some distractions.

My throat wasn't hurting anymore. I was intubated during my initial surgery, and I guess it took a really long time, so my throat was raw for a while. Now, I could finally talk to Nik when he came in without being in pain. The nurse said I could use more morphine, but I didn't like the way it made me feel.

Every damn time Nik came to visit me, he would comment on my IV. Guy can't turn it off. He hadn't gone back to work yet. I was worried. It had been about a week and a half, I think. I wasn't sure. My sense of time was still really messed up. The flowers Lars sent were still fresh, so it couldn't have been that long. Right?

"I got a surprise for you," Nik said. "Can I download an app on your phone?"

"Sure," I said, clumsily unlocking my phone with one hand.

Nik got out his credit card.

"Are you buying something?" I asked.

"Yeah. There is a monthly fee, but it's the only place I could find it."

"Find what?" I asked. "Porn?"

"No," he laughed. "You'll see."

"Hey, how's it going?" I heard Mandi ask as she came in.

"Pretty good," I said. "What did you bring me this time?"

"Am I that predictable?" she asked holding up a bag full of candy and snacks.

"If I develop diabetes, I'm blaming you."

"Mandi!" Nik said with a huge smile. He excitedly gave her a big hug. "Any news?"

Mandi had become our conduit to the outside world. The shooting was all over the news. Nik and I were avoiding it all. Mandi kept an eye out and let us know what was going on.

"It still looks like they are going to work out a plea deal," she said. "The prosecution is pushing for him to be charged as an adult, but that's very unlikely because he is so young. They dropped the domestic terrorism charge. They are still considering it a hate crime."

"What about you though?" Nik asked. "Is anyone after you?"

"About that...I came here to say goodbye."

"Oh? Did you change your mind? Are you moving to Australia to be with Traci?" Nik asked.

"No."

"You couldn't work it out?" Nik seemed really invested in them staying together.

"Nik, I still love her. I always will. The circumstances won't allow us to be together. I need to make peace with that. So do you."

"Are you in trouble? Did you get found out?" Nik asked, concerned. "Where are you going? Will I see you again?"

"I can't really talk about it, but don't worry, you'll see me again soon. I'm just going to be gone for a while," she said, cracking a reluctant smile. "It's a good thing. I'm finishing something that I started a long time ago."

"Will you be safe?" Nik asked.

"I'll be fine. I won't be alone. You focus on taking care of yourself and taking care of Jaimes. Please, tell me you'll take care of yourself. Tell me that I don't have to worry."

Mandi gave Nik another big hug.

"Of course, I'll take care of myself. Don't worry. I love you, Mandi. You be careful."

"I will."

"You better."

"And you! You!" Mandi looked over at me. "You appreciate this boy, okay?"

"Always," I said.

Mandi came over to me and kissed my forehead.

"I'm so glad you are doing well." Mandi got a little teary.

I didn't want her to feel any worse than she already did, so I put on a smile. Part of me was bitter, but the only one responsible at the end of the day was the guy with the gun. I just got caught in the crossfire. If the kid was a better shot, Nik would be dead.

"I'll get through," I said. "Nik is keeping me company."

"Tell me if there is ever anything you need," Mandi said. "Anything at all. I'll figure out a way. Okay?"

"Okay," I said.

"Goodbye," Mandi said.

"Goodbye," I said.

She gave Nik one more big hug. Nik kissed her forehead.

"I'll be alright. You be alright, too," Nik said.

"I'll try."

Then, Mandi left. Nik was stunned. He blinked a few times like he was having a hard time realizing what had happened.

"Get me some gummy bears," I said. "I can't open the damn bag myself."

Nik didn't seem to realize, right away, that I had said something.

"Sure...of course."

He got some gummy bears from the bag Mandi brought and set some out for me.

"You said you had a surprise for me?" I asked.

"Yes! I think you'll like it. Open up your phone again."

I gave him my phone and he started to cast to the TV.

"You remembered?" I laughed as the costume drama from the Boy Love room started playing on the screen.

"I was worried you would be the one who didn't remember. Drunk bastard. But you said you wanted to find out what happened. There are 60 episodes. I thought you'd appreciate that. You'll probably be here for a while."

"This is great," I said. "I'll pay for it though. I know you haven't been back to work. When do you plan to go back?"

"I'm not well enough to go back. HR is arguing with the insurance company about whether or not I should be paid or paid half or not paid at all. I keep having to fill out stupid paperwork and getting my therapist to sign stuff. It's a mess."

"Maybe Mandi should brick all their printers."

"The hospital?"

"No, the insurance company, silly."

"I'm going to miss her," Nik said.

"Me too."

"Let's watch TV," Nik suggested.

He took out two sets of headphones and a little adapter.

"Great! I really do want to know what happens."

Patient

"It's not my imagination, right?" Jaimes asked. "That's a blow job reference."

Nik went back to the line and read the English caption. "How about saying it on my knees."

"Yes, and then he laughs. He's offering the other guy a blow job."

"Oh, my goodness, you're right," Nik admitted.

"And then the guy he offers a blow job to puts a spell on him so that he can't talk. So obvious."

"You have such a dirty mind."

"Sex isn't dirty," Jaimes said.

"Blow jobs are dirty."

"Only when you do them right."

"Damn, Jaimes. You must be hard up. You haven't had sex since the first night of con."

"Who says?"

"What? Please tell me you aren't having sex in the hospital."

Jaimes started laughing, "Your face! So funny. No, I'm not hooking up in the hospital supply closet with the cute night orderly because getting the IV pole in there with us was too difficult, so we used the bathroom over there." Jaimes pointed.

"You didn't."

"You're hilarious. C'mon, I can go a few weeks without sex."

"I have no evidence of this," Nik joked.

They kept watching the show.

"This is when they fuck each other," Jaimes said.

Nik paused the show. "What? They got lost on the mountain. That's why they were out all night."

"You missed the bit with the head band? You missed how his homophobic brother reacted?"

"You really have a sixth sense for these things, don't you?"

"I mean. It's so obvious to me. Those two are lovers. They love each other. It's so blatant. How can anyone watch this and not get it?" Jaimes asked. "You'd have to be completely oblivious."

"Jaimes. What do you want out of life?" Nik asked.

"Huh? Where is this coming from?"

"Sometimes when people get hurt like you did, they start thinking about those things. So, I'm curious."

"Well, one thing I thought about was that I haven't traveled anywhere far away," Jaimes answered. "I mean, maybe, after physical therapy, I'll take some time off and go somewhere. I'll definitely start doing more freelance work. Maybe do some book covers, that sort of thing."

"That sounds wonderful."

"When we're both well enough, let's travel together," Jaimes suggested. "Is there anywhere you really want to go?"

"I'm not sure but traveling with you sounds great."

"What about you?" Jaimes asked. "Anything you want to do?"

"I'm not sure, but there is something I need to say. I was worried I'd never get the chance. It's something you really wanted to know, and I didn't tell you."

"What's that?"

"When you got drunk, the reason I was so upset was because I knew that when you told me you loved me, it didn't mean anything. You were saying you loved me, because you were drunk. I realize now that I wanted you to mean it. I wanted it to be real, so I was angry because it wasn't."

"I meant it," Jaimes blurted out. "I love you. I've loved you for a long time. You didn't know that?"

Nik shook his head. "No. I thought you just wanted to..."

"You were wrong," Jaimes said emphatically. "I love you."

"You do? But what do you mean? When you say that, what do you mean?"

"What do you think I mean? I care about you, and I want you. When you're hurt, I hurt. When you're close to me, I want to touch you. When you're gone, I miss you. I love you."

"We can't pretend anymore, can we?"

"No."

"You can be patient with me, right? We can be patient with each other. We can take our time."

"Of course, but do you know what else I want to do before I die?"

"What?" Nik asked with anticipation.

"Lars sandwich."

Nik burst out laughing. "I can't believe you said that."

"Nik, I can barely move. Kiss me already."

"Of course."

"Stop looking at my IV."

"Sorry."

"I love you."

"I love you, too."

Book Three: Lonely Lies

Pancakes

From Jaimes' point of view.

"So, going home is hard now. I keep trying to be patient. I promised him that I would be patient. But it sucks. I have to make sure he doesn't see me topless, and I don't wear T-shirts anymore. I quit waxing my chest, thinking maybe that would help, but it didn't.

"I thought when I got home, we could be together, you know? Finally fuck. Be a couple. All of that. It's so much worse than it was before. He's even on medication that makes him uninterested. At least he cleans his room now. He even got obsessed with buying new furniture and decorating. What the fuck is up with that?"

"Um...buddy? Not to be rude, but that's a much longer answer to, 'Your place or mine?' than I was expecting."

"Oh shit, I'm sorry."

"I'm going to...go over there," the guy said, retreating.

I was drunk and fucking frustrated. I wanted Nik so bad. But I knew if I pushed it, even a little bit, it could be a memory he hated – another memory he hated.

So, I got shitfaced and tried to forget about it. I was off my pain meds, so I could finally go out drinking. At least nobody recognized me here – yet. I was waiting for the dreaded, "Hey, aren't you the guy who got shot?"

"Jaimes? Is that you? I didn't know you came here."

Oh no. Here we go.

"Yes. Yes. I'm the guy who got shot!" I responded, slurring my words and being much too loud.

I turned around and realized it was Lars.

"Oh sorry. Hi."

"How are you and Nik?" Lars asked, standing there with a drink in his hand. I thought of saying that we were fine or something and blowing him off or fucking him in the bathroom, but instead I fell into him crying.

"Oh gosh, that bad, huh?" he said, putting his drink down and holding me up. "Let me take you home, okay?"

"No. Don't make me go home. I don't want to go home. I can't stand it."

"My poor, poor boy." Lars patted me on the back.

"Lars is everything all right?" the bartender asked, seeming concerned that I was bothering him.

"It's fine. He's a friend," Lars answered.

"Good. He obviously needs one," the bartender said. "I'm going to settle your tab, okay, man?"

The bartender was cutting me off. I think he wanted me to leave. I gave him my card.

"I have nowhere to go," I told Lars. "Can I...just for tonight?"

"My couch is a little short for you."

That was a hint. He obviously didn't want to deal with me all night.

I missed Mandi. I missed Traci. In a way, I missed Nik. No, I missed him the most.

"Don't make me beg," I said. My voice was odd. I meant to talk him into letting me stay at his place. But despite myself, I made it obvious that I wanted more than that.

"Jaimes, shape up," Lars said, using his elder queer voice. "You need pancakes."

"Pancakes?"

"Yes, Jaimes, you need pancakes. Let's go get pancakes."

"Pancakes."

Tea

From Nik's point of view.

Jaimes was staying away from the apartment a lot. He sent me a text saying he was going to be gone, completely out of the blue.

The apartment was very quiet without him. I don't know what was worse, feeling completely alone or being constantly reminded of the worst day of my life.

"I won't be home tonight or tomorrow," I said out loud, staring at a text message he sent me.

"You can't handle being around me either, can you?" I muttered to myself.

I didn't respond. I accepted it.

I didn't cry anymore. I literally couldn't. I hadn't cried since my psych ramped up my meds.

Playing video games didn't really pass the time anymore. I tried to watch TV, but I wasn't really paying attention. I just sat there.

I got another message on my phone.

"Let's get coffee."

"Sure."

I sat there, at the coffee shop, sipping my apricot mocha latte. I was in a haze. I could barely make myself look at him. It was like I was dreaming.

"You've been having a hard time," he said.

"Yes, but I'll live."

"Let me see you. Look at me. Aren't you happy to see me?" he asked.

"Of course. It's nice to see you again," I said, briefly glancing up at him. "It is. I'm glad you're okay."

I wasn't lying, but it was more complicated than that. Being around him was difficult. The timing was awkward. The situation was bizarre.

"I'm so sorry about what my sister did to you," Shawn said. "I didn't want any of that to happen."

"Believe it or not, I've been in a similar situation. You remember Mandi? She took revenge on my behalf once, a long time ago."

"Yes, I remember Mandi," Shawn said, drinking his tea. "The difference is that you didn't deserve what happened to you. I wanted to let you know that. You didn't deserve what I said to you, either."

I closed my eyes for a moment. It meant so much to me for him to say that. Despite myself, I craved his forgiveness. I needed his forgiveness.

"Thank you. I know this can't be easy for you," I said, continuing to stare into my coffee.

"I'm fine," Shawn assured me. "I bought a tiny house and adopted a dog. I started meditating and got into nature. I decided to turn it around and feel amazing now, like magic."

"I'm so happy to hear that. Must be nice."

"I look back now, and I realize that I was unreasonable. Our relationship was not healthy. I was thinking in a black-and-white way. Everyone around me was either an angel or a demon," Shawn explained. "That's why I reacted the way I did."

He was right. We had become very close very quickly. If I couldn't spend time with him, he would become distraught. He would talk about how perfect I was, how beautiful I was. But when I disappointed him, he became angry.

"I appreciate you saying that. I should have been more honest with you. I'm sorry."

"Yes, you should have, but the way I reacted was wrong." Shawn played with his empty teacup. "I was wrong. I regret it. I regret breaking up with you."

Why did he have to say that? Screw you, Shawn. Screw you and your great life. Why did you have to say that?

"You do?" I asked, weakly.

"Forgive me." He put his teacup back on the saucer and reached his hand out to me.

I let him take my hand. What was I doing?

"I..." I caught myself. I stopped myself from saying it. I had said it so many times before. It was a habit to tell Shawn that I loved him when he took my hand. "I forgive you."

What was I saying?

"Hey, why don't we watch a movie and get some pizza or something?" Shawn suggested. "Your roommate's not around, is he?"

Why wasn't I saying no? I needed to say no.

"Sounds great," I said.

Banana

From Jaimes' point of view.

"For a couple days, no more," Lars said. "This isn't ideal."

He was being too nice. I wasn't even sure why. I was lucky that he found me at the bar. I wasn't very careful with myself these days.

I didn't know how to deal with it all. I could barely use my left arm. I needed to relearn how to do almost everything. Nik was unwell. Mandi and Traci were gone. I had to be honest with myself. I had no one. I was frustrated. I was alone. Hook ups felt different. I was still easily startled. I was a hot mess.

I wished that I could go back home to my parents for a while, but I guess being on national television as the victim of an anti-gay hate crime let that cat out of the bag. They didn't even visit me in the hospital. I knew why. It was a hell of a coming-out story, but inconvenient.

"Don't worry. I'll be gone in the morning. I really appreciate this," I said, trying to get comfortable on the couch.

It wasn't working.

"I told you that the couch was too short. You can take the bed. I'll take the couch."

"It's your home. I can't do that," I insisted. "I'll sleep on the floor."

"The bed is big enough. Sleep with me," Lars suggested.

"That would be..." I wasn't sure what to say. Nik and I weren't exclusive. Right now, our relationship was nothing like that, but Lars and Nik had been together many times. "I don't know how Nik would feel about that."

"Us sleeping in the same bed?" Lars laughed. "I think he'd want me to take good care of you."

Why didn't I see it before? Lars was doing this for Nik. He was taking care of me for Nik. For some reason, once I realized that, it gave me a license to get what I wanted. I stopped holding back.

I stood up and walked over to Lars, I got into his space until he took a step back. "Then take good care of me."

Lars immediately got a telling smile on his face. I suppose he'd been waiting for months, since he and I were in bed together waiting for Nik to bring us condoms. I called it off back then – to take care of Nik.

I tried to go out and fool around as if nothing had changed, but that was bullshit. Everything changed the moment Nik and I admitted that we had feelings for each other. But right at that moment, all I wanted was to get my fucking dick wet.

Nik and Lars meant something to each other. Somehow, that made me want Lars more. I could tell he was excited by how forward I was being.

"Safe word?" I asked as I took another step forward.

"Banana."

Fine

From Nik's point of view.

"Oh, this is the good part," Shawn said, pointing at the screen. "Once she's been cured of being a mutant and isn't ugly anymore, he abandons her."

"That's the good part?" I asked.

He took the remote and played the scene back again. "He was the one who loved her when the world rejected her. She's beautiful to the world now, but no longer beautiful to him."

"He's an asshole," I said, raising my voice. "If he really cared for her, he would never abandon her. He was using her. So, what if she's different now? Leaving her now, after this happened to her, is horrible. This is not the good part."

"You seem invested," Shawn said, amused. "It's a well-written scene. That's what makes it the good part. I agree with you. Of course, he's being awful to her."

"I'm sorry."

What was wrong with me? Why did I apologize?

He paused it.

"What's gotten into you?" he asked.

"I told you, I'm not okay. I haven't even gone back to work. I can't stop thinking about it."

"About what Ava did?"

"No."

"About what happened to your roommate?"

"Yes."

"He's fine. He lived. Forget about it."

"No, he's not fine. There is no fine," I muttered as if I was talking to myself. "I hate it when a family asks if a patient is going to be fine, because even if I'm not the one who has to tell them, I know the real answer. They want to be told that everything is going to be the same. It's not. It never is. His arm was shattered. His shoulder no longer works right. He lost so much blood that his heart stopped. He turned pale. His lips turned blue. I took the scissors from the kit and cut his T-shirt. His chest was..."

"Stop talking about it," Shawn demanded, interrupting me.

"His chest was smooth and still," I said, finishing my sentence. "And that crap about whatever doesn't kill you makes you stronger? Also, bull. Complete and utter bullshit."

"What did I say? I don't want to hear it."

I was holding his hand again. I shouldn't do that. I took my hand away quickly, moved away, and tried not to look at him.

"I'm here now, Nik. Everything is better now. Forget about him. I know that I hurt you, but I won't abandon you. I never did."

I had spent weeks living with someone I could hardly stand to look at and talking to a therapist who asked me questions that he didn't believe the answers to. My best friend in the whole world moved away. I wanted to be close to someone so much.

"I love you," I said.

"I love you, too."

Shawn extended his hand and glared at me, waiting for me to take it. I did.

Maybe this was good. How could I keep Jaimes on the hook? How selfish would that be? He deserved better than me. He deserved his carefree life.

Shawn was confused and sad when he said those things to me. If you really love someone, you work things out, right? Jaimes told me that once.

I tried to convince myself, but I couldn't. Who was I kidding? I knew what was happening, but there was nothing I could do. I was too weak. I was too lonely.

When the movie was over, Shawn turned off the TV and moved closer to me.

"I missed you," he said.

He looked at me in a way that I had become familiar with. I knew what he wanted.

"I missed you, too," I said. "I just..."

He put his finger up to my mouth. "You forgave me, right? We're back together."

My mind was screaming at me. Just say no. Say no. But that's not what I said.

"Yes."

I meant it.
Of course, I meant it.
Jaimes would be free. I wouldn't be alone anymore.
"Yes," I repeated.
It would be different this time. Shawn said it would be.
"What do you say?" Shawn asked, climbing on top of me.
I knew the words he wanted to hear.
"I'm yours. I'm for you."

Rest

From Jaimes' point of view.

"Good gracious," Lars panted. "I'm spent."

We both laid on our backs on Lars' bed, our chests heaving and full of sweat.

"Are you sure?" I asked.

"I'm too old for this," he joked.

"Going to take a nap, old man?" I asked, smiling.

"Yes, I'm going to take a nap. Aren't you?"

"Give me five minutes."

"Oh, to be young."

"How old are you anyway?" I asked, knowing it would piss him off.

"Forty-two."

"What? Seriously? Your profile says you're 33."

"I lied."

Christ! Lars is 42? I guess we all had our deep dark secrets.

"Thanks, old man." I looked over at Lars with a grin, but only for a moment before the situation started weighing on me again. "I really needed this, but I still don't know what I'm going to do."

"Rest," Lars told me with seriousness. "Let yourself rest."

When he reached out to hold my hand, I couldn't grasp it. I had very little grip.

It had been over two months. I was told that my recovery had only just started. When I first took off my shirt, Lars tried not to react, but I could tell he was horrified. My scars are very deep, and I lost a lot of muscle from lying in the hospital for so long.

They would have sent me home, but my case was complicated. I was told that they had considered amputating my arm during my emergency surgery and had to consult several specialists to decide. It wasn't only my arm that was affected. I had also lost some of my coordination and fine motor skills. For a few days, early on, I couldn't think straight. I could hear people talking around me, but their words made no sense. It was horrible. I was terrified.

"Let yourself rest," Lars said again, continuing to hold my hand gently.

"I'm worried about Nik. You two are really close, aren't you?" I asked, finally addressing the elephant in the room.

"It doesn't matter. He's in love with you."

"He told you that?" I asked, surprised.

"I knew it the moment he threw gummy bears at your head."

That seemed like so long ago. I wished we had figured it out earlier, before all this madness.

"What am I going to do?"

"Stay here for a couple days if you need to. I don't mind."

"I couldn't possibly impose on you like that," I said, trying to keep it together.

"Don't worry about me. Apparently, letting you stay has benefits."

"Shameless."

"Nik used to call you that," Lars said. "Shameless."

"He was jealous of me, I found out. He thought I took life so easy. He finally, finally seemed happy and then this happened. He told me...he said he wished he was the one who got shot. I'm like, 'That's ridiculous. I wouldn't have known what to do and I would have had to watch you die.' He got excited and told me...I swear to God, 'So, you understand that you're the lucky one.'"

"Oh dear."

"Obviously, they don't need phlebotomists in physical therapy, or he would know better. It's fucking torture. Sometimes I wish they chopped this damn thing off."

"At least it wasn't your right arm," Lars joked, obviously trying to lighten the mood. "That would have been a loss for mankind."

"You think so, huh?" I laughed. "Do you work tomorrow?"

"No, I get weekends off now."

"Good. Get your sweet ass over here."

Finished

From Nik's point of view.

Being with Shawn was different than it was before. It must have been the medication. I wanted to give him what he wanted so badly. I closed my eyes and thought about the way being with him used to make me feel. I tried to replace my discomfort with intense memories.

I opened my eyes to look up at him. He was so beautiful. I touched his face. He kissed my wrist, and I smiled. I knew he couldn't read my mind. All I needed to do was lay there until he was done. It wasn't so bad.

I ran my hand over his chest. I still knew every inch of him. I wanted to feel elated. I wanted to feel desired. Instead, I felt nothing more than the motion. I might as well have been brushing my teeth.

It didn't matter. I was for him. I put both of my hands up to his face. He bent over and kissed me. Then he held my arms down as he finished.

The moment he got off me, I walked to the bathroom to take a shower. He followed me to clean up. We were both very quiet. I felt like I had done something wrong.

"Sleep here tonight," I said.

"I can't. I have to take care of my dog."

"Your dog? Of course, your dog. I forgot about your dog," I said apologetically. "But, before you go, can we lay down for a while? Just lay down together?"

"I told you already, if I don't get home, my dog will pee on the floor."

"Oh, okay. Could you come back? I don't want to be all alone. Jaimes is gone."

"Why do you keep talking about your slut roommate? You didn't let him touch you, did you?"

"No, of course not. He's just a friend."

"Friend? I thought you hated him. I never liked the way he looked at you. You're still broken up about what happened to him. Why?"

"I literally watched him die. Of course, I'm still broken up."

"I know. It was all over the news. You're a damn hero," Shawn said sarcastically. "You brought him back to life. Blood everywhere. I probably should have used a condom."

He started to put his clothes on.

"Please don't talk like that," I said.

I impulsively rubbed my forearms and hands for a second, like I was washing them. I hoped he didn't notice.

"And don't worry. I was tested recently," I added.

"Tested? Why would you be tested? What have you been doing?" Shawn asked, accusingly. "I almost forgot. You had sex with that old man."

"I...um..." I hung my head.

"Didn't take long. You waited a month or so to debase yourself like that," he said, continuing to get ready to leave.

"I was lonely."

"You were lonely? So, you went whoring around? Was it just him? The one in the video?" Shawn asked. "Were there others?"

"Yes," I said, taking a step back from him.

"Really?" he said, sounding hurt. "Really? Fine. Fine. I'm not angry. I'm worried about you. That's not you. You aren't that type of person. I know you. Whatever you did, that's over now. You're for me. That's what you told me. You wouldn't lie to me, right? You love me and only me."

Why did I let him come here? What was I doing? What was I thinking?

"Please! I don't want to be alone tonight," I blurted out.

"Don't be silly. We have the rest of our lives. I have to go take care of my dog. I'll message you in the morning," he told me as he walked out the door.

I was still standing there in a towel. It was late. I went to my bedroom, took off the towel, and crawled into bed. There was a wet spot from Shawn having sex with me. It felt slimy and cold. I got out of bed and ripped my sheets off. I went to the linen closet to get new sheets, but then looked over at the door to Jaimes' bedroom.

I went into his room and crawled into his bed. I hugged one of his pillows. I wanted to feel close to him. I tried to cry. I couldn't. I wanted to scream. I didn't.

I waited to fall asleep. I breathed in deeply and imagined that Jaimes was with me, holding me.

Sleep was escape.

Morning

From Jaimes' point of view.

I woke up, sleeping on my stomach with my head between the pillows.

I didn't have a change of clothes, and I had half a mind to go buy something. I didn't want to go home. I'm sure Nik was playing video games or shopping for fake flower arrangements or something. I should, at least, let him know I was going to be gone for a couple more days. I mean, I didn't want him to worry.

I found my pants and took my phone out of my back pocket.

What the hell? I had more than 20 notifications. They were all from Nik. A wave of fear swept over me. I immediately opened them.

"It will never happen."

"I could never be with a slut like you."

"Did you have fun fucking a random piece of ass?"

This wasn't Nik. It couldn't be. Maybe he completely lost it?

"You give gay men a bad name."

"You're the reason the world hates us."

"Have you lost count?"

"Shallow piece of shit."

"You don't deserve me."

"Leave me alone forever."

"Never talk to me again."

"You're disgusting."

"I wish you died."

What the fuck was going on?

"I'm with Lars," I texted. "Did someone take your phone? Where are you? Are you safe?"

"Lars!" I called out. "Something is happening with Nik. I have to leave right away." I started putting on my clothes.

"What's going on?" Lars asked, walking out of the bathroom in a towel. I handed him my phone.

"I think that someone who doesn't like me took his phone. That's not him," I insisted.

"It's Shawn," Lars said flatly, giving back my phone.

"Shawn?" How the hell would Lars know it was Shawn? "Are you sure? I thought it might be Ava. It reminds me of that stuff written on that dating app sock account."

"Yes. I'm sure of it. It's Shawn. I'm going with you," Lars insisted.

His tone scared me.

"Is...is Nik in danger?"

"He might be, yes."

"Physical danger?"

"I'm not sure, but we need to get Nik away from Shawn," Lars said, getting dressed quickly. "Your car is still at the bar, so I'll drive."

"Okay."

"Nik didn't tell you a lot about Shawn, did he?" Lars asked after we got into his car and on the road.

"Not really. I know that he broke up with Nik and cut him off when he found out Nik dated women."

"He didn't simply find out. Shawn made Nik go through all the pictures on his phone and delete them if Nik was with other people. That's when Shawn found a picture of Nik with his ex-girlfriend and lost his temper."

"What? That's what was going on? Jesus Christ. How did I not know?"

I remembered when Nik and I were setting up his dating profile. I had to take new pictures of him because he couldn't find any without Shawn in them. He didn't even have any recent pictures of just him. They were all with Shawn. It seemed strange, but I didn't think too much about it.

"Nik is in denial. Shawn is a truly frightening person," Lars explained.

"I knew Shawn was messed up. I didn't realize he was that messed up." I started feeling a lot better about telling Nik that Shawn never loved him. "Nik is really messed up right now, too."

"I haven't seen him since you were in the hospital. I didn't want to intrude, so I stayed away."

"Thanks for the flowers, by the way," I said, realizing I never said it before.

"You're welcome. I sent the flowers as a farewell gift. I assumed you and Nik got together and everything was fine because Nik wasn't coming over anymore."

"That's not quite what happened," I explained. "He um...he told me he loved me and kissed me...on the forehead."

"On the forehead?"

"I was confused. Were we dating or were we close friends? I was in the hospital. I was recovering. He was there with me almost all the time. I signed some paperwork so that my family couldn't swoop in and take over. They're dickheads, by the way. I gave Nik the legal power to make medical decisions. I updated my will – and I still didn't know if we were dating."

Lars kept shaking his head. I'm sure he thought it was as absurd as I did.

"Anyway, at some point, he started checking out," I explained.

"What do you mean?"

"Staring off into space, saying weird things."

"Like what?"

"Everything would be fine, then he'd look over at me and stare off. He wouldn't move or say anything. He looked scared. Eventually, he would calm down, but he usually left after that. One day this happened, but instead of calming down, he started to panic and called the nurses in as if there was an emergency. So, he started taking medication."

"I'm not that surprised, unfortunately," Lars said. "Our demons build up over time. He's been through a lot. Human beings are only so resilient."

"It was awful, and it got worse when I went back home. I had to wrestle scissors out of his hands once, which was fucking hard to do with only one good arm."

We were almost at the apartment at this point.

"They increased his dose after that," I explained.

"I'm so sorry. I didn't know."

Lars parked in my spot. I noticed that Nik's car was still in the lot.

We ran up to the apartment. Nobody was there.

The sheets were ripped off of Nik's bed. His dresser drawers were open, and clothes were missing. My bed was slept in and the lamp in my bedroom was broken. It looked like it had been smashed against my dresser.

The shower had been used recently, and Nik's toothbrush and deodorant were gone.

"Fuck! Fuck life!" I cried out in panic. "He's gone. He's gone."

Breakfast

From Nik's point of view.

"I can't find it," I said, searching my bag for the third time. "I'm sure I brought it with me. I take it with breakfast."

"Don't worry about it," Shawn said. "You don't need it."

"Yes, I do."

"No, you don't."

I couldn't find my medication.

"Do you think I would be taking that stuff if I didn't need it?"

"I got you out of there. I rescued you from that life. You'll be fine now. Trust me."

Trust him? What would he know? How would he know what I was going through?

"I need to go to the pharmacy."

"No," he said matter-of-factly. "You're not taking that poison anymore. I threw it away."

I ran over to Shawn's garbage can. It was full of yogurt cups and take-out containers. I rummaged around in the garbage. I couldn't find it.

"Where is it?"

"Gone."

"Shawn, you shouldn't have done that."

I knew it would take several days of not taking my daily dose before the medication was out of my system. Who knows? Maybe I would be okay with Jaimes not around. Maybe this was all for the best.

"You're with me now. Forget about him. Forget about that degenerate and you'll be fine."

"I can't."

"He's the one who's hurting you. Forget about him," Shawn insisted, raising his voice. "You're here with me now. You're safe."

"Safe?"

"He's a bad influence on you. Why can't you understand that? He is only motivated by sex. Once he has sex with you, he'll be done with you. He will

145

throw you out like garbage, like everyone else he's had sex with. He doesn't love you."

"Why are you saying these things?"

What does he know about Jaimes and me?

Shawn was sitting on a couch that doubled as part of a dining set. The table was folded up. The house was very small. The bedroom was a loft. The kitchen, dining room and living room were one space. The dog had his head on Shawn's lap.

"Listen to me carefully," Shawn said sternly. "He's grooming you. He's a liar. Your roommate and that old man are sick."

"I wish you would stop talking about Jaimes and Lars that way. That's not true."

"See? You're defending them. You used to complain about your roommate all the time, and now you're defending him. What did he do to you? He twisted you all up. Everything is his fault. All of it."

I knew that I should have been angry and yelling at him for saying those things. Why wasn't I?

"What do you mean, 'Everything is his fault?'" I asked, quietly.

"Jaimes took a picture of you. He masturbated while looking at it. Did you know that? What do you think he wants from you? But you're not like that, so to convince you, he needed to change you. He brought home a different man every night. He talked you into going on that dating app. He even introduced you to that old man who offered to violate you the moment he saw you.

"That old man. He's the sickest one of them all. I hate that you let him touch you. I was upset, but I can forgive you. I left you alone. I shouldn't have done that. You had a moment of weakness, but you're not like them. You're different. You told me a long time ago that you wanted one person to love, and that was me."

"You're right," I said.

What was I saying? I didn't do anything wrong. Jaimes and Lars were my friends. How did he even know all these things?

Maybe Ava told him? Maybe she was telling him what she saw from the cameras in my apartment? No, it had to be him that was watching me. It was Shawn. That's how he knew these things. He never really let me go.

All of this was his plan from the start.

All of this was wrong.

"Can I have my phone back, please?" I asked.

"No. If you have your phone, you'll talk to them. Then, they'll continue to bring you into their superficial lifestyle. They'll use you like those men on the boat. I'm doing this to protect you. I'm saving you. Why can't you understand that? I'm protecting what's mine."

"This..." I had to say it out loud. I had to. "This is wrong."

I should have been incredibly worried, but I didn't feel it. Just like I didn't cry anymore, I didn't worry anymore.

I didn't worry when Shawn smashed a lamp because I slept in Jaimes' bed. I didn't worry when Shawn insisted that I move in with him immediately. Leaving my car behind didn't make me worry. Shawn taking away my phone. Shawn throwing out my meds. Getting back together. Everything.

I knew it was wrong, but I didn't feel it, so I ignored it.

"Wrong? Nik, come here," Shawn insisted, holding out his hand to me. "You don't have to be alone anymore. Don't overthink it. Be with me. You wanted to lay down for a while, right?"

"Yeah," I said.

That was all I wanted. That was what I needed.

Shawn climbed up the ladder to the bedroom and took off his shirt and pants.

I stood there for a moment, looking up at him from the main floor. I could leave. Why wasn't I leaving?

"Get up here. Let me hold you."

As I climbed each rung of the ladder to the loft, my feet felt heavy. I knew I was making a horrible decision, but I did it anyway.

I took off my pants and my shirt. I got into his bed and pulled the covers over myself. He crawled in behind me and pulled me close. He was warm and soft. He was my beautiful boyfriend.

I held his arm. "Thank you," I said.

I could have stayed there forever. I felt warm. I felt safe. I felt loved. I forgot about everything else.

"I'd do anything for you. Do you understand?" Shawn said. "You're mine, and I would do anything for you." He pushed his body forward so that his erection rubbed against me.

"Can we just lay here for a while?" I asked, desperately.

"Don't you want me?"

He pulled his hand out from under my arm and brought it up to my neck.

"Do you have any idea the things I've done for you? I love you more than life," Shawn said, putting pressure on my throat and holding my head back so that he could whisper into my ear. "Nobody loves you more than I do."

He was telling the truth. He was. Why should I force myself to worry? Why should I make myself miserable?

"I love you," I said, pulling down my boxers. "I'm for you. I'm yours."

Deal

From Jaimes' point of view.

"I told you to only call me at this number if it was an emergency. This better be an emergency."

"I need you to find someone's address," I started to explain. Lars and I were in his car, ready to go. I had the phone on speaker so Lars could hear.

"You need me to find someone's address? You couldn't do that yourself?" Mandi said over the phone.

"It's Shawn. I need to know where Shawn lives. This is an emergency, okay? He took Nik."

"What! Hey, Blondie!" It sounded like she was calling out to someone else in the room. "Here, you're on speaker. Tell Jaimes where your brother lives. That little shit broke our deal. He took Nik."

"Oh no," I heard someone in the background say. "My mom bought one of those tiny homes for Shawn. I'm looking up the address now."

"Ava? Is that you?" I asked incredulously.

I remembered Mandi saying that she wouldn't be alone so that we shouldn't worry. I now understood why she didn't tell us who it was.

"Yes, it's me," Ava confirmed. "How do you know that Shawn took Nik?"

"We aren't 100% sure, but someone took Nik's phone and texted me all this bullshit about me being a slut, and then when I went back to our apartment, it was messed up and Nik was gone. It looked like he packed some of his stuff and left," I explained. "Look, Nik isn't doing well right now. And to be honest, I'm fucking terrified."

"I have the address, are you ready for it?"

"Sure."

Ava rattled off the location, and Lars started driving.

"You go tell that ginger little shit that he's going to prison!" Mandi shouted, seething.

"You are not sending him to prison. He's my little brother. Do you have any idea what would happen to someone like him in prison? You can't do that."

"He hired a hit man, Ava. What do you expect me to do? He promised to stay away from Nik, and he didn't. He broke the deal," Mandi yelled back.

"I'm calling my mom," Ava said.

"Shawn hired a hit man?" I asked. I couldn't believe what I was hearing.

"He hired the person who shot you," Mandi explained. "Shawn found out about that kid yelling at Nik at the convention. He took the opportunity to hire the kid to shoot you."

"You're telling me this now? You're seriously just telling me this now? You are fucking unbelievable, Mandi," I fumed. "So, he found out that quickly? He hired him that day? How is that possible?"

"He never stopped stalking Nik," Ava said. "I thought I put a stop to it, but I was wrong. I'm sorry."

"You're sorry?! I almost died!" I was beyond angry.

"We'll talk about this later," Mandi said. "There is a lot you don't know."

"Obviously!"

"Go save Nik," Mandi said with a very serious tone. "Shawn is..."

"Shawn is very manipulative and possessive," Ava interrupted. "He's my brother, but he is who he is. Shawn is an incredibly good liar. He had me fooled. Help Nik. You need to get Nik away from him."

I heard a crashing sound in the background.

"What is going on?" I asked. "Are you okay?"

"Oh yeah, sorry," Mandi said, sounding farther away from the phone. "You called at a bad time. We're in the middle of something."

"We really need to leave," Ava said. "It will be really bad if we get caught."

"You don't want to spend the night at the U.S. embassy?" Mandi laughed.

I heard another crash. It sounded like a metal file cabinet falling on concrete or something.

"That's not funny," Ava said.

"Gotta go!" Mandi shouted. "Say hi to Nik for me!"

It sounded like she was kicking something made out of sheet metal or beating it with a stick. Jesus Christ, Mandi! This is what you left us to go do? Pal around with Ava and break shit?

"I hope Nik is all right," Ava said. "Be careful."

Right as the call disconnected, I could hear Mandi in the background yelling, "You should have deleted it jackasses! So sad! Stay mad!"

"What was that about?" Lars asked. "Are they out of the country?"

"I don't know. I don't care," I said. "Apparently, without telling us, Mandi teamed up with Shawn's sister and made some stupid deal to protect Shawn from getting arrested for literally trying to kill me."

I was happy to not be driving. I don't think I'd ever been angrier in my entire life. What gave Mandi the right to make those decisions for us?

"Normally, I'd try to think of something insightful to say, but I have no idea how to respond to that," Lars said.

I didn't need him to try to give me some life lesson. I needed some time to calm down. I put my right hand over where the second bullet hit my left arm.

Nik was never the target. It was me. That kid wasn't a horrible shot. He was only a few inches off. Knowing that changed me. It was like there was this fear that was in the pit of my stomach this whole time waiting for me to realize, truly realize, what had happened to me.

I tried to put up a front, but I was struggling.

"You know, my friends warned me about who I might find on dating apps," Lars said, breaking the silence.

"You should have listened. You know, if you want to bail, I'll understand."

"Nah, it's worth it."

"Why? I have a talented right hand?" I tried to joke.

"It's worth it to help family."

"Nik is family?"

"Yes, he is," Lars explained. "That's the code we used to use, back in the day. We couldn't openly talk about it. Many of us were rejected by our parents. So, we made new families and would ask, 'Are you family?'"

"So, if he was straight, we'd go get breakfast?"

Lars started laughing. He looked over at me briefly and shook his head. "At least you haven't lost your sense of humor."

"It gets me through," I said, rubbing my arm.

No

From Nik's point of view.

"What is wrong with you?" Shawn demanded after he was done.

"What do you mean?"

"You laid there like a wet fish. It's that poison you were taking. It's damaged you."

"I'm sorry."

"It doesn't matter. The longer you are with me, the more things will get back to normal. You weren't thinking about your roommate, were you?"

"Of course not," I lied. "I'm going to take a shower."

"Fine."

Shawn put on his pants, climbed down from the bedroom, and turned on the TV.

I went into the bathroom. The shower was small. I liked it. I felt like I was hidden. I turned on the water. I made it much too hot. It hurt, just a little bit, just enough.

What was I going to do? Was this my life now? I didn't like it.

Where was my head at? I couldn't give up.

I needed to get my phone. I could call my parents and hide back home for a while. I could run away. If I wanted to, I could leave. Right? I promised Mandi I would take care of myself. I promised her.

"Hey, Nik. We don't have a lot of hot water, so don't be in there all day," Shawn called out to me.

Too bad. The water was already cold. I stayed in the cold shower, trying to think of ways to get my phone back. Maybe I could tell him that I needed to call my psych or the insurance company?

"Why are you still in there?" Shawn yelled. "Come watch TV with me."

"Sorry!"

I got out and grabbed a towel to dry off. I looked at myself in the mirror. My skin was red, but it wasn't that bad. The burns were superficial, but bad enough to twinge as the towel rubbed against the skin of my back.

"I promised Mandi," I muttered under my breath. "I promised Mandi that I would take care of myself. I'm such a liar."

I got out of the bathroom. Shawn's dog ran over to me and was sniffing around. It was so funny and awkward. "No doggie," I laughed.

I climbed the ladder to the bedroom where the clothes were.

Shawn didn't notice my skin. Good. I found something to wear and put it over my body. Good. My skin was covered up.

I tried to convince myself that this wasn't so bad. It was so much easier to go along with it than to fight it. I didn't want to be alone, and I didn't know what Shawn would do if I tried to leave.

We were both broken. We could be broken together.

As I started climbing down from the loft, the dog started barking and I heard knocking at the door.

"What's going on?" I asked.

"I'll deal with this," Shawn said, throwing on a hoodie.

He went outside, shutting the door behind him.

I climbed down the rest of the way and tried to listen, but the dog was still barking. "Shh, doggie."

"Is Nik in there?" a voice asked loudly.

It was Jaimes.

"No. What are you talking about? I haven't seen Nik in months. Has something happened?" Shawn asked, pretending to be concerned.

"Let us look around, and then we won't worry. How about that?" someone else asked.

Was that Lars?

"I'm not letting you into my home. I'm sorry. My dog is already upset. If she bites you, I'll be in trouble. He's not here. If he's missing, you're wasting your time talking to me."

"Nik! Nik!" Jaimes shouted. "Are you in there? Say something."

Why wasn't I yelling? Why wasn't I shouting? It was Jaimes and Lars, they came to help me.

Wait. My phone. I had to find my phone. I started searching everywhere.

"I told you. He's not here. I think I've been very patient with you. What exactly are you accusing me of?" Shawn asked, "Why do you think he would be here?"

"Some texts were sent from his phone that seemed to be from you," Jaimes said.

"That's it? That's your evidence?" Shawn scoffed. "Look, I don't know what's going on between you and Nik, but it has nothing to do with me and I want you to leave."

Where was my phone? I needed to find my phone. I was tearing up everything. Shawn watched me unlock it. He must have gotten into it if he sent Jaimes messages. This was bad.

"We're not leaving," Lars said.

"What are you going to do?" Shawn asked. "Look, I'm calling the cops."

Lars started laughing hysterically.

What was going on? I could hear them, but I couldn't see what was happening.

"What's his problem?" Shawn asked.

Lars continued to laugh. "That's Nik's..."

"Wrong phone, dipshit," Jaimes interrupted. "Now where's Nik? You tell me right now, or I'm going to fuck you up beyond recognition. You think the cops are going to come save your ass before I make paste out of your pretty-boy face? Huh? Try me."

"You're good at pretending, aren't you, Jaimes? Acting like a tough guy. He probably thinks you actually care about him. He's not as easy as your usual conquests, huh? You're nothing. You're nobody," Shawn ranted. "He's mine. He's not yours. Leave! Now! Or you'll regret it, both of you. Do you have any idea who I am? You touch me and you're dead. Dead. And you'll stay dead this time."

I calmly walked out of the house. Everyone was silent for a moment. Even the dog had quieted down.

"Nik! Nik, are you okay?" Jaimes asked, taking a step towards me.

"No," I said weakly.

"Tell them! Tell them that you love me, and you don't want them," Shawn insisted. "Tell them what you told me."

I was frozen. I had made promises to Shawn. I told him I loved him. I told him I forgave him. I made him think that we were together. I was a horrible person.

"I don't know what to do," I said. "What am I supposed to do?"

"You heard what I said!" Shawn turned around to plead with me. I could tell he was hurt and angry. He wasn't acting. He was desperate. "Tell them that you're for me. Only me. Tell them."

"Nik, come with us," Lars said. "We should go."

"No," I said.

"No?" Jaimes was in shock. "Nik, Shawn isn't a safe person to be around. Please, let's leave."

"Shawn, can I have my phone?" I asked. Shawn finally gave it back to me. "Thanks."

"You would never leave me. Tell them!" Shawn started to tremble. "You're not like them. You wouldn't lie to me, use me, and leave me, would you? You're not that kind of person, are you?"

My beautiful boyfriend started crying.

"Of course, not," I said, desperate to comfort him. "I promised not to hurt you."

What have I done? Lars and Jaimes had horrified looks on their faces. They were speechless. Did they realize now what an awful person I was?

I told the people around me whatever I needed to in order to get what I wanted. That was the type of person I was. I was a liar. I was weak. I was hopeless.

"I'm sorry, Jaimes. It should have been me," I said. "Everything would be better if that kid was a better shot. The bullets were for me."

"No, they weren't," Shawn said. "Of course, they weren't. Don't say that! They were for that irredeemable degenerate slut."

Shawn pointed at Jaimes.

"I finally found you, and you were living with him. You were living with a dirty pervert who wanted what was mine. Mine! Those bullets were for that disgrace. That worthless piece of shit should be dead. One in the head and one in the heart. He's supposed to be dead."

What did Shawn say? How did he know who the bullets were for? I didn't want to accept what I just heard. Time seemed slow as I replayed the words in my head. The bullets weren't for me.

"It was you," I said, staring at Shawn in disbelief. I was looking at my beautiful boyfriend that loved me so deeply that it drove him crazy. I could have, I would have, stayed with him. Even though I knew our relationship was messed up, I was ready and willing to be with him out of guilt, obligation, and loneliness.

I thought that I couldn't live with myself if I hurt him again, but I had to.

"You did this to me, Shawn? You did this to me? Why?"

"Did what to you? I didn't hurt you. I hurt him," Shawn pointed at Jaimes again. "I did it all to protect you. I heard you say that you wanted to be him. To *be* him! That's not who you are. I know you. I know you better than anyone in the whole world. I had to do something to stop him from changing you."

I knew Shawn was sincere. He really thought he was doing the right thing. He really thought that he loved me.

"The picture? The video? You were listening in. It was you spying on me," I said, finally, slowly admitting to myself who Shawn really was. "It makes sense because I know you are the kind of person who would do that."

I kept staring at him. He was changing in front of my eyes. I tried so hard to replace what I saw with who I wanted him to be. I wanted him to be that innocent, beautiful boy that I couldn't believe would even give me a second look but who pursued me as if I was the beautiful one.

"We missed one, didn't we?" I asked Shawn. "We missed one of the cameras. You've been listening in, waiting for me to be alone. You planned this, didn't you?"

"I needed to teach you a lesson," Shawn explained. "You needed to know that you couldn't keep secrets from me. You know now what will happen if you lie to me. You know that now. I fixed it."

He didn't love me at all. Did he even know what love was? Was he even capable?

"You meant it when you said you were for me! Tell them!" He was yelling very loudly now. "Why aren't you telling them! I told you to tell them!"

"I meant it. I really did, Shawn. I didn't lie. I meant it when I said it. But you're the one who's sick." I started to shake. "You're the one I need to be saved from. I'm leaving. I'm leaving with my friends."

"Leaving? You can't leave!" Shawn shouted, seething and screaming in my face. "After everything I did for you, after everything I gave to you! How could you? You monster! You promised me that we'd fall in love, but I had to wait. I waited for you, for so long, and found you. You're mine. You've always been mine. Say you're sorry."

He started crying and took a step back as if he couldn't stand to be near me anymore.

He was waiting for me to beg his forgiveness. I knew what he was doing. He was putting on a show now. I knew what he wanted, but I didn't do it. I didn't run to him. I didn't plead with him. I didn't reassure him. I stood there.

My noncompliance enraged him.

"You tried to hurt my friend," I said. "There is no coming back from that. None. I will never be with you, ever again. Never. Never in a million years. I want nothing to do with you. I don't love you. I don't want you. I never want to see you again."

By the time I was done talking, he had become a different person. He wasn't my beautiful boyfriend anymore. His face was contorted and shaking. His eyes were red against his pale skin. He looked like the monster he was.

"I should have realized how damaged and worthless you really are," Shawn cried. "I guess that's who you are deep down, huh? Some cum-filled dick socket that gets passed around at parties for everyone's fun. I bet you secretly loved it. To think, I felt bad for you. My mistake. Disgusting, dirty, perverted, cheap piece of ass! I hate you! Once a whore, always a whore!"

Shawn got 200 dollars out of his wallet and threw it in my face.

"Nik," Jaimes said. "We need to go right now, because if we stay here a second longer, I'm going to beat the living shit out of this man and I might not stop."

"No need," I said and punched Shawn in the face.

157

Out

From Jaimes' point of view.

I had to stop them, of course. I doubt either of them had been in a real fight in their life. Part of me wanted to take bets on who was going to break a thumb in their fist first. But I couldn't let it happen.

I simply stepped in between Nik and Shawn. I could stare down Shawn like nothing. What a coward.

"I'm going to get my stuff," Nik said, going into the house.

I stood there looking at this guy who literally tried to have me killed, not to mention driving the love of my life insane.

"You did that to Nik," Shawn said. "You've ruined him."

"You're delusional," I replied stoically.

"I still won. You'll never be together."

I was impressed by my own self-control.

His nose was bleeding. Good shot, Nik.

"You think this is winning?" I asked, shooting him a smirk that clearly warned him that he should choose his words carefully. I felt my skin get hot. I wanted to hurt him, so badly. I was physically weaker than I'd been in ages, and I only had one good arm, but I knew damn well if I lost control, Shawn would be on the ground before he knew what happened. My legs worked fine.

"He'll crawl back to me, you'll see. He knows that he's mine. I might take him back if he begs and if you don't dirty him up too much."

As I started to make a fist, I heard a voice calling out from the parking area.

"Shawn, get in the car."

"Mom?" Shawn looked over toward the voice.

"Mom?" Both Lars and I asked almost simultaneously.

"I said, get in the car. Ava told me what you did. I'm cleaning up your mess. You'll be on a plane by the end of the day," the woman said. She was wearing a tailored blue pant suit and crossing her arms.

"But Mom!" Shawn whined.

I couldn't believe it. He sounded like a toddler.

"It's either the car or prison," she said, in this oddly blasé tone as if she was telling him that they had plenty of ice cream at home. "1...2...3...4..."

Was she seriously counting to 10? Lars and I looked at each other, wondering if we had slipped into some parallel universe.

"But my dog!" Shawn pointed at the door to his house.

"We'll rehome your dog. Now get in the car before I'm tempted to let the police deal with you," she said. "5...6...7..."

"Fine!" Shawn stomped over and got into the back seat of a car sitting in the lot. Judging from the model, his family did not hurt for cash.

"Are you the young man who was shot?" the woman asked me.

"Yes," I answered. I was taken aback by the way she looked at me. She seemed genuinely upset. I suppose I would be upset, too, if Shawn was my son.

"I'm very sorry for what happened to you. We're going to send my son far away. We'll compensate you. I appreciate your discretion."

I blinked for a second before nodding my head. I wasn't sure what else to do. It was all surreal.

Nik came out of the house. Her expression changed when she saw him. I don't think she liked him very much.

"I trust that you'll stay away from my son?" she said pointedly. "Absolutely no contact. Never again."

"Don't take this the wrong way," Nik said to Shawn's mother. "But I hope I never see your son again for the rest of my life. I'm sorry for everything that happened. I wish I handled things differently."

"Me too," she said. "Me too."

"I can take care of the dog," Nik said, "and I'll clean the house up."

After all this, Nik wanted to help out. The hell? After this woman's children ruined his life, he is the one apologizing! Sometimes his insistence on being the good guy was endearing, and sometimes it was pathological.

"On second thought, no, I don't think so," I said, taking a step toward Shawn's mother.

"Jaimes, please, let it go," Nik said quietly as he stood behind me. "You don't know what you're doing."

"No. This isn't right. Shawn should go to prison. I know you talked to Mandi and Ava, but whatever deal they made with you, I didn't agree to it."

"Don't make her mad," Nik said, sounding alarmed. "Let it go."

"Let it go? How can I let it go?"

I practically ripped the side of my shirt, taking it off to reveal my arm and shoulder.

"This is what your son did to me! I can barely do my job anymore. I jump at loud noises. Nik can't function without being so drugged up that he's a goddamn zombie. Your son should be in prison. He is dangerous. He is obsessed. He is not a goddamn child."

I looked over at Nik cowering with his arm over his face.

"He can't even look at you!" Shawn laughed. "Live in hell, faggot."

I ran toward the car, and some big guy stepped in front of me and pushed me to the ground with no effort at all.

Lars ran over to me to see if I was all right.

"You're not going to win this one," Lars said. "Not today."

Shawn's mom walked over to me before I had the chance to get up.

"You have two choices. You can go to the police right now and give them whatever evidence you think you have. By then, Shawn will be out of the country. There will be no extradition. You won't get your justice, and I will bury you and everyone you care about," she said, looking down at me. "Or, you keep your mouths shut, and you and Nik will be handsomely compensated for the inconvenience my son has caused you. Either way, I'll keep Shawn in a residential facility so that he can't hurt anyone. Weigh your options."

"A what?" Shawn rolled down the window to shout at his mother. "It better be nicer than the last place. They didn't even let me play video games. It was so fucking boring. The doctors better believe me this time! I'm not a liar. Nik is mine! He belongs to me! He loves me. He would never hurt me. He's just confused. His head is messed up right now. One day, he'll remember what we mean to each other. He will. I know it."

"We'll send someone for his things later today," she said, simply ignoring her son. With that, she walked to the car, she got into the backseat beside her son, and the big guy drove them away.

Lars helped me stand up and put my shirt back on. Nik walked over to us. Then, the three of us stood there for a while, speechless.

"I'm sorry," Nik finally said. "I'm so sorry."

"It's not your fault," I said.

"Yes, it is. All of it," Nik insisted. "Don't tell me it isn't. I know the choices that I made that led to all of this. Let me feel bad. Please, don't pretend to know things you don't."

Lars put his hand on Nik's shoulder. "You made some bad choices, but you're a good person," Lars said. "Your friends know this. I hope you realize it too."

Nik hadn't cried for almost two months. He was crying now, just a little bit. His eyes were wet.

"I'll try, but it won't be today. I'm not ready for that," Nik said. "I'm not ready."

"What do you need?" Lars asked.

"Can you help me with the house?"

"You...you want us to help pack up Shawn's stuff?" Lars asked. "That's what you need?"

"We can burn things," Nik said, laughing through his tears.

We went into the house. It was a disaster. I guess Nik was trying to find his phone and ransacked the place.

So, we fixed it up. That's what Nik said he needed, so that's what we did.

Even though we were tempted, we didn't actually burn anything. The dog was really interested in us, and Nik really liked to play with her. I started to think that Nik taking care of the dog would be really good for him.

At some point, I finally took a shower. There was hardly any hot water, and I still didn't have a change of clothes, but it was nice to feel clean. I used Shawn's pretentious bodywash. I probably smelled like fair trade rainforest berry oatmeal or something.

Eventually two guys showed up with a truck to take the things away. It was mostly clothes and jewelry and things like that. They took his computer and game console, but they left all the furniture, towels and bedding and things like that. One of the guys drove Shawn's car away.

"I found the keys. They're mine now," Nik told one of the men. "Tell your boss that I'm keeping the house and the dog."

"I'll tell her but that doesn't mean it's going to happen."

"She'll agree to it," Nik said. "And tell her not to worry. None of us will be a nuisance. We know better."

"You seem confident," I told Nik once the guy was gone. "So, you're moving out?"

"Yes," Nik said. "I'm moving out."

Alone

"Why don't I go get some take-out," Lars suggested, holding up the two hundred dollars he found on the ground. "Chinese food sound good?"

"That sounds great," Nik said.

"Good idea," Jaimes agreed. "Thanks."

Lars left. Nik and Jaimes sat in Shawn's tiny house.

"I'm sure she'll give me the house," Nik said. "She cares about appearances. I'm sure she'd rather throw money at us than worry about any attention from this."

"It's a bold move, but I don't blame you. You've been through so much shit. You deserve something nice."

"I don't deserve an award for screwing up. I decided that I would finally do the right thing. I don't want to be alone, but I need to be alone. I need to figure myself out. I need to work through it all. I wish, so much, that things were different, but I need to be alone."

"I know," Jaimes answered. "I know this is hard for you."

"Don't get me wrong, you and Lars can visit. I'm going to try to make more friends. I just need to get my head on straight."

"Not too straight," Jaimes joked.

Nik laughed and held Jaimes hand, the hand that was too weak to reciprocate. "I don't want to keep you on the hook. I don't want to hold you back. I don't even know if I'll ever be well enough to be with you. You're free. Okay? Completely free.

"I'm so sorry for what happened today. It's easy to blame it on Shawn, but I went along. I didn't want to be alone. No matter the cost, I didn't want to be alone. Now, I realized that's what I need. I need to be alone even if it hurts."

"I'm proud of you," Jaimes said.

Nik smiled. "Thanks."

"I need the opposite. I need to finally really be with someone," Jaimes said. "Please, tell me if that bothers you. Be honest with me."

Nik grinned. "You and Lars did it."

"Yes. A lot. We did it a lot."

"I'm happy for you. It's about time you two got together."

"You're really okay with it?"

"Of course. I want you to be happy. I love you."

"I love you, too," Jaimes said. "You're family."

"Family? Are we destined to be like brothers?"

"That's not what I meant, but maybe we are. I mean, it doesn't matter if we eventually get together or not. I'll be here for you either way. I was scared today. I was scared for you. Please, take care of yourself. Care about yourself. Please."

"I'll try. It's difficult for me. I don't know why. It's difficult for me to say no. It's difficult for me to say things out loud or even to know what I want. I need to work on that somehow."

"Well, what do you want right now? Besides Chinese food, a tiny house, and a dog."

"I want to kiss you."

"That's dangerous. One kiss?"

"Yes."

"Then what?"

"I want you to hold me," Nik said. "I want to be held."

"Sure."

"But you want something else, something I can't give you."

"So what? You mean much more to me than any of that."

"A tiny house and 200 bucks," Nik said, lying down on the couch and putting his head on Jaimes' lap. "That's what I'm worth."

"Shh. You know damn well you're worth much more than that," Jaimes' said, putting his hand through Nik's hair and kissing him on the forehead.

"We should have sent Lars out for sandwiches," Nik joked.

"That would have been hilarious."

"Does he even know we make that joke?"

"Joke?" Jaimes laughed. "You mean, does he know that we are making plans? I mean, we all know who the meat is in this situation."

"Shameless."

"Oh gosh, I think the dog peed on the floor," Jaimes said, pointing.

"Oh no, doggie," Nik said, getting up to clean up after the dog. "I have a few things to figure out, don't I?"

"Yes. You do. So do I."

"We'll be okay."

"Yes, we'll be okay."

"Just not today."

"No, not today."

Book Four: Making a Living

Crime

From Nik's point of view.

"This is all confidential, right? Even in court?" I asked for the hundredth time.

"Even in court," she said. "However, if this involves you being a danger to others, particularly children, I'm a mandatory reporter."

"How about crime? Like crime, crime?"

"If you are using illegal drugs, it's important that you tell me. I can't be compelled to disclose that to law enforcement. Is that what this is about?"

"No."

"It's important that you feel able to discuss things with me freely, but don't feel compelled to discuss anything you are uncomfortable disclosing."

"It's just that I want to talk to you about something that is illegal," I explained. "Very illegal."

Damn it, she got that look on her face again, as if she knew what was going on even when she didn't.

"Are you involved in prostitution?" she asked.

Seriously? But she was better than my old psych, so I suppose I would deal.

"No."

"I wanted to make it clear that if you were, you could tell me, and that would be privileged information."

"That's not it. You see, Shawn, my ex..." I started to explain, but then stopped talking. She was going to think I was delusional. I was worried that she would put me on the wrong meds if she thought I was making all this stuff up. This sucked so much.

"Yes?"

"You're going to think I'm crazy."

She blinked at me a couple times. "Try me."

Every once in a while, she seemed to slip up on the overly professional act. She was new. I'm pretty sure she got stuck with me. Like, I imagined that her fellow doctors all got together, and she got the short straw.

"My ex hired someone to kill my old roommate, and his mom paid us off to keep quiet about it."

That rendered her speechless. "Wait, your roommate was the one in the news, right?"

"Yes. My old roommate, Jaimes."

"You are telling me, that someone paid that boy to shoot Jaimes." She seemed painfully out of her depth all of a sudden. "Why?"

"My ex, Shawn, was obsessed with me, because I was his first. After we broke up, he made his sister think that I was a terrible person, so they spied on me by using hidden cameras in my apartment. When I had sex with Lars, they used footage from my hacked webcam for revenge porn. But then my roommate and I became close, so Shawn got jealous and thought Jaimes was corrupting me or something. So, when that kid publicly threatened me because he thought I was a pervert, Shawn found him and paid him to shoot Jaimes. Then Shawn tried to get back with me, but that broke some sort of deal he made with his sister and my best friend, so his sister told his mom. And his mom paid us off and sent him out of the country."

Oh no, she was scratching her eyebrow. She didn't believe me. She always scratched her eyebrow when she didn't believe me. She should never play poker.

"Anyway," I continued. "I feel guilty about taking the money. I mean, it seems wrong."

"If you feel guilty, is it possible to make a different choice?"

"No. She didn't give us a choice. It was either take the money or she would hurt us. She threatened us. But that's not the whole story."

"There's more?" she asked, incredulously.

"My friend from high school extorted money from the boat-guy, too."

"Wait, your high school friend extorted money from the man who assaulted you when you were a teenager?"

"From the owner of the boat, who isn't...I told you, I don't know who...actually...whatever. She extorted money from a bad rich guy using an early version of ransomware to lock him out of his computers so he couldn't easily destroy evidence. He paid her, but instead of unlocking his computer, she turned him over to the FBI."

"Okay," she said, blinking a few times.

"Anyway, last week I got a letter in the mail from Mandi. Inside was a sealed envelope and a note. The note said to put it in a safe place and not say a word about it. The envelope said not to open until a certain date, which was a few months ago. Well, I opened it and there was a card inside with numbers on it. I really don't know what it is, but it's the same number of digits as a bank account and routing number."

"You think it's money?"

"Yes! More money! Like, everyone is giving me money. It makes me feel strange, as if accepting the money is excusing all the things that happened to me, that happened to Jaimes, or even somehow being guilty myself. I don't know how to deal with that."

"I see."

"You don't believe me, do you? You think that my mind is creating elaborate stories and false memories as a type of defense mechanism to deal with my trauma. I've heard that shit before."

"I would be lying if I said the thought didn't cross my mind. Regardless, they are your experiences, I'm here to help you work through them."

"So, are you saying that it doesn't matter if it's true or not?" I asked, confused.

"I'm saying that it's not my job to believe you or not believe you. You said that you felt guilty for accepting the money. Would you like to discuss that?"

It didn't sound like she was going to try to put me on antipsychotics like my last psych. Thank goodness.

"Yes. It makes me feel like all I am, is a victim, as if that's my job...literally my job. I want to get back to work. I used to be the guy they brought in when nobody else could get a good stick. I was very good at my job. It's not about having money. It's about feeling good about myself."

"So, that's a goal? Returning to work?"

"Yes."

"Are you able to see a path toward that goal?" she asked.

"No," I started to cry. "No and I'm scared. I'm scared that I'll never be able to work again."

Invitation

From Jaimes' point of view.

"C'mon Lars! It'll be fun. Super fun," I pleaded.

"I'm not going. I would feel very out of place. Everyone there will be nearly half my age. They will probably think I'm your sugar daddy."

"Aren't you?" I joked.

"No. No, I'm not, young man," he said, clearing the table.

"You did make me breakfast."

"Is that the only reason you come around?"

"Of course not," I said with seriousness. I gave him a quick kiss.

"Jaimes, my lovely talented Jaimes," Lars said sitting down and holding my hand. "Am I really the person who goes to these types of things with you?"

I was dreading this conversation, but I knew it was inevitable at some point. "It's not like I'm bringing you to meet the parents. It's just a class reunion. I don't want to go alone."

"You should bring Nik," he suggested.

Here we go again. At first, I appreciated that he accepted how close that Nik and I were, but now I felt like he was trying to pawn me off. I had to face it. I was more serious than he was. To him, I was just a fling.

"I'm not sure he'd be up for it."

"That boy needs to get out of that tiny little house. He spends all day playing video games and dressing his dog up in weird outfits," Lars said.

"Hey, Cosplay Dog is very popular. At least he's doing something. They seem to have figured out his meds, too. He was plain creepy for a while there."

"You should take Nik. If it gets too much for him, you can always leave. It's not like you actually like any of those people."

"That's not completely true, but to be honest, I think I like the people who weren't my friends better than the people who were."

"That's healthy," Lars laughed.

"I was a jackass in high school," I admitted. "If anything, I'm going to apologize and maybe get slapped."

"Slapped?"

"I was a shitty boyfriend."

"I find that hard to believe," he joked.

"That's not funny. I wish it were. I dated girls to keep up appearances."

"You did? Gosh, I didn't date in high school. High school for me was..." Lars took a deep breath. "An absolute nightmare I don't wish to dwell on."

I could imagine that Lars had it bad. I'd seen a few old pictures of him. He was this short, sort of nerdy guy. I knew he was estranged from his parents and his two sisters. I guess he had an aunt that still gave him news about his family now and then. He really didn't talk about it much.

"It would be uncomfortable for you to be there, wouldn't it?" I asked, admitting defeat.

"It would. Once I left home, I never looked back," Lars explained. "I'm glad to leave high school in the distant past."

I wanted to think that our age difference didn't matter, but sometimes we simply couldn't relate to each other. For him, high school was 25 years ago, not five.

"I'm sorry," I said, walking up behind him and giving him a hug with my good arm. I was suddenly sad. It felt like he was pushing me away. That's not what I wanted.

I nuzzled his neck. I knew it made him smile.

"I want you," I said.

The double-meaning wasn't lost on me. I wondered if he could tell. I wondered if he really knew what I meant. Shame on me for getting so attached.

"I want you," I said again, this time whispering into his ear.

Lars was the one I wanted.

Gentleman

From Nik's point of view.

"A reunion? I thought you hated high school," I said.

"I did, in a way, but I want to go. It'll be fun to be myself around them for once," Jaimes said.

"Ask Lars."

"He already said no. He said he'd feel like an old man."

"Old man? He's only 34 years old."

Jaimes gave me this weird look. "Well, actually..."

"He's not 34? We had a birthday party!" Lars lied about his age. No way. "How old is he?"

"He's going to kill me if I tell you."

"I slept with him. Doesn't that mean I get to know?"

"43."

"Holy crap!" I said much too loudly for a quiet coffee house in the middle of the afternoon. "43? Robbing the cradle, is he?" I laughed.

"Don't say that, please." Jaimes almost sounded angry.

"I'm sorry. I didn't mean anything by it. I think you two are great together."

I did feel jealous sometimes, but I meant it. I was happy for them. It made me worry less about Jaimes to know that Lars was in his life. I wasn't always in the best state to help him.

"I don't know if we're going to stay together much longer," Jaimes said.

"Why? Did something happen?"

Damn it. First Mandi and Traci. Now Lars and Jaimes.

"It's the age difference. I don't think he'll ever think of me as long-term."

"Do you think of him that way? As long-term?"

Part of me really wanted him to say no. I mean, there was still a little seed of hope that we would end up together.

"Yeah, I do." He sounded upset. "He's kind. He's adorable. He's wise. He understands what it's like not to be able to go back home. I'm comfortable with him and we're very..." Jaimes paused. I think he was looking for the right word.

"...compatible." I said finishing his sentence.

Jaimes was blushing. That never happened. Jaimes was blushing. He was so cute.

"I knew you two would be *very compatible*," I said, trying to hold back a giggle.

"How would you know that?"

"I've been with Lars, or did you forget?" I lowered my voice to not be rude. "Or the year where I listened to you having sex almost every night?"

Jaimes leaned in over his flat white, as if he was going to tell me a secret, and whispered, "Did you ever, you know, while I was doing it?"

What the heck was I supposed to say to that? "You ... you bastard."

"You did! You so did!" he shouted. He made a loose fist with his right hand and shook it back and forth a couple times to be extra vulgar.

"A gentleman would not have asked that question," I said with feigned offense.

"Your face!" He pointed and laughed.

Maybe if Lars and Jaimes broke up, it could open the door again for us, but I didn't want to be the type of guy that swooped in. I wanted Jaimes and Lars to be happy. If they were happy together, I wanted them to stay together.

"Does Lars know how you feel?" I asked.

"I think so. I'm worried that he thinks we've gotten too close. As I said, I don't think he sees me that way."

"You need to be sure. You don't actually have telepathy. Don't let things end without knowing."

I didn't want to be the reason they weren't together. I didn't want to feel like I stole something from them.

"Have you been dating?" Jaimes asked, seeming to want to shift the conversation to me.

"I went on a date a week ago," I said. "With a girl I met online."

"How did that go?" he asked, excitedly.

"I think I might be gay," I said, pretending to be serious.

I can't believe I managed to say that with a straight face. Jaimes completely lost it. I loved that we could make each other laugh.

"No, seriously, how did it go?"

"She seemed nice, but we didn't really hit it off. I think she was more excited about Cosplay Dog than me. I don't think I made a very good impression."

"Oh no."

"My new psych put me on something new. I told you that, right? It's an antianxiety medication. I had to slowly work up to the full dose, and I'm still getting used to it. I probably shouldn't have gone on a date."

"Why? What happened?" he asked.

"You know how most people have filters?"

"Filters?"

"Like, you avoid saying things that pop into your head because it would be rude."

"Okay."

"I seem to be doing less of that," I explained.

"Probably not the best time to go on a date."

"True."

"You didn't comment on her weight or something, did you?" Jaimes asked.

"No, but I told her that all I do is stay home all day and play video games, that I was a huge overmedicated unemployable mess, and that she'd probably only like me if she was attracted to pathetic men and wanted to take on a project. I explained that I was currently living on short-term disability insurance and didn't know what I was going to do once it ran out."

"Oh boy."

"At least I didn't comment on her weight. I mean, she was kind of chubby."

"What?"

"I mean, she was attractive, in a fertility goddess sort of way."

"Jesus Christ."

"I'm serious. Not everyone who's attractive is thin like you." A flash of his chest came across my mind. Damn it. I'm fine. I'm fine. Redirect my thoughts. "I was totally thinking of having sex with her during the entire date. I had to go to the bathroom and adjust myself. Her breasts were huge."

"You need to stop talking. You're really oversharing."

"Am I?" I took a large sip of my pomegranate mocha latte.

My psych warned me about this, but I didn't always realize when I was doing it. I didn't feel as nervous about what I was saying.

It was still dangerous to look at Jaimes. I had to look away from him right now. If he kept talking, I could get my mind off it. I would be fine.

"Yes, you're really oversharing," he explained quietly. "I mean, you're talking about your date's breasts and your erection."

"Yes, I'm finally getting erections!" I said too loudly.

Jaimes cringed.

"I also miss boobs. I haven't touched boobs since con, and she was behind me most of the time."

"Jesus, Nik," he lowered his voice, trying to get me to lower mine as well. "So, you got your sex drive back."

"Yes. I asked her for a pity-fuck, she said no," I explained.

"You didn't actually use that word, did you?"

"Yes."

"Please tell me you're joking." Jaimes looked legitimately horrified.

I wasn't.

"Anyway," Jaimes said, trying to change the subject. "Do you want to go to my five-year high school reunion with me?"

"Sure."

"And don't worry, if you decide you want to leave, we'll go," Jaimes assured me.

It was like he could read my mind.

"That sounds good."

"Wait. Cat-girl was behind you most of the time?" Jaimes asked.

Oh gosh, he didn't miss that. Funny.

"Oh, I shouldn't overshare," I said, pretending to be serious. Jaimes had been trying to get me to describe my encounter with the couple at con for a very long time. At this point, it was fun not telling him. "I'm a gentleman you know."

"Perfect gentleman."

Comfort

From Jaimes' point of view.

I loved fucking this man. I suppose his skills came from years of practice. I thought I had a good intuition, but he was somehow superhuman. It had been a while since I was with the same guy so many times. It was brilliant to be so comfortable and so knowledgeable about each other.

I craved the intensity, but I wasn't used to being so emotional. Wasn't I the carefree one? Wasn't I the experienced one? Wasn't I the unaffected one?

But here I was, crying in Lars' arms after sex. I was overwhelmed. I never got overwhelmed. I was the one who gave aftercare. I was the one who wiped others' tears away and built them back up.

I couldn't imagine being this way with anyone else, even Nik. Lars pulled the covers over us. He stroked my hair. He held my hand. I wanted to tell him I loved him, but I knew he didn't want to hear it. I was a silly boy.

When did I become the silly boy?

"A little too much?" he asked after a while.

"I'm fine. Give me a moment."

"Take all the time you need, young man."

"Lars, would you be angry if I told you that I loved you?" I asked, barely believing that I'd said it.

His body tensed up in a weird way. My face was buried in his chest so I couldn't see his face.

"Angry? Never. Why would you think I'd be angry?" He sounded hurt.

"Because that's not what you want, so saying it seems like a dick move."

"You think I didn't suspect?" He squeezed my hand a little more tightly. "I'm so sorry, Jaimes. You are a wonderful, amazing young man. I care about you deeply. I cherish you. I do. Being in love is not quite that. I don't want to see you hurt. I'd be shattered if I hurt you."

"I know. That's why telling you was cruel, but I needed to know for sure. You know, in case it was mutual. Just in case... It was a selfish thing to do."

"Good god, Jaimes, you're breaking my heart."

And that was it.

That's how our relationship ended.

I couldn't stop crying.

I loved him so much, but I knew the moment I said it out loud, it would be over. Fuck. Why did I have to say that? Because Nik told me to?

Nik thinks I'm the lucky one. Is it lucky to be cared for and not loved? Is that lucky?

I was laying there, naked, in bed with the man I desperately wanted and sobbing like a child. His touch, which was meant to comfort me, was pain.

Voice

From Nik's point of view.

"What should I wear?" I asked Jaimes over the phone.

"Whatever you want," Jaimes answered. I could hear someone in the background. Was he at the gym or something?

"C'mon, give me an idea," I begged. "Or maybe we can go shopping together."

"Get off the phone," some guy in the background demanded.

"Why don't you get down there and suck my cock?" Jaimes shouted and then started talking to me again. "Sorry, about that. Yeah, we could go shopping. That money still burning a hole in your pocket?"

It sounded like he moved the phone away from his mouth again. "I said, suck it, twink bitch."

"Are you busy? I can call later."

That was definitely not Lars. Jaimes seemed strange. Did he seriously take my call while having sex with someone? Is this really happening?

"I'm not busy," Jaimes said. "Someone else is busy. Keep talking to me. Please, keep talking."

I could hear his breathing change. Was he getting off on my voice?

"Jaimes. This is really uncomfortable," I said. "You're being an asshole."

He laughed. "Trust me, I'm not the asshole in this situation." He moved the phone away again. "Turn around and show it to me!"

"The fuck is wrong with you? I'm hanging up."

"Prude."

I ended the call and stared at my phone for a moment before putting it down. Did that just happen? I hated this feeling. I knew that sometimes he took teasing me too far, but this was beyond not okay. And since when did he talk to people like that?

I was so angry. What did he think that was going to do to me? Of course, I was turned on, and it felt horrible.

That absolute piece of shit.

I went over to my computer, put on my headphones, and started to play loud music. I tried not to close my eyes because my imagination was going places that I didn't want it to go. How could he do this to me? Did he not understand what he just did?

Cosplay came over and put her head on my lap. "Doggie!" I petted her on the head. I scratched her under her chin. She liked that.

Then it dawned on me. Lars and Jaimes must have broken up. That was still no excuse. Shameless asshole.

My mind kept going back and forth from imagining Jaimes' strong, lean, naked body and seeing his lifeless one. I wanted to rip out my brain. The phone call replayed in my mind. The way he told me to keep talking was on repeat. I tried to sing along with my music to drown it out.

Music. Doggie. Doggie. Music.

"Nik? Nik?" I could feel headphones being taken off my head. I was lying on the floor. "Are you with me? Should I call your psych?"

I looked up and there was Jaimes' face, looking down at me. "You're here?"

"You seem out of it."

"Did you think that was funny?" I asked, sitting up.

"I..."

"Answer the question! Did you think that was funny?"

I stood up and got into his face.

"The phone call?" he asked, as if he didn't know what I was talking about.

"How could you?" I screamed. I started hitting his shoulders.

"Holy shit. Calm down."

"I didn't want that. You creep. You jerk. Why did you have to do that?"

"Nik. Stop."

"You deserve it. Thoughtless. Careless. Shameless jerk."

He grabbed my left wrist with his right hand. I didn't like how it felt. I hit him in the face with my right fist.

He pushed me back onto the floor and stepped back.

"What the fuck is going on? I'm calling your psych." I heard the door to my house slam.

Cosplay came over to me. She licked my face. I gave her a hug.

"What happened Cosplay? What's going on?"

Oh no, what did I do to Jaimes? I got up and ran to the door, he was sitting on a patio chair on his phone.

"What happened?" I asked him.

He looked over at me and I could see that his lip was swollen and had a small tear.

"Did I hurt you?"

"It's hard to block two hands with one," he said, with venom.

"I can't believe I did that. I'm so sorry."

Jaimes put the phone in his pocket.

"It went to voicemail," he scoffed. "Don't worry. I can take a punch. I probably had it coming."

"Don't say that. I can't believe I hit you. I feel like crap."

"I get it. Sometimes I take the joke too far. I came over to apologize. You didn't come to the door, so I came in to check on you. How long were you laying there, anyway?"

"What do you mean? I just got off the phone with you."

"No, you didn't. It's been over an hour since I talked to you," he explained.

"Shit. Shit. Shit. I don't want to go back on my old meds," I muttered. "This is bad."

"You've been doing good recently, right?" Jaimes asked. "What happened?"

"I'm sorry." I didn't know what else to say.

Jaimes had started to shake. He put his head in his hands. "I can't deal with this. I can't deal with this right now."

He got up and started to leave.

"You and Lars broke up, didn't you?" I asked, calling after him.

He stopped, turned back toward me, and nodded.

"Let's get out of here. Let's go shopping. Let's go to the mall. I'll buy you something nice. I'm worried about you," I said, talking fast. "And I shouldn't be alone right now."

We were quiet for a while then. I wondered if he realized why I couldn't be alone. I almost blurted it out, but I didn't want him to freak.

"I'm not okay," Jaimes finally said.

"Neither am I."

"I'll drive."

Eyes

From Jaimes' point of view.

It was absurd. We were sitting in a booth in the food court, mall music in the background, sipping sodas and picking at gigantic slices of pizza.

"I really lost it, didn't I?" Nik finally said, breaking the silence.

"Yes, you did." My face hurt more than I wanted to admit.

"I was upset when I realized what you were doing. I was shocked. It was unexpected. It made me feel very uncomfortable. You know what I mean? I got this picture in my head of you..."

He paused and sipped his soda. He looked like he was going to die of embarrassment. I would have let him off the hook, but my face hurt.

"...doing it. You know, thinking about your body."

Nik was literally on drugs that made him spill his guts, and he looked humiliated. This was too much.

"Nik, if you don't want to talk about it, you don't have to."

At this point, I wasn't sure I wanted him to explain.

"I have to. If we keep hanging out, I have to. So, I was thinking about your body, and I saw your corpse," Nik explained.

I knew that he didn't like me wearing T-shirts. I knew he didn't want to see my body. I knew that being around me reminded him of the day I got shot, but he had never used the word "corpse" before.

"For a while, I saw it every time I closed my eyes," Nik continued. "Sometimes in the shower, where there aren't any distractions, I can't help but see your blue lips and your still chest. Every little detail of your lifeless body is burned into my brain. If I look down, and the angle of my vision is just right, I'll get this vague glimpse of you dead. At the hospital, sometimes that's how I would see you, like literally, that's what you'd look like."

This seemed like the worst fucking place to talk about this. Families were walking around us. Kids were pestering their parents for toys and candy. Why was he talking about this here?

"Is that why you got the nurses that one day?" I asked.

"Yes."

"The drugs helped. Right?" The side effects were so awful. I realized now why he was willing to take them.

"Yes. They helped a lot. Now I'm worried that the new ones aren't going to work well enough. I mean, I hit you, Jaimes. I hit you. I feel so horrible."

"I forgive you. I mean it. As I said, I can take it. Is this why you moved out?"

"Yes. Well, one of the reasons."

"Should I be staying away from you?" I asked. I suddenly felt oddly aware of my body and how close I was to Nik.

"I'm okay right now. I'm not even sure why everything hit me so hard. I have some ideas, but they're all really gross. I mean, I was really turned on, too, but I was upset and angry about it."

Dear god, don't overshare. I didn't want to know where that was going. I was not really prepared for Nik being some closet necrophiliac or something.

"Why did you hit me, though?" I asked.

"When you held my wrist, I panicked. I'm sorry. It's awful to think that I'm not safe to be around. I mean, how am I ever going to get back to work and to my life? I had some hope before this happened, and now, I'm starting to think I need to give up. I'm starting to think I need to give up on quite a few stupid ideas. I have to be realistic, don't I? Wanting what I can't have is too damn exhausting."

Nik started to cut his pizza into pieces.

Wanting what you can't have. I knew something about that.

"Not giving up is overrated," I said. "I wish I had given up on what I wanted, so that I could have kept what I had."

"Are you talking about you and Lars? I'm so sorry. You must be upset, and here I am being impossible."

Leave it to Nik to be going through hell and still be more concerned about me.

"What happened between you and Lars?" Nik asked.

"I told him that I loved him," I explained. "He told me I was a great guy."

"Oh."

That's all Nik said. For a knowing moment, our eyes met. Then, he stared down at his food.

I ate my crappy pizza. I sipped my watered-down soda. I listened to all the mall brats, the walkers and the spoiled kids surrounding us and getting their shitty overpriced fast food.

I sure as hell wasn't going to be a crybaby in the fucking food court. So, I left it at that.

Clothes

From Nik's point of view.

"What do you think?" I asked Jaimes once I walked out of the changing room. I turned around to show off the suit I was wearing. It was tan with a white shirt and a loud tie.

"Are you sure you aren't gay?" Jaimes joked.

"So, you like it?" I asked, sticking out my tongue at him.

"I love it, but you don't have to be all formal."

"Why not? What are you going to wear?" I asked. "Pick something out, I'll pay."

"One of these suits is a whole month's rent. I can't do that."

"I don't pay rent," I said. "I pay property taxes."

Jaimes chuckled, but it didn't sound like laughter. He looked miserable. I wanted to give him a hug, but we were at the mall. I didn't want to attract attention. Disapproving looks were the last thing I wanted to deal with. I got angry so quickly now.

"Are you insisting?" Jaimes asked.

"I am. You find something. I'll go get measured for this."

"You're going to get it tailored? Money bags."

I went back into the changing room and started taking off my clothes. I caught my reflection in the mirror. I was so out of shape. I suppose a steady of diet soda and chips while sitting on my butt will do that.

I was usually such a rail. I should start working out with Jaimes, I thought. Damn it. Brain. Stop it. La La La La La, I muttered to myself to stop thinking about Jaimes working out.

I got my old clothes on and left the changing area. Jaimes was chatting up the sales guy.

"Hey, Jaimes, find anything you like?" I asked grinning and obviously insinuating something. The sales guy raised his eyebrows and looked like he was about to walk away.

"Sir," I said, before he could leave. "I'd like to get measured for this suit, if you could help me."

"Certainly, come this way," he answered.

I stuck my tongue out at Jaimes again. He shot me a look, as if I was being obnoxious. I guess I was.

The guy told me how to stand and started measuring me. I actually hadn't been measured for a suit before. It was a little awkward.

"We aren't a couple," I blurted out.

"I make no assumptions," the guy said, continuing to do his job.

"I don't want to be a cock block."

He sighed and kept doing his job.

"Oh sorry, am I being inappropriate?" I asked sincerely.

Damn meds. I blamed the meds.

"A bit," the salesmen said.

"Oh. Sorry. Seriously, I'm sorry," I said. I felt bad. I had no social skills anymore, apparently.

"If you must know, I'm happily married," the guy said after writing down my waist measurement.

"My friend wasn't bothering you, was he?"

"No, but I did get a whiff of desperation," he said as he measured my inseam.

Oh, this guy was brutal.

"He's actually going through a difficult time," I said in a low voice.

"Sorry to hear that," the guy said. "You're all done. Once you've made all your selections, they'll help you at the desk."

"Thanks."

I walked back over to where Jaimes was looking at clothes. "Find anything?"

"You realize, I'm looking for clothes. I'm not looking for a fuck."

"Of course not. I'm sorry. Gosh, who's the oversensitive one now?"

"I am." Jaimes closed his eyes and took a deep breath. "I told you. I'm not doing well."

I wasn't used to him being this direct or vulnerable. He was usually cracking jokes. That was how he dealt with things.

"I'm having a bad day, too. Could you try not to be upset with me?" I pleaded. "We can talk later."

"Okay, okay."

"This is supposed to be fun." I picked out a gray pinstriped suit. "How about something like this?"

"No, it clashes with what you picked out."

"Do we have to match?" I asked. "They are going to think we're a couple if we match."

"I don't want us to clash," Jaimes said. "It has nothing to do with that."

What was going on? He seemed hostile. He wasn't just annoyed that I assumed he was trying to pick someone up.

"What's wrong?" I asked.

"What's wrong? What do you think?" He glared at me. "I don't know, maybe I had a breakup, and my only friend can't look at me without having nightmares. You don't get it, do you? I don't have any other friends. I have good fucks. Apparently, that's all I'm good for."

"We're in a store," I said, looking around. "Could you stop swearing?"

"I don't give a shit."

"We can go back to my place if you aren't up to this, and we can talk."

"Me simply existing hurts you, doesn't it?" he asked, his voice cracking. "Being around me hurts you, doesn't it?"

I didn't know what to say, but I had to do something. I couldn't stand seeing him so upset and not doing anything about it. So, I grabbed him. I wrapped my arms around him.

My body was pressed up against his chest. I tried to hear his heart and feel his breath, so I was reminded that he was alive. He put his arm around my shoulders.

"I can take it. Don't worry," I told him. "I love you, very much."

"You're a great guy," Jaimes joked.

"Brutal."

We both had a little laugh.

I gave him a squeeze and then let him go. I was surprised, really, that I could be that close to him and still be okay. My brain was weird.

"That's quite enough you two," the salesman said in a mildly sing-song voice. He was holding up a suit. "May I suggest the brown herringbone?"

When we were done picking out clothes, we went to the bulk candy shop. I got a huge bag of mixed chocolates. Jaimes got licorice and gummies.

"Do you want to come back to my place?" I asked as we walked to his car.

"I have a deadline," Jaimes said. I was pretty sure he was lying, but I wasn't going to call him out on it.

"Are you getting lots of work?"

"Besides my highly paid freelance gig?"

Shawn's mom was laundering her compensation to Jaimes through an ongoing contract position at one of her firms. I think Jaimes was struggling with the ethics of the whole scheme, just like I was.

Her people helped me set up Cosplay Dog as a business, and then paid me enough money for "artistic works" to buy the house with quite a bit left over. She used a picture of Cosplay in a superhero costume for an advertising campaign about life insurance.

Mandi said that a good forensic accountant would see right through it, but a crappy one would miss it. I had no idea that a "forensic accountant" was a thing. I wasn't comfortable with any of it, not really. I couldn't spend the money fast enough, which wasn't a smart move, but, oh well.

"Yes, besides that," I said.

"I did a book cover for someone's e-book."

"You did? Send it to me, I want to see it." I smiled.

"Sure. Hey, is it safe for you to be alone tonight? I mean, are you asking me over because you need someone around?" Jaimes asked.

It sounded like he understood.

"You should invite some other friends over," he said before I could respond. "Lars and I are still on good terms, you know. You should invite him over. Do whatever you want."

Holy shit, was he suggesting I have sex with Lars? Those Lars-sandwich jokes seemed sort of messed up all of a sudden.

"I'll be okay," I lied.

"Are you sure?"

"Yes," I said.

It was what he wanted to hear.

Thirty Minutes

From Jaimes' point of view.

I dropped Nik off at his house. Before he went in, he walked over to the driver's side of my car and gave me a kiss near where he hit me.

That was the third kiss he ever gave me. He kissed my forehead at the hospital. He kissed me on the cheek on the day Shawn left. Now he kissed me on the other cheek.

We were moving fast.

I chuckled at my own sarcasm and turned up the radio. With effort, I was able to use my left hand to roll the window down and rest my arm on the car door. My physical therapist had gotten a bit short with me last session.

"Use it or lose it," he told me.

Harsh.

I had work to do, but it had been a long fucking day. I didn't really want to work. I wanted to feel better. At the stop light, I turned off the radio.

"Call Pete," I said.

The phone started ringing through the car onboard.

"Hey."

"Do you have thirty minutes?" I asked.

"When?"

"Now."

"How soon can you get here?" he asked.

"About fifteen minutes."

"Sure, but make it twenty, and don't use your phone when you're at my place. I knew you were taking a call, but I can't have people taking pictures and stuff. You understand."

"Sure."

"And rough talk is fine, but not getting rough."

"I know."

He ended the call.

Paying for it was the final indignity, I guess. I used to make fun of guys who paid. Like, what? Does nobody want you? I wasn't as sought after as I used to be, but that wasn't why I decided to pay. Hookups are easy to find, even when you're scrawny and only have one good arm.

Paying was simple. No confusion. No misunderstandings. No pretense. Why the fuck not? I had the money.

When I got there, someone else was leaving. The look on his face was ridiculous. We're both here, jackass. You don't have to be embarrassed.

I knocked on the door. Pete, obviously not his real name, looked at me with the chain locked and then let me in. "You're a little early, give me a minute," he said.

I sat down on the couch while he went to the bathroom.

His place was nice. I mean, it was spotless. Pretty sure that was good for business. He had hardwood floors covered in fancy throw rugs and furniture that seemed pretty ordinary, but once you thought about it, was likely functional.

He had two high-backed chairs with open backrests. I imagined those could be interesting.

When he got back, I could tell he noticed my fat lip, but of course he didn't say anything. He didn't ask what happened. He didn't ask if I was all right. He didn't make a comment about seeing me twice on the same day.

He asked what I wanted. I told him, paid him, and he gave it to me. Then, I left.

I was halfway down the hallway when I heard another guy knocking on his door. Christ, this guy was popular. I wasn't sure if I should be happy for him or a little concerned. Like, what kind of hours does this guy keep? How many appointments a day? Does he give himself a day off full of spa treatments once in a while?

"I need you to leave," I heard Pete say.

Oh no. I turned around and saw the new guy pushing against the door so Pete couldn't close it. The chain lock was still engaged, so the guy couldn't get in.

Was this really happening? What a fucking shitty ass day.

"Hey, he told you to leave," I said, walking slowly toward the new guy.

That was usually enough to get most guys to stop whatever the fuck they're doing. I mean, some guys like fights, but most sane people would realize that whatever the hell they had in mind wasn't worth a trip to the hospital.

"Stay out of this," the guy said. "You don't know him like I do."

"Look. I realize that I don't know what's going on, but this is his apartment and he asked you to leave. So, let him close the door, okay? I want to make sure that nobody gets hurt. None of us wants that, right?"

My new job title was hostage negotiator it seemed.

The fucking asshole ignored me and put his foot in the door.

"I'm calling the cops," Pete said, stepping back into his apartment.

"You think the cops are going to help a whore like you? Call them, and I'll make sure they arrest you," the guy called into the apartment, keeping his foot in the door.

Now, that was disrespectful.

I had no idea what kind of fighter this guy was. He was sort of hefty, so I had no clue how strong he was. My body was still completely shot. I couldn't raise my left arm at all without considerable effort and it has a limited range of motion. If this escalated, it could be very bad for me. Of course, for all I knew, he was armed. I could end up in the lake. Maybe he would shoot my other arm, make it a pair.

So, fighting him was probably a bad idea.

I could stand around and wait for the cops to show up, so I could give them a statement.

I could leave, I guess, but that seemed like a shitty thing to do.

I could start recording what was happening, but that would provoke the guy. He would probably wreck my phone. I mean, my phone was a Flying Horse Warrior approved phone at this point. Losing it would be a damn shame.

Oh, Mandi! I laughed.

"What are you laughing at?" the new guy asked angrily, his foot still in the fucking door. "Stay out of this."

I started walking away, then turned around the corner so I was definitely out of his sight for a moment.

"Caleb, give me back the money," the new guy yelled into the apartment.

Ah, this guy knew his real name, huh? I calmly walked back into the main hallway and leaned against the wall safely out of the new guy's immediate reach.

"What are you doing back? Mind your own business!"

The guy started to shove his shoulder against the door, trying to break the chain lock.

"I told you. I don't want to see anyone get hurt," I said loudly. "You're trying to get into my friend's apartment, and he asked you to leave."

"Your friend? What, are you his pimp or something?" the guy asked.

"I don't owe you shit!" Caleb shouted.

A stream of rusty orange liquid sprayed onto the new guy's face through the opening in the door.

This stuff was noxious. Immediately my eyes started stinging and watering. I began coughing uncontrollably. I couldn't see anything, but I heard Caleb's door close and lock.

My eyes wouldn't open. Holy shit. I think I underestimated Caleb. Also, I couldn't breathe. I had to get out of the hallway. Jesus Christ. Am I going to die?

I tried to feel my way out of the building but ended up falling down the fucking stairs. I was a crumpled mess on the second-floor landing, but at least I could breathe.

I still couldn't see. I tried to move, every bit of me ached, but I was pretty sure nothing was broken.

Just my fucking luck, the cops showed up. Those bastards scraped me up and threw me up against the wall. I still couldn't see.

"Put your arms over your head! You know the drill, right?"

Oh god, no.

"I can't," I tried to say but my throat was sore.

I put my right arm over my head.

"Put *both* arms over your head," cop-guy practically yelled, sounding impatient.

"I can't." Maybe they couldn't understand me, or maybe they didn't care.

I raised my left arm as far up as I could, which wasn't very far. I felt someone grab my left wrist.

"Please, no!" I tried to yell at him the moment I realized what he was about to do, but I had no voice. "No!"

When the officer lifted my left arm up over my head, it felt like he took a jagged handsaw and jabbed it into my shoulder. Pain shot up my arm and through my entire body. I cried out, but the sound I made was a hoarse, almost inhuman sounding, groan.

"What the fuck was that?" cop-guy asked.

"Maybe he's enjoying it," another officer answered. They both laughed.

That was funny. Really funny, assholes. It literally hurt less to be shot. I could feel myself lose my sense of balance. The pain was excruciating.

I could tell that they searched me, but I could barely feel their hands because my mind was too busy screaming at me to put my fucking arm down. I started slipping in and out of consciousness. The next thing I knew, I was in the back of a police car, handcuffed.

"I'm injured you fucks," I yelled. My throat was still raw, but I knew they could hear me now. "I'm injured, take me to the ER."

I was laying down on my side in the back seat. My weight was on my left arm. I tried to open my eyes, but they couldn't focus properly. I started screaming. It sounded like a cat dying. I kicked the car door out of frustration.

"Mandi! Nik!" I cried. "Help me! Please help me."

"Did he say he was injured?" cop-guy asked.

"They always say stuff like that," the other one, who sounded older, answered. "He's probably drugged out of his mind. He's just a faggot John. Don't worry about it."

"I need to go to the hospital, please!"

There was nothing I could do. Nothing. I'd never felt so scared and helpless in my life. Literally dying was more pleasant.

"You'll regret this! You sadistic fucking pigs. Take me to the hospital."

"Shut up, cock sucker," the older officer said. "I'm sure you'll get plenty of play in prison."

"Prison? For what? You closet case. Does your wife know?" I yelled. "Take me to the fucking hospital."

I tried to flip myself onto my other side, but it hurt so goddamn bad, I realized I might mess myself up even more. "Please, take me to the ER. You fucked up my arm. C'mon!"

"The station is calling me," the younger officer said.

"What? On your phone?" the other one asked.

"Yeah."

"You're fucked. You're fucked," I yelled then cried, "Thank you! I know you can hear me! Thank you! Oh my god, thank you. I knew you would save me."

One Hour

From Nik's point of view.

"So, after we went clothes shopping, I invited Jaimes over, but instead he went to a prostitute, but then this guy was hassling him..."

"Hassling Jaimes?" she asked.

"No, the guy was hassling Caleb, the prostitute, and Jaimes was worried about him. So, Jaimes used one of Mandi's programs on his phone. It starts an open line with Mandi and me and creates a recording, but the phone looks like it's off. It's for emergencies. So, we could hear the whole thing.

"Anyway, there's this weird sound like hairspray or something and Jaimes starts coughing. Then it was really loud and noisy, then quiet, and five minutes later the cops showed up. Well, the cops...they..."

"Take all the time you need."

"They...um," I paused for a long time.

"What did the police do?"

"They demanded that he put his arms up, but he can't and then I hear this horrible sound, it seemed barely human. It must have been Jaimes, because the cops were making a joke out of it...a sick sexual joke. Then there was a lot of rustling, doors opening and closing, and it sounded like they were dragging something. I realized they had dragged Jaimes into the car when I heard the door close.

"Then Jaimes started begging them to bring him to the hospital, but they kept making fun of him and saying that he was on drugs or something. It was horrible. He kept begging them to take him to the hospital, and they kept refusing."

"How did that make you feel?"

"It was horrifying. I felt so helpless. Anyway, Mandi had connected the line to the station nonemergency number, an internal affairs hotline, a couple investigative reporters, a lawyer she knows, and a city council member, and a police oversight..."

"How many people?"

"A lot. Anyway, so the station calls the cops and tells them to bring him to the emergency room."

"So, the police brought Jaimes to the hospital?"

"To the ER, yes. Now he's in the hospital."

"Is he there right now?"

"Yes. That's why I wanted to talk to you as soon as I could. I haven't gone to see him. I'm really worried I'm going to say things I don't mean. I'm worried I'm going to get weird because I'm in a hospital. He's there all alone. I feel like shit, but I wanted to talk to you first. I really appreciate you squeezing me in."

"Could you tell me more about what you're worried about?"

"Well, earlier, yesterday, I lost an hour. I'm worried that's going to happen again."

"You...you lost an hour? What do you mean?"

"I called Jaimes, and he was getting a blow job while he was talking to me on the phone and making sexual jokes. I got really turned on and upset and then tried to get my mind off of it by listening to music. Then suddenly, Jaimes was in my house. Like he teleported there or something. I was so upset at him and so disoriented that I hit him."

"You hit Jaimes?"

"In a completely whatever-sort-of-way that won't force you to report me to the police way."

"When you hit him, was he hurt?"

"Only a little. I gave him a fat lip."

"Do you have the urge to hurt him again?"

"No, not at all."

"Okay, so you told me that you lost an hour. Are you sure?" She seemed alarmed.

"Yes. Right after I got off the phone with Jaimes, he just appeared. He told me it had been more than an hour."

"Have you experienced anything like that before or since?" she asked, very concerned.

"No."

"Can you describe what you were thinking right before it happened?" she asked.

"I was thinking about Jaimes when he was healthier and then I was thinking of him when he was dead. I mean, I don't want to explain."

"Is there something about your thoughts that caused you not to want to share them?"

"They were sexual thoughts," I said, glaring at the floor.

I hate therapy.

"I'm going to ask you a couple questions, and I don't want you to be alarmed by them. Simply answer honestly and as best you can. I'm trying to figure out what may have happened. Okay?"

"Okay."

"Afterward, you said you were disoriented. Did you feel a loss of balance?"

"At first, but then I was fine."

"Did you feel exhausted afterward?" she asked.

"Maybe?"

"Were you able to understand speech and to talk normally?"

"Yes. Oh, you're making sure I didn't hit my head, right? It wasn't that. My GCS was probably about 13. I'm also pretty certain it wasn't a seizure." I think I knew the checklist better than she did. "Sorry, med people make the worst patients."

She cracked a smile. "If you only experience it once, it's unlikely we'll understand what happened. There's a variety of things that it could be. It could have been a seizure, or a narcoleptic event, you could have fallen asleep, or maybe had a particularly long dissociative episode. If it happens again, going to the ER isn't an overreaction. Okay?"

"Okay."

"Is there any other reason that you feel uncomfortable visiting your friend in the hospital?" she asked.

"He blew me off to go to a prostitute. He even lied. He said he had work to do. That hurt. That hurt a lot."

"Do you plan to talk to him about how that made you feel?"

"I should, shouldn't I?"

"It's not my place to give advice. But I can say, whatever you choose, it may be helpful to attempt to prepare yourself for the experience. You know, make peace with the possible outcomes."

"Yeah."

Possible outcomes? Like me losing my temper on my friend who's in pain and traumatized right now?

"And don't neglect the possibility of explaining to your friend what your worries are."

"I don't want to upset him more. He and Lars broke up. His class reunion is coming up. It looks like he might be put in the middle of another court case. We both have the worst luck."

"Well, I hate to do this, but I have another client coming in soon. I'll give you some homework for next time."

"Homework?"

"Write down some of the good things that have happened to you in the last few months. Even if they are small. Think of at least five."

"Five things? I'll try." It sounded a bit silly. "I'll do my homework."

Gosh, that's something Mandi says. I wanted to hang out with Mandi when there wasn't a crisis. That would be nice.

"Thanks again for seeing me. I know you're busy."

"I'm glad to do it when I'm able. I hope everything goes well today."

I walked out of her office and the building. I realized that I could walk to Jaimes' room from here if I walked across the hospital campus.

I got out my phone. "Can I visit? What room?" I texted.

I started walking toward the building I knew he was in. Of course, I knew where it was. I used to work here. I missed working. It seemed strange, I was always looking forward to days off and now I just wanted a reason to get out of bed.

"Nik? Is that you?" I looked up to see Haydan running across the courtyard. Oh gosh, she was the one who helped me when the whole email thing happened. I almost forgot that half the staff I was walking past had seen my dick. Jeez.

"Haydan! How have you been?" I asked.

"Living a boring life," she said, sort of joking. "I'm happy to see you. I was worried. I saw what happened on the news. You're a damn hero."

"I don't feel that way," I said, lowering my head.

"So, you transferred out, right? How's the new place?" she asked.

"Actually, after my friend was hurt. I wasn't able to go back to work."

"I'm so sorry. That bad, huh?"

"Yeah."

"Occupational hazard, I guess," she said. "You know, I never got a chance to get your number before you left. We miss you at trivia night."

Don't cry. Now that I could cry, I cried all the time.

"It wouldn't be awkward?" I asked, getting out my phone.

"Because you don't work here anymore, or because we've seen your penis?" she said with a straight face. "We're medical professionals. We can handle seeing dick."

"I appreciate that," I laughed.

"Here, let me give you a hug. You look like you need a hug," she said. "You don't work here anymore so we won't get in trouble with HR."

She gave me a friendly hug. It was nice. It was really nice.

"Thanks," I said. I looked at my phone. Jaimes answered me with his room number. I was relieved. Part of me was worried he didn't want to see me.

I gave Haydan my phone number.

"Well, my friend is waiting, and I bet you have to get back to work," I said.

"Your friend? Are you visiting someone?" she asked.

"Yeah, actually it's the guy that was in the news. The one who got shot. The cops messed him up last night."

"The police?"

"Long story."

She just shook her head.

"Well, I hope he recovers well. That sounds really terrible."

"Thanks. Oh, can you call me quick, so then I have your number?" I asked.

"Sure."

"H – A – Y – D – A – N" I said. "Right?"

"You got it."

Cast

From Jaimes' point of view.

I wish I had that casting thing that Nik got me last time I was in the hospital. It wasn't like I had a chance to go back to my apartment and get it. I was full of morphine and bored out of my mind. A lawyer that magically showed up was looking into what happened to Caleb.

I was waiting for Nik. I told him last night I was admitted into the hospital, but he didn't text me back until now.

"If you don't feel like coming, don't worry about it," I had written but didn't send.

Fuck it.

I wanted him to come. I could be selfish. I erased it.

"Please come visit me. We should talk," I wrote and erased.

"I miss you," I wrote and erased.

"I'm lonely and scared," I wrote and erased.

"Are you still angry at me? I said I was sorry," I wrote and erased.

I hadn't shaved or waxed since Nik got weird about my "smooth chest" forever ago. Christ I was hairy. They had immobilized my left arm completely, so I was all wrapped up in weird ways. I felt so uncomfortable.

Spa day with Caleb. That sounds enjoyable. I should have asked him who does his waxes.

"Hey," someone said, walking into the room. It was Nik.

"Nik!" I was overexcited. "Nik, come in. Come in."

He walked in sheepishly and just stood there.

"Pull up a chair," I suggested. "They took a bunch of x-rays last night and are bringing in some experts again. I'm going to need another surgery. The police showed up half a dozen times trying to get the doctors to say I was injured falling down the stairs instead of by the cops. I guess Caleb used some sort of pepper spray they use for bears, like real bears. Apparently, it works on both kinds."

That was gold, why wasn't he laughing?

"Nik?"

He finally walked over and pulled a chair close to the bed and sat down next to me.

"I heard the whole thing," he said. "It was terrible. I heard you call out for us to help you. It was horrifying. I'm so sorry this happened to you. I'm also angry, and I'm hurt."

His speech sounded rehearsed.

"I really did have a deadline," I said weakly.

Fuck. Who am I trying to kid?

"Seriously, Jaimes? That's bullshit. We were both going through a hard time. I invited you over and you made some excuse and then spent your time with a prostitute. How do you think that makes me feel? But you had this awful shit happen to you, so it's like I feel guilty for being upset. It sucks."

"You're jealous of Caleb?"

What? He wasn't jealous of Lars, but he was jealous of someone I paid. Does that make sense?

"No. I'm angry you lied to me. I'm hurt that you went to get a screw instead of staying with me when I was sad and hurt and fucking suicidal. You asshole."

"Nik? You said you were okay. I can't actually read your mind. I asked you. You told me you were okay."

Suicidal? Christ.

"Obviously I wasn't okay."

I wanted to get angry and call him a liar, but he looked horrible. I simply couldn't.

"You aren't stupid." Nik continued ranting. "I was so messed up I lost time. I lost control of myself so badly that I hurt you. I felt like crap and then you scolded me for assuming you were trying to get with the salesman guy, as if I was thinking too little of you or something? What the hell? And you totally were. I wasn't imagining it."

Yeah, when the married guy thought I was "desperate" that didn't hit a nerve or anything.

"Nik, calm down please. I was upset about breaking up with Lars. I'm sorry. But I also thought that being around me might make things worse for you. It was all a little too much. I'm sorry."

"And what? Are you paying for sex now?"

Well, that comment was only a matter of time.

"Do you have a problem with that?"

"Yeah, I do."

At least he was being honest.

"Like, I'm sure Caleb is a nice guy and nobody's forcing him to do anything. I hope he's safe and happy, but I don't like it. The way you talked to that guy you were with, when you were on the phone, I couldn't stand that either."

"That was Caleb. It was play, Nik. It was just play. I didn't know it would upset you so much. I'm sorry I took the call and said those things."

How could I be so stupid? Of course, he might be sensitive to talk like that. Damn it.

"That was Caleb? That's why it was different," Nik said. "It felt wrong."

"Wrong? C'mon don't give me that shit. We're both adults. We agreed on everything. Don't make it sound like something awful."

He better not take it too far. I wasn't in the mood to deal with his fucking judgment. I was so goddamn sick of it.

"That's not what I meant. I used to be your roommate. I know how you are with people. That wasn't like you. You are so torn up about Lars, you want to turn yourself off. Please don't."

"Turn myself off? What are you talking about? I am sorry I didn't stay with you, okay?"

I was telling the truth. I wished that I would have stayed with Nik and not been bear sprayed and assaulted by police. That was true.

"You're right. I miss Lars," I explained. "Being with him was sweet and wonderful and stress free. I hadn't had anything like that in a really long time. I am gutted that it's over. I'm worried that we can't all be friends anymore and that I screwed that up, too. That's why I wanted you to invite him over."

"It felt like you wanted to get away from me."

"No. Don't you think that maybe I wanted you to be comforted by someone who doesn't give you nightmares? Did you think of that? Maybe I was worried that Lars wasn't doing that great right now either."

"Oh. I'm sorry. I just..."

"I know. I'm sorry, too. Remember, a long time ago, we promised to be patient with one another? Let's be patient with one another now, okay?" I suggested.

To think, that was a simpler time.

"Okay."

"Last night was terrible," I told him. "I was in pain and felt helpless, but I knew you and Mandi were listening and would save me somehow. Seeing you now means a lot. I know this can't be easy for you."

"I'm sorry I didn't come to you right away. Everything happened so fast. When I realized you had gotten safely to the ER, I realized that the staff were taking care of you. I didn't know how well I would deal with it. I didn't want to get in the way. I couldn't sleep well. This morning, I went to see my psych. She seemed really worried about me losing time like that."

"Did she have any ideas?"

"Disassociation or narcolepsy," Nik answered. "In other words, she doesn't know, but I think I figured it out. It's nothing to worry about."

"Okay. What have you figured out?"

I was curious, even if it was something really weird. I wished he'd come out with it. So frustrating.

"I'm sorry. Can we talk about something else?"

You've got to be kidding me.

"Sure," I said.

Whatever it was, it was still really messing with him, but if he wanted to talk about something else, I would talk about something else.

"I was hoping to get one of those TV cast things in my room again."

Nik grinned and took a black box with a cord attached out of his pocket. "I knew you'd want one. I got some ear buds too. There's a new movie about these two male friends who are super friendly and fight dragons. You can tell me at what point they have sex off screen and never talk about it."

"Nik, I love you."

"I love you, too."

He set everything up, and we watched a movie together. Later, he went out and brought us food. He stayed with me until he was worried about Cosplay, and then he went home.

What was I going to do? I already screwed up one friendship by pushing it too far. This was the way it was going to be, it seemed. I needed to accept that Nik and I would never be together.

For fuck's sake, I was his trauma. I was literally his trauma. Everything about me reminded him of the worst experiences of his life.

The universe hated us. The universe had a shitty sense of humor. The universe sucked.

Trip

From Nik's point of view.

"It looks amazing. They did a great job," I said.

Jaimes was wearing his new suit. They had to retailored it to fit around his immobilized arm.

"It looks weird. One arm is bigger than the other," he said.

"Well, it was either that or take the sleeve off completely. I can go get a scissors and cut it off ..." Oh, that didn't bring back memories or anything.

We were both quiet for a moment.

"That's okay. It looks fine," Jaimes said. "And you look stunning and nerdy."

"Exactly what I was going for," I said, smiling.

We found ourselves in Jaimes' car. He was driving. I wanted to make conversation, but I wasn't sure what to say.

"You do look very nice," I said.

"Thanks. You, too."

"I'm supposed to think of five positive things that have happened to me recently and report them back to my psych."

"That sounds silly," Jaimes said.

"That's what I thought," I agreed. "But I suppose it could be fun."

"Five things?" Jaimes laughed. "Didn't one of your Cosplay Dog posts get a thousand likes?"

"Yes, okay, now we need four more."

"Well, think of one."

My mind was blank. C'mon, anything? Was my favorite cereal in stock? Did my favorite band put out a new single?

"Haydan gave me a hug," I said.

"Haydan?"

"An old work friend. She gave me her number, too."

"Oh?" Jaimes asked.

I could tell he was imagining setting us up. Quit being my wingman, Jaimes.

"I didn't call her though. She wanted me to go to trivia night."

"Is that a bad thing?"

"I get too nervous in bars," I explained. "I mean, I was able to go to trivia night for a while, but then they moved where it was. I think they are still at the new place."

"Is there something about that bar you don't like?"

We were way past me keeping my mouth shut, weren't we?

"It's the sound. It's a smaller building. People get drunk and they laugh. It's really the only thing I can't handle. I'm a lot better than I was right out of high school, but that's the only thing I still can't deal with. So, when she invited me, I was happy, right, but like, of all the things for her to mention. I'm trying hard to make friends. It was such a kick in the teeth. I suppose..."

"Wait, that's why you don't go to bars?" Jaimes asked.

"Yeah. Kind of sucks. I mean, the whole gay bar scene, I can't do."

"I didn't know that was why. I mean, am I understanding you right? I don't want..." He seemed nervous about asking.

"It reminds me of the boat," I said.

"That's the only thing?"

It was obvious that he wanted to ask about something but didn't want to upset me. I hated it when people walked on eggshells around me. Understandable, I guess.

"Yes. I mean, I don't even really remember much. Drunken laughter, that stuck in my head. I mean, I remember some other things, but they don't hit me. Realize, stuff like this doesn't make sense. Shawn would sometimes try to upset me on purpose and fail."

"He did what?" Jaimes asked angrily.

"He talked about it all the time. He kept pushing me to remember details and he'd make stuff up. When he talked about me being passed around at parties and he threw money at me? That's what he was doing. He was trying to trigger me. That's why I hit him."

"Is...is that what happened?" Jaimes asked, hesitantly. "You were..."

"No," I interrupted. "I mean, maybe? I don't remember. I seriously have no idea. I was drugged out of my mind."

"Jesus Christ," Jaimes said. "Shawn sure is a sick fuck."

"Not going to disagree, but could you just not?"

"Not what?"

"Insult Shawn," I said.

I wasn't sure why, but it bothered me.

"He...he literally hired someone to kill me. Are you fucking serious right now? Shawn is a sick fuck. He's a murderous piece of shit. He's an abusive, obsessive, manipulative stalker."

"Please stop. Please, I'm asking you to stop."

I didn't want to hear it.

"What is wrong with you, Nik? You know it's all true."

"I know it's true, but what does that make me then? Huh? I'm the one who dated him. I'm the one who stayed with him."

"Quit taking the blame for everything. Damn it, Nik," Jaimes said. "Do you ever get angry?"

"Of course, I do."

What was Jaimes getting at?

"Then stop fucking asking yourself what it makes you. You blame yourself for everything. You blame yourself for getting on the boat. You blame yourself for going out with Shawn. You probably blame yourself for me getting shot. Just stop it. None of that shit's your fault."

I didn't know what to say. "Are you done?"

"Look, Nik, I'm about to face some people that I was completely awful to. Okay? All that shit is on me. I'm not boat guy. I'm not Shawn. I've never shot anyone. But I was an asshole. I pushed people around. I used people. That was because I was messed up, not them. I had issues, not them. Someone tripped and dropped their books? Target. Some girl thought I was cute and looked over at me? Target. Random, stupid luck," he ranted.

"It's not that simple. We're not talking about schoolyard bullies."

Is he making this about him? He didn't know what he was talking about.

"Aren't we? Those college kids that got you on the boat, they targeted you. You don't think they knew what to say to random teenager X to talk you into it? It's not your fucking fault. And Shawn. Do you think that you made him that way? He has a fucking screw loose. He's a bad guy. If it wasn't you, it would have been somebody else. Did he see you alone and make some excuse to ask you to help him with something, then act shy? Did he butter you up?"

"Shut up."

I didn't want to hear it.

"If you think you were actually his first, you're fucking delusional," Jaimes kept ranting, not skipping a beat. "Nineteen-year-old who can pull off that shit isn't a virgin. I bet you my left nut he was even fucking around while you were dating."

"Are you done?" I asked again.

I never considered that Shawn might be lying about that. Was Shawn only saying that to make me feel guilty? Was that possible?

Whatever. Jaimes kept crossing the line with me.

"What's your point?"

"My point is that I'm sick of you beating yourself up. I'm sick of you not standing up for yourself. Your old work friend doesn't know you can't go to the bar. Tell her you don't like bars and suggest doing something somewhere else. This isn't rocket science. If there is something I do that makes you sad, just fucking tell me and don't sugarcoat shit. Tell me. If I ask if you are okay and you aren't, say no. Just say no. Don't fucking lie to me. I'm sick of seeing you hurt. I can't stand it."

We were traveling down the highway. He was looking forward, of course. He was driving. He got so emotional. I wondered what was going on in his head. Maybe seeing his old classmates was a bigger deal than I realized. Maybe all our problems were getting to him.

Whatever, he was going too far.

"I've told you all the things that bother me. It's not easy to talk about this stuff. You're being a dick right now."

"All the things?" he asked.

Was he really pressing me right now?

"Then why did you get all weird about Caleb?"

"We're talking about Caleb now?"

I was tempted to blast the radio and ignore him for the rest of the trip.

"Well, we're on the road for another," he looked at the navigation, "five hours, so might as well talk about Caleb."

"Which time I got weird about Caleb? You'll have to be more specific."

I hated talking about Caleb.

"Any of the times. When you got all pissy about me paying for it? When you got all weird about me talking rough to him? When you literally hit me?"

Jerk. I was trapped in a car with him.

"Pissy? I'm not a big fan of prostitution."

"Sex work," Jaimes corrected.

"Whatever. Maybe that has something to do with me being a human trafficking victim? You think? Did I tell you I was paid? Found 200 dollars in my pocket and some meth. That's why Shawn threw 200 dollars at me."

"See? What are you talking about right now? Don't you fucking dare put me in same category as those pieces of shit. Hiring someone like Caleb is completely different. You watch porn constantly. You're such a hypocrite."

"I know it's not the same. If I thought it was the same, would I be hanging out with you? Defensive much?"

"Do you blame me? Of course I'm defensive. So, if it's not the same, what's your problem?"

I blanked for a moment. He scoffed at me, like I didn't have an answer.

Boy, he was something else today.

"It's impersonal. That's why." I finally answered him. "Just because someone agrees to it doesn't mean they want it. I'd never want to be with someone who didn't want me. Honestly, the idea of it upsets me, but it's not like I get a flashback or anything. What? You want to know about every subject that upsets me? Vivisection upsets me. I'm not a big fan of snakes. Holocaust denial is terrible. I'm not good with heights."

"C'mon, last time it came up, you were all whimpering and saying you couldn't talk about it. Let me ask. Save the sarcasm, okay?"

"I already told you. It worried me because you seemed different."

"It worried you that much that I seemed different? You were worried about me?"

"Yes. Very. Still am."

"You weren't worried," he insisted. "You were mad."

"Didn't you just scold me for not getting angry? Well, I was angry at you and worried about you. Not the type of angry you want me to be, huh?"

"Explain to me why. Why were you so mad? You keep saying you don't want to talk about stuff, but maybe if you hit me, I have a right to know why."

"You're still mad that I hit you?"

"Yes."

Five hours of this. Great.

"I told you why. It made me uncomfortable."

"Very specific."

"Do I have to spell it out?"

"Yes."

Five hours. Five hours of this crap.

"Okay. What if I suddenly put my hand down your pants without asking or talking about it first? How can you not realize that's not okay?"

"I didn't touch you."

"You didn't have to. You might as well have. You told me to keep talking like you were getting off on my voice. I did not agree to that."

"Oh shit. I did, didn't I? I'm sorry."

Finally, he got it.

"Yes, you did, and I'm having all these thoughts about your chest, plus you sprang this on me, plus you're acting weird, and then your..." I hated this man. Why did he have to push me all the time? "I don't want to talk about it."

"Christ! Are you being serious right now? This is what I'm talking about. I know this stuff is difficult, but like, you're constantly leaving me wondering what the fuck is going on. I end up having to guess. I thought maybe the rough talk brought back bad memories or something."

"What?"

Holy shit, how long was he thinking this? That didn't even cross my mind.

"No. Not at all. Not even a little bit."

"Then why the fuck are you getting all weird about the rough talk?"

"If you really must know, the reason I don't want to talk about it is because we're in a car and I'm wearing fitted pants and using a seat belt."

Now, I got to wait until he gets it.

"Huh?"

Silence.

Then, Jaimes burst out laughing.

"Thanks for understanding. Well, that was the last of my dignity."

"Wait, wait," Jaimes said, still laughing hysterically. "When you said that the reason you passed out was gross..."

"Acute epididymal hypertension and vasovagal syncope."

"What? What does that mean? I don't speak that language."

Did I really have to spell it out for him?

"I was aroused...but I didn't, you know...and I fainted and fell asleep."

"You're kidding?" He was laughing so hard he was wheezing. "That can actually happen?"

"I mean...not by itself...but..."

"Do you need me to pull over to a rest stop or something? You could lay down in the back for a while?" Jaimes joked. "Or, you know, the seat reclines. There're wet wipes in the glove compartment."

"I hate you, so much."

"Too bad I don't have two good hands, or I could help you out and keep driving."

"Sadist."

Name

From Jaimes' point of view.

The event was at a country club banquet hall.

When we finally arrived, I was nervous. Nik was still grumpy. I was tempted to keep joking with him, but it was hard to know when he thought it was funny and when he'd had enough.

He looked amazing.

"How should I introduce you?" I asked.

"Nik?" he laughed. "Did you forget my name?"

"I mean, who should I say you are?" I clarified.

"Fuckboy," he joked. At least his sense of humor was back. I straightened his tie.

"No, seriously."

"Friend, I suppose. Do I have other options?"

Nik looked up at me with doe eyes. Jesus, what was he asking? I wanted to kiss him.

"My good friend, Nik," I explained. "My old roommate. The guy who saved my life. Plus-one."

He straightened my tie and my left sleeve.

"Good friend works," Nik answered. "We don't need to mention the whole lifesaving thing."

"All right."

"But they are going to assume we're a couple anyway."

"That's fine. I don't mind, do you?"

He didn't answer, he just grabbed my hand and started practically skipping toward the door.

"Hey, why don't we have a code word if either of us wants to bail?" he suggested.

"Banana," I said.

Nik chuckled.

"I went to a pretty large school. For all I know, nobody will recognize me, and we'll have a nice meal."

"They might recognize you from the news," Nik suggested, opening the door for me.

"Maybe."

When we got in, a few people were milling around. I didn't recognize anyone right away.

"Hello! Find yourself!" a lady called out to us from behind a table full of nametags.

I stepped up to the table and looked around. Ah shit, they used my first name. I picked up my name tag, and Nik gave me this huge side eye.

"Bartholamew?" Nik asked.

"Surprise!" I said, smiling. "Jaimes is my last name."

"Oh. Wow. I didn't know."

"I just realized, I don't know what Nik is short for," I said, putting on my name tag.

Nik grabbed one of the name tags for plus-ones and wrote something on it. He held it up, smiling and then put it on his chest.

"Nikola. Neat. I always assumed it was Nicholas."

"Nope. Nikola," he said, still grinning.

"So now," the lady said, "fill out one of the introduction cards and give it to the doorman. He'll introduce you to the room."

"What a cool idea," Nik said, picking up one of the cards. "Here, I'll fill it out."

"Bartholamew," he said slowly while writing it and looking at my name tag for the spelling.

"Jaimes has an 'i'," I said. "J – A – I – M – E – S."

"I knew that!"

He filled out the rest of the card and started to walk toward the doorman. His grin was too large. I got suspicious.

"What did you write on there?" I asked.

"Nothing," he chuckled.

I grabbed for it, and he tried to keep it out of my reach.

"Let me see it, you little bitch," I laughed.

He started running so I ran after him. I was able to trap him in a corner by the large doors to the banquet hall.

"What did you write on there? Give it to me."

He was holding the piece of paper over his head. Since I was taller than him, I was able to reach over with my right arm to try to grab it, but I had to get very close to him to reach. Then he switched hands to keep it away from me.

"No fair," I protested.

Taking advantage of my bad arm, so obnoxious.

"Call me a bitch again," he whispered in my ear.

"Give it to me, bitch," I whispered back to him mischievously.

He dropped the paper on the floor, grabbed the back of my head and kissed me. I forgot where I was. I didn't care. Holy shit. What just happened? When did he get so bold?

I returned his enthusiasm by carefully parting his lips with my tongue. He ran his fingers into my hair and made a light fist, pulling my hair and controlling me.

I could hear someone clearing their throat to get our attention. We both came to our senses, stopped, and looked up from what we were doing. My classmates and their dates in the lobby area were all staring at us.

"Sorry, I guess we got a little carried away," I muttered.

The person who was clearing their throat was the doorman. He walked back to his post by the door. "Bartholamew Jaimes and his fuckboy Nik," he called out into the banquet hall, reading off the card he must have picked off the floor.

I stared at Nik incredulously. "You didn't?"

"I didn't think he'd actually say it!" Nik laughed.

What had gotten into Nik? He wasn't nervous at all. He was bold. He was cracking jokes and laughing. I wasn't sure why. Maybe this was his old self? Was this what he was like in high school before the world had other ideas?

"Well, let's go find a place to sit," I said as I took Nik's hand and walked through the door to the banquet hall. People were sitting around tables and standing around. Nearly everyone was looking at us.

I stopped and scanned around the room, some of the faces I remembered from basketball. I saw a few kids that I used to pick on, at least I think it was them. I didn't notice any of my ex-girlfriends. Everyone looked a bit perplexed. Nik was standing beside me, still holding my hand.

"Do you want to stay?" he asked.

"I guess we should. We came all this way."

We found a small open table. By the time we sat down, the crowd stopped looking at us and carried on.

"I'm so sorry," Nik said, staring at his place setting.

"It was hilarious, don't worry about it."

"No, I mean..." he trailed off.

"The kiss? Don't be sorry. It was wonderful and unexpected."

"It was not well-timed. It's just, you were so close."

Since when did he want me so much? Did I simply not notice? First, we had that weird conversation in the car and now this. I could walk into a bar and figure out who's up for it in a few minutes and this was lost on me?

"We are very close, aren't we?" I smiled.

Just then, Nik got this horrible, startled look on his face.

"No! Don't!" Nik shouted as one of my basketball teammates slapped me on the back to say hello.

I grimaced.

"Oh, um, sorry," the guy said.

I looked up. I recognized him. His name was Jon.

"It's okay, but that's my injured arm. Please don't do that again."

"Injured? Sorry to hear that, what happened, man?"

"I was shot." What was I going to do, lie?

"Shot?" Jon asked. "Hunting accident?"

I guess he didn't watch the news.

"I'd rather not talk about it, to be honest."

"Right on," Jon said. "Nice seeing you and your...friend."

Jon bucked his head back to acknowledge Nik. Nik sort of waved.

"Didn't expect that, but like, good for you. Whatever floats your boat."

Jon hit Jaimes on the other shoulder, and then he left.

Nik seemed to get a kick out of Jon's reaction.

"That wasn't so bad, I guess," Nik said, with a smile. "Could be worse."

I looked around the room again. It seemed like most folks were actively avoiding us.

Why was I even here?

Nik and I kissed, really kissed, for the first time and we're sitting on uncomfortable chairs surrounded by people I barely really knew.

"Is that Jaimes?" I heard a voice ask.

"Of course, it's Jaimes."

"Who is he with?"

"His boyfriend."

"What?"

"His boyfriend. They kissed in the lobby."

"Hot."

"Rude!"

"Hot and rude."

I looked over at Nik, who seemed to have also overheard the conversation. He had his hand over his mouth, trying not to laugh. He took a deep breath. "I think she might be having thoughts," he said giggling. "Sandwich thoughts."

"Shh." I was trying not to laugh. "C'mon, we're really pushing it."

I couldn't believe that I was the one trying to rein Nik in.

"I suppose. I'll get us something to drink," Nik suggested, getting up. "I'll behave."

I thought maybe I should go with him, but I doubted that anyone was going to start shit, and I didn't want our little island of isolation to be taken over.

Another one of my teammates walked by. He tried to avoid eye contact. It dawned on me that these were my best friends, and they were treating me like I was barely there. I didn't think it would bother me, but it did.

Nik came back after a little while with two cans of soda.

"I didn't dare take the punch. Neither of us can drink at the moment, and I don't trust this crew not to spike it," he said as he sat down. "Hey, someone recognized me from Cosplay Dog, believe it or not."

"Oh really? That's cool."

"She was surprised I was dating you. I wasn't sure what to say. I mean...we aren't. I said we were good friends and she laughed, like I was bad at lying."

"Could we?" I finally asked. After all this time, I finally asked the question.

"What?"

"Is it possible for us to be a couple?"

"I don't know. I, seriously, don't know," Nik answered, opening my soda for me and then opening his own. "And that's why I'm sorry. I'm terribly sorry. I shouldn't have kissed you like that without being sure."

He was practically in tears suddenly.

I took a sip of my soda and then held his hand again. "It's okay. We'll figure it out."

Nik nodded.

I could hear all the people around me milling around and reminiscing. They were talking about where they went to college, their jobs, where they were living, all of those things. A few people had already gotten married. A few already had kids. They were all telling stories and laughing. We sat there, sipping our sodas.

I could have gotten up and approached some of the people I knew, but it became clear that all I was, was the elephant in the room.

I was popular in high school. I was really good at basketball. These were the people who had, at one time, literally chanted my name. Now they wanted nothing to do with me. I felt invisible.

"I don't want to be here," I finally admitted. "I really don't want to be here."

"Pancakes?" Nik suggested. "Banana pancakes."

"Lars has taught you well."

"He really did teach me well," Nik joked as he stuck his hand in the air with two fingers sticking out, pretending like he was massaging someone's prostate.

"I can't believe you did that!" I wheezed.

"I wanted to see you smile," Nik said. "Now, let's get out of here."

So, we retreated. We got up and left. What a waste of money. What a wake-up call.

"At least Jon came over," I said once we got near the car.

"He seemed nice," Nik said.

"You know, it would have been easier if they had been shocked by us or even started shit. They simply didn't care."

"You said, yourself, the person you were in high school wasn't you."

Once I got into the car with Nik and we shut the doors, I broke down crying. I would have never thought I'd react this way to simple indifference. What the fuck was wrong with me? When did I become such a crybaby?

"I guess. It makes perfect sense," I said, trying to compose myself. "The people who were my friends never knew me. I'm sure they figured that out quick. The people I was awful to, why would they want to talk to me? It makes sense, but it feels terrible."

"Well, I don't feel so bad about being obnoxious then," Nik said. "I can't believe he actually said fuckboy."

"That was pretty funny," I said. "Shameless."

"I learned it from you. I learned to be shameless," Nik smiled. His eyes were bright. "I'm not even joking."

"So, pancakes?" I confirmed, starting the car.

"Sure."

Work

From Nik's point of view.

I was still reeling. I wasn't sure what had gotten into me. I didn't just kiss him. I was very forward. Perhaps it was a potent combination of antianxiety medication and sexual frustration, maybe a little jealousy.

We were in front of all his classmates, too. I never would have guessed that's how it would happen. Gosh, did I have an exhibitionist streak I didn't know about?

Jaimes was checking into the hotel. I offered to pay for it, but since it was his class reunion, he insisted. By the time we were done at the restaurant, it had gotten pretty late.

Jaimes told me a bunch of stories from high school. I think that helped him deal with how he felt. I think I understood why it hit him so hard.

Those were the people who used to cheer for him. Some of them were teammates. He had all sorts of stories about them. I was always an outcast in high school. Jaimes belonged. Now, he wasn't one of them anymore. It was like none of that ever happened. They didn't even care enough to react. He was no one. I'm sure it didn't help that his own family basically did the same thing. They simply stopped caring.

Jaimes was accustomed to going into a bar and immediately being recognized and sought after. That didn't happen anymore either.

He tried to make things work with Lars, and that ended.

He must be so lonely. I was so worried for him.

He got the keys, and we started up to the room. We had separate beds this time. That was probably a good thing. Everything had changed so much.

When we were roommates, it was all about him being too sexual, too forward, and teasing me. Now, I was worried that I would take advantage of him. I was worried I would make him think that being with me was a possibility when it wasn't.

It was all too sad. I had to stop thinking about it.

"Do you want to watch TV?" I asked.

"Sure. Let me change into my pajamas. The suit is getting heavy."

"But hey, we both have nice suits now. I'm sure we'll find other places to wear them." I wanted to look on the bright side. "Wait, let's take a selfie."

"A selfie?"

"Yeah, us all dressed up."

We needed a picture of us on the day we first kissed, I thought, but I didn't say that out loud. I guess I was getting used to my new meds. I wasn't saying everything that popped into my head anymore.

Once we were in the room, we stood in front of a clear area of the wall and leaned into each other to both get into the shot.

"And a silly one. We need a silly one," I insisted.

We both stuck out our tongues, and he gave me bunny ears.

"There, got it."

"What do you want to watch?" Jaimes asked, taking off his tie.

"You should decide this time. You always leave it up to me."

"You ever watch old basketball games?" Jaimes asked.

"No, but I guess I could," I said, really, really not wanting to do that. Was he joking?

"Your face!" He pointed and laughed. "Do you even know the rules?"

"It has something to do with throwing a ball into a basket."

"Yes, good enough." He was thoroughly amused.

"Gosh, you can't play basketball anymore, can you?" I asked, immediately regretting saying it. Was that a rude question?

"I can. Not as well, but I can. I mean, I haven't played seriously since high school anyway. I wasn't good enough for college. I guess that I could have tried out, but I would have ended up on the bench the whole time anyhow. It's not a big deal. The most frustrating thing is typing. The occupational therapist says that I might be able to start using a regular keyboard decently at some point, but right now I'm using a touch pad. I'm getting pretty good at it, but it's not as fast."

"I'm sorry I wasn't around more," I said. "I wish I could have helped you more."

"You were dealing with some pretty awful shit. Jesus, no worries."

He got out his pajamas. He used to sleep in boxers and maybe a T-shirt. He switched after the shooting because I asked him to.

"I'll change in the bathroom," Jaimes said.

219

"Thanks."

I started to set up the TV thing. Once I had it all set up, I started taking off my suit. While I was taking it off, Jaimes came out of the bathroom in button-up pajamas.

"I really appreciate you wearing that."

"It's not a problem," Jaimes smiled. "I'm glad you seem to be doing better."

"I am doing a lot better, I really am. I'm thinking of trying to get back to work."

"Really? That's great."

"My psych and I had this idea that I'd volunteer at the hospital and see how I do, you know, being around everything again and then go from there."

"That sounds like a great idea. Low stress, right? Just volunteering," he said as he piled up the pillows on one of the beds.

"Yeah, basically. I'd be bringing toys to kids and stuff, pushing around the book cart, that sort of thing."

"I never really understood why you didn't try to go back to work a while ago. I mean, I realize you couldn't. I'm not questioning it, but I don't quite understand why."

Jaimes got into his bed and leaned on the pile of pillows that he had created.

"Anything having to do with medical stuff, at all. I can't deal with it," I explained.

"Medical stuff?"

"Yeah. I work with blood all day. I mean, I used to work with blood all day and blood's a thing for me now and you have to have very steady hands. Any sort of nervousness and you're blowing sites or having to dig around. Right now, I'm not sure I can even be in the room and be calm."

"But you visited me in the hospital," Jaimes said.

"Yeah."

"You visited me even though it made you feel terrible?"

"Yeah."

I wasn't going to lie.

"Wow. Okay."

"In a way, it was a good thing. Wanting to visit you helped me get over that initial anxiety, you know."

"What happens if you can't be calm?" he asked.

"Then I don't go back to work. What do you think it means?"

I was stripped down to my boxers. I crawled into the other bed with the remotes and put a couple of pillows behind me.

"Is there something else you'd want to do?" Jaimes asked.

"Not sure I can pay the bills making dog outfits. Cosplay Dog is a labor of love," I smiled. "And money laundering."

"Don't remind me."

"I suppose, at some point, I could get a retail job or work at the coffee shop or something. You know, if it doesn't work out at the hospital. That'd be tough, but better than staying home all day."

Nothing like being one of the best at something and then not being able to do it.

"I'm hoping it doesn't come to that," I added.

"I understand, at least a little bit. I was worried I wouldn't be able to go back to work for a while, too, until they set me up with the touch pad and the right software. I was thinking, great, four years of college down the drain. Now, I have to worry about speed. I used to do things a lot faster. It's really frustrating."

"I can imagine."

Gosh, I don't think we ever really talked like this before. I mean, we knew basically what was going on with each other, but I don't think we ever calmly talked about the practical things. Maybe the car ride cleared the air.

"So, what do you want to watch?" I asked.

"You decide, you always pick neat stuff."

"Okay. Let's see." I looked though the movies on my phone.

I wondered if it would be funny to put up a basketball movie, but I really didn't want to watch one.

"There's one about a train that travels around the world in the snow."

"Nope. No! Not in the mood for that one."

"One about repo men that collect organs from people delinquent on their medical bills after transplants. It's a musical."

"What? No. How about a superhero movie or something?"

"Ah, sure." I cast a movie onto the TV.

"Subtitles again?" Jaimes complained.

"I can find something else."

"This is fine," he said as the movie began. Right at the beginning, they had a sequence with computer-generated Chinese dragons.

"Jesus Mary, this is really beautiful. Like aesthetically amazing," Jaimes commented. "I wish we were watching it on a better television."

"See, I know what you like. I mean...I didn't mean it like that."

Now I did it.

"Sit with me," Jaimes said.

"I...um..." I wasn't sure that was a good idea, not because I didn't want to, but because I wanted to. I really wanted to.

"I'm sorry. I know that's a thing," Jaimes said apologetically. "Let's just watch the movie."

"What if it doesn't work?" I blurted out.

"What are you talking about?" Jaimes asked.

I stopped the movie.

"What if we try to be together, but find out we can't? What would happen?"

"I'd still love you and we'd still be friends," Jaimes said. "Whatever happens with us, that's never going to change."

I turned off the TV, and I walked over to Jaime's bed.

"There's only one way to find out," I said nervously. "There's something I need to do."

Restart

"What are you suggesting?" Jaimes asked.

"I need to know what my mind does," Nik explained. "Lie down in the middle of the bed. Don't do anything. Okay? If it gets too weird..."

"Banana."

"Yeah."

"Okay. I trust you," Jaimes said, moving one of the pillows to the middle of the bed and laying down.

Nik pulled down the covers so that they were covering Jaimes' lower legs. He crawled up onto the bed, kneeling down beside Jaimes and looking down at his chest.

"So far, so good," Nik said and started to unbutton Jaimes pajama top, starting at the bottom.

"I need to remove your shirt," Nik whimpered.

"If this is too much, please don't push yourself."

"I'm alright. I need this. I need to deal with this."

Nik continued to unfasten the shirt one button at a time. Once it was unbuttoned, he opened it up to reveal Jaimes' chest.

"I'll skip the part where I take off your hair with duct tape," Nik joked.

"I appreciate that."

Nik put his right hand on Jaimes' left side and his left hand on top of Jaimes' chest.

"See? Your heart is between my hands," Nik said, smiling.

"My heart is in your hands?"

"Between my hands, so the electricity goes through your heart."

"That makes sense."

"Focus on me. Look at me."

"I am."

"Do you remember me saying that?"

"Yes, I tried but I couldn't. Now I can."

Nik started trembling as they looked into each other's eyes.

"Are you okay?" Jaimes asked.

Nik nodded. "You're alive. You're warm. Your lips are pink."

Nik closed his eyes but kept his hands on Jaimes.

"I'm here," Jaimes reassured Nik. "I'm still with you."

Nik lowered his right ear onto Jaimes' chest.

"Your heart is beating so fast."

"Of course, it is. You're close to me," Jaimes said. "Can I hold you?"

"Please."

Jaimes wrapped his right arm around Nik, who was still listening to his heart.

"Did you find out what you needed to?" Jaimes asked.

"Yeah. You're going to have to take me from behind so I can't see you."

"What?" Jaimes asked, breaking the solemn mood. "Are you being serious right now? Be clear, all right? Is that really what you want? I can't believe you said that with a straight face."

"I'm joking, well sort of joking. I'm actually doing much better than I thought I would. Though, it might not hurt for you to be behind me, I guess."

Nik kept his ear to Jaimes' chest.

"Of course, it wouldn't hurt, I know what I'm doing," Jaimes joked. "Well, I usually do. I'm worried I'll accidentally do the wrong thing. That's not something I'm used to."

"I'm willing to try to figure us out if you are," Nik said, lifting up his head. "I want to be able to look at you. I want to see you. I don't want it to be some impersonal thing. I don't. What's the point of that?"

"But are you good, right now?" Jaimes asked. "Do you see me the way I really am? Alive and well."

"Yes. Listening to your heartbeat and your breathing helped. Feeling how warm you are helped."

"You restarted my heart."

"The defibrillator did, yeah."

"No, you did, you restarted my heart" Jaimes said with sincerity as he touched Nik's face.

"Who are you? Are you serious? So sappy!"

"Kiss me."

"What's the magic word?"

"Bitch."

"Maybe something else."
"Fuckboy."
"Try again."
"Boyfriend."
"I like that."

Book Five: Truth Dies

Magic

From Nik's point of view.

"Then you had sex, right?"

"Like it's any of your business, Mandi," I protested.

"You told me that you and Jaimes are finally together! Of course, I want to know. Do we not talk about that sort of thing anymore?" she asked, setting her liquid-candy-bar of a drink down on the table.

"No, Jaimes and I didn't have sex. We made out and then we watched the rest of the movie. Then we slept. In the morning, we drove back home."

"But you're dating right?"

"Yes," I answered. "Sex and dating aren't the same thing, Mandi."

"So, Jaimes is not having sex right now at all?" she asked incredulously.

"Not your business."

"Nik, what are you two doing to each other? How far have you gone?"

"That's none of your business, either. Mandi, I haven't seen you in months, and all you want to know is the porn of my life?"

"I don't want a play-by-play. What I'm saying is that you two seem to keep denying yourselves. It's going to get to a point where you're making yourselves miserable."

I wasn't making myself miserable. I was miserable, damn it. I was not well enough. I couldn't magically be okay.

"I don't want to talk about it," I said.

"Nik? It's me, Mandi. You can tell me anything."

"Really?" I fumed. "Are we the type of friends that tell each other everything, because last I checked you found out that my ex tried to literally murder someone I cared about, and because I didn't know what he did, I got back together with him."

I was trying to keep my cool. I missed Mandi so much. I did. I really didn't want to lose my temper, but I couldn't help it. I just saw red.

"Screw you! Screw you, Mandi!" I yelled. "Want to hear some stories about Shawn and me? Huh? Are you curious? Do you want to know what sex with him was like?"

"Nik?" she whimpered. "You don't understand, I..."

"What? You wanted to protect me? You aren't my mom! You could have fucking said something."

"No, I couldn't. I really, really couldn't. You need to shut the hell up," Mandi said through gritted teeth. She stood up, leaned over the table, and grabbed my shoulders. Then, she whispered in my ear, "You made a deal with a really scary person. You know that."

"Like, I had a choice." I pushed my forehead into her shoulder as hard as I could. The whole place was quiet. I'd made a scene. "You better let me go, right now," I spat, clenching my jaw.

She slowly let go of my shoulders and sat back down. She looked scared. Oh no. Did she think I was going to hurt her?

"I'm sorry I yelled at you," I said, shaking.

"You have a right to be angry."

"You're damn right, I do."

I got up to walk out.

"But Nik, I need to talk to you! It's important!"

She followed me and tried to grab my arm.

"Don't you dare touch me! Don't call me! Stay away from me!"

I left.

Mocha

From Jaimes point of view.

Nik sent me a text. "Pick me up. I'm at the park."

"What happened? I thought you were with Mandi," I texted back.

"Please pick me up."

"Are you okay?"

"No."

My phone started ringing. It was Mandi.

"What's going on?" I answered.

She was crying.

"Nik got really angry at me. I'm worried about him. You should check on him."

"He already asked me for a ride."

"I needed to make sure he was okay."

"You don't sound good either. What happened?"

"He blames me for him getting back with Shawn. He told me to stay away from him. He's my best friend in the whole world."

She was distraught.

"I'll talk to him," I said, walking to my car. "Things have been pretty bad lately. He tried to get back to work recently, and it was a disaster."

"Oh no, poor Nik."

"Are you going to be all right?" I asked, starting my car. I routed the call into the onboard so I could drive.

"I'll be okay," she answered. "Jaimes, I know this might be a weird time to mention it, but did Nik tell you about a letter that I sent him in the mail?"

"No. He didn't tell me about a letter."

"It's really, really important that it doesn't get lost."

"What is it?"

"A big deal. A really big deal. At some point, I need it back. I need to talk to Nik about it. Please trust me."

"I trust you."

"At least someone does."

"Look. I wasn't very happy about you not telling us what was going on, but I know you must have had your reasons."

"I did. Shawn would have...we couldn't..."

"I know that you're our friend and the shit Shawn did is not your fault. It's Shawn's fault. I'm sure Nik will calm down. He just needs time."

"I hope you're right. It's also important that we keep up our deal with Shawn's mom. Really, really important. Don't mess around. Please."

"Okay. Don't worry. I get it."

"I don't think Nik does. He said some stuff at the coffee shop he shouldn't have, not in public like that. Please, make sure he stays on board."

"Okay," I reassured her.

I found a place to park and quickly found Nik. We often went to Rainbow Coffee. We would walk to the nearby park on nice days. He was staring off with his hands folded in his lap, sitting on a bench. His eyes were red, and his face was wet.

"Mandi's worried about you," I said, sitting down beside him.

"Let her worry. I wish she would stop trying to save me. She never asks me what I want. She decides for me. She'll never stop thinking of me as some idiot kid."

"Having someone who cares about you the way she does is not a bad thing. Take your time, but you should talk to her. She's really upset."

"She called you?"

"Of course, she called me."

"I lost my temper. That never used to happen. She looked at me like she didn't recognize me, like she was afraid of me. You know, like when we were at the con and I said those terrible things to her. Something she said set me off, and I lost it. I hate this. I have a right to be angry. I don't have the right to treat her like that."

"What did she say that made you so angry?"

"She was annoyed that I didn't want to talk to her about personal stuff. When she said that I should be able to tell her anything, I blew up on her. I told her that if she would have told me about Shawn and what he did, I wouldn't have gotten back with him."

"You were having this conversation at the coffee shop, in public? Nik, you have to be careful. You know that, right?"

"Yeah. I guess we got paid, huh? Do you know what I almost did? I thought, why don't I take all the money out. I could fill out all the paperwork and get it all in cash, then spread it around the park."

"Nik," I said, looking around to make sure we were reasonably alone. "It's not about the money. Even if we gave it all back, the deal wouldn't be off, you know that. C'mon, Mandi is terrified."

"What? I know I yelled at her but..."

"Not terrified of you. She's terrified of Shawn and Ava's mom. Anyway, we shouldn't even be talking about this here. We should go home."

"I left my marshmallow mocha latte at the coffee shop."

"Do you want to go through the drive-thru and get another one?"

"Yes." He cracked a slim smile. "I do."

"Will it make you feel better?"

"Like magic." He finally looked up at me. "You know, that's what Shawn told me. That he turned it all around like magic. I should have realized he was full of crap. That's not how it works."

"No such thing as magic?" I asked.

"Well, marshmallow mocha lattes are pretty damn good. Maybe if I take the full dose. Worth a try."

"Mandi said she needs to talk to you about a letter she sent you."

"So, an extra-large marshmallow mocha latte then."

Upstairs

From Nik's point of view.

Jaimes and I laid down in my bed like we often did. It was a really comfortable bed.

"You're right. I should apologize to Mandi," I said.

"I already sent her a text saying you were sorry and that you were okay."

"Did I say I was sorry? Did I say I was okay?"

"Are you?"

"Yes."

"Okay then."

"Don't speak for me without asking, please." I was getting sick of not being consulted. "I'm serious."

"Sorry. Mandi was incredibly worried."

"It's fine. I get it. We should tell her she can come over tonight. I don't want to leave things like this."

"I'll let her know," Jaimes said.

The original plan was for Mandi and me to spend the day together since she was in town. Then the three of us would have dinner and watch TV or play games at my place. Jaimes had work to do, so it made sense. He'd get his work done during the day and hang out with us in the evening. But I messed it up.

"I think you two have a lot to talk about," Jaimes said. "Maybe if I'm around, it'll be easier."

"I think so. I don't think I would have lost my temper if you were there with me."

The idea was a little funny. For a long time, it was difficult for me to be near Jaimes, but now being with him made me less nervous. The more I was with Jaimes, the easier it was. If anything, I was more uncomfortable thinking about how I was in Shawn's house and in Shawn's bed.

"I like being with you," I said.

"I can stay. I have work to do, but it can wait." Jaimes held my hand under the covers.

"Move in," I said. I wanted to ask him for a while, but it suddenly seemed urgent.

"What?"

"Move in."

"Okay."

"Okay?"

"Yeah, Okay."

"Did that just happen?" I rolled over to look at him.

"Yes," Jaimes said with a big smile. "It did."

He kissed me on the forehead. I kissed him on the lips.

"Do you think the house is big enough for the both of us?" I asked.

"We'll make it work."

"Maybe if I get a job, we can buy something bigger."

"Buy a house together?"

"Yes," I said. "Buy a house together."

"You realize, we could go anywhere as long as I have fast internet."

"I guess you're right. I wanted to get back to my job so badly, but I'm free now, aren't I?"

"Right, maybe you could find a remote job like me," he suggested.

"I'm still nervous about the video. Even with the troll site down, I don't want to start a career that would end badly if someone found it."

"How about porn?"

"Very funny."

I knew he was joking, but I couldn't think of anything else off the top of my head either.

"I can try to get ripped again and get a bunch of tattoos, and you could start curling your hair," he joked.

"How about I get ripped and get a bunch of tattoos, and you start curling your hair and wearing stockings."

"Stockings? I don't think so. Are you actually into that?"

"Would you do that for me if I was?"

"Maybe for your birthday," he joked. "For you, sure. Not for porn. Not for anyone else."

"I don't think porn is for me. I hate that those personal things were consumed by strangers," I said. "I still feel like I've been gutted and put on display."

"I realize you don't want me to know the details, but I keep thinking, how could it possibly be that bad?"

"Remember when I played things out to help work through defibbing you?" I asked.

"Yes. Of course, I remember."

Now I waited for him to get it.

"Holy shit. I thought you were just talking about stuff before having sex."

"No, not just talking about it," I confirmed.

"Maybe we could learn another language and live in a different country," he suggested, trying to lighten the mood.

"With my luck, we would accidently move across the street from Shawn."

Jaimes laughed. "Don't be silly, Nik. Shawn's mom is rich. We couldn't afford to live in that neighborhood."

"You have a point there. So, where do you want to go?"

"Canada?"

"But they speak English in Canada."

"Quebec?"

I was laughing, but at some point, I knew we would get serious. I wanted to be with Jaimes, and I wanted to be anywhere but here.

We heard a knock at the door.

"Is that Mandi?" I asked. "She's early."

Jaimes checked his phone. "Yes, it's her. Look. She sent a text."

He held up his phone so I could read it. The text read, "Act normal and don't mention the bug sweeper."

"You're kidding me!" What sort of madness was Mandi getting us into? "Well, I guess we have to get dressed then."

Jaimes laughed. "Maybe we should move to a nudist colony."

"A Canadian francophone nudist colony?"

Cosplay started barking.

"I think Cosplay vetoed the plan," Jaimes joked.

"We could get a map, put it on the floor, and see where Cosplay pees on it," I suggested as I put on my clothes.

I noticed that Jaimes was putting on his clothes more easily now. His left arm was getting stronger and after months of physical therapy he had a better range of motion. I used to help him dress when we were together, but now he did it himself without too much trouble.

Jaimes had started working out again too and looked well. I was less worried about him than I used to be. We were going to get-togethers with Lars and his friends now. That was fun.

He started going to a spa every couple of weeks with Caleb, of all people. When Caleb got out of jail, Jaimes gave him a spa day as a got-out-of-jail present, and they kept going. They invited me along, but I didn't need my nuts waxed, thank you very much.

I finally got downstairs and opened the door. Mandi was standing in front of me, looking upset.

"I'm sorry I got so angry at the coffee shop. I've been having a hard time, you know, but I shouldn't have taken it out on you."

As I was talking, Ava and some guy in a black suit quickly came into the house. The guy was holding what appeared to be a scanning device of some sort. Before I could protest, Mandi gave me a huge hug.

"I'm so sorry. I can't keep lying to you. I'm so sorry."

I pushed her arms away. "What do you mean? Lying to me? About what? What now?"

I was sorry that I yelled at her, but I wasn't quite ready for that.

"The house seems to be clear," the man said. "All I'm picking up is our phones."

Mandi was my friend. I kept telling myself this. But what bombshell was she going to throw at me now? What piece of information was so disturbing that she looked like she was going to faint? This wasn't her at all. She was fierce. She was capable. I guess the stress was getting to her. It had to be.

"We're going to bring down Shawn's dad," Mandi said, finally walking into the house.

"What? Shawn's dad? What does he have to do with anything?" I asked, confused. "I've never even met Shawn's dad."

"Yes, you have," Ava said. "You met him a long time ago."

"I'm telling you. I've never met Shawn's dad. I don't even know what he looks like."

235

"We all need to sit down and talk," Ava insisted.

There wasn't very much room downstairs to sit, and Cosplay wouldn't leave us alone. So, we went upstairs, and all five of us sat on the bed. It was awkward.

"As you know, Ava and I have been working together," Mandi started to explain, "and we eventually compared notes about what happened seven years ago and..."

"Seven years ago? No. Stop talking." I desperately tried not to lose my temper again. "I've had enough. Do you understand? I'm sorry Mandi, but I can't take this anymore. I can't."

"I'll give you a choice, then," Mandi said, wiping her eyes. "I can keep you in the dark. That's what I planned to do, but then you got angry at me for keeping secrets. So, here I am. Do you want to know or don't you? I kept quiet before and that didn't turn out well, did it?"

"Wait, can we talk around him?" Jaimes asked, pointing at the man that came in with Ava and Mandi.

"No, you can't," the man said bluntly. "Anything pertinent to the case, I'm going to report."

"What case? Who are you? Why are you here?" I asked. "Why are Ava and some strange guy here? They should leave."

This was my house, damn it.

"No," Mandi said. "They stay."

"Why? Why is it up to you? Why do you get to decide? It's my house."

"The only reason I can be here is because he's here keeping an eye on me. And this involves Ava's family, so..."

"Involves? And how exactly are you two involved with each other, huh?" I asked, pointing at Ava and Mandi.

"Friends. We're friends now." Mandi glared at me.

Just friends? My ass.

"How can you be friends with her? Help me understand how you could possibly be friends with her."

"Nik, I know you are extremely angry," Ava said. "I don't expect you to forgive me, but there is a lot you don't know. Shawn was manipulating me. He led me to believe that Jaimes was hurting you and was being controlling, and that's why you broke up with Shawn. We set up cameras supposedly to collect evidence and to help you."

"Shawn broke up with me," I protested. "He found out I had a girlfriend in high school and absolutely lost it."

"I know that now, but I didn't then. He made it seem like he was trying to cover something up, all while feeding me misleading information meant to steer me toward a particular conclusion. He made you out to be an absolutely horrible person while pretending to defend you.

"I only realized much later that he was obsessively watching you, and that the plan, the entire time, was to hurt you. He acted like he was worried we were taking it too far, all while doing awful things behind my back. He used me. Everything was part of his plan to make you vulnerable. Everything he said and did was an act."

"But that's not it! He wasn't trying to hurt me. In his mind, he was trying to save me," I ranted loudly. "He believes his own crap. He lies without even realizing he's lying. It's a reflex to avoid pain. It's like taking his hand off a hot burner. He says whatever he needs to say to avoid that pain. You make it sound like he's so calculating. He isn't. He just takes every single opportunity to feel better, even if it's only for a moment. Nothing else matters, and there is nothing he won't do to feel in control. When he pretends to be tough and uncaring, that's the act, that's the lie. He's afraid, all the time. That's why he needs to be in control, it's because he's scared to death of being unloved and alone. That's why he won't let me go. That's why he's doing all of this!"

"Jesus Christ, Nik." Jaimes looked stunned.

I was saying too much. Oh well.

"Look, Nik, it doesn't even matter what exactly went through his head. That's what ended up happening," Ava explained. "I lost myself in the whole thing. I don't expect you to forgive me, but please trust that I'm a good friend to Mandi, and I want to do what I can to make it right."

"Sorry if I'm bitter," I said clenching my jaw. "I remember a time before all this when my best friend was dating a lovely girl named Traci who was sweet and kind, and the worst thing that I had to worry about was Jaimes pissing off the neighbors. Everything went to hell because of you. Do you understand? I can't even do my job anymore."

"Nik, please," Mandi said, upset.

"Why!? Tell me why? Why aren't you happy in Australia right now? Why are you here crying about crap that isn't even about you that happened seven years ago? Go live your life, Mandi, please! Why do you care about Shawn's dad? Why are you hanging out with Shawn's sister?

"Shawn is poison. He was so bad for me, Mandi. Me and Shawn, together, we are so messed up. Beyond messed up. We're fucked up in exactly the right ways to feed on each other. You don't even know. You can't know. I lived it. I lived through it. Please, let me forget about all of it. Please, let me run away and never come back."

"Is that what you want?" Mandi asked. I could tell she was struggling.

"Yes. I want you to be happy. I want you to be happy instead of dealing with my problems. You shouldn't have to deal with any of this."

"It's not that simple," Mandi protested.

"Yes, it is! I want you to be happy. You keep going through hell for me. Stop it. Go! Go do amazing things with your life. Forget all about me if you have to. I can't stand seeing you miserable because of me. Go to Australia, buy a huge bouquet of flowers or something, and win her back."

We stared at each other for a long time. We were best friends. This was terrible. It was all garbage. This wasn't the way it was supposed to be.

"I would rather have an icepick through my eye than enter this conversation," the man said, "but she doesn't actually have a choice."

Mandi nodded. "It's either this or prison."

"Seriously? You've...that's not funny..." I said, so shocked I was barely able to speak.

"No, it's not," Mandi said. "It's not funny at all. I've turned state's evidence. That means that I admitted guilt. To avoid prison, I'm required to provide certain information and assistance to the prosecution.

"Depending on how everything plays out, I might even have to testify against really scary people. I could never live with myself if Traci was hurt because of the shit that I did. But if I had a choice, I would be with her. I would have followed her anywhere in the world. I would have started a family with her. But I don't have a choice. Cool crimes are still crimes."

Mandi was a mess. She was fighting back tears. Her whole face was puffy and distorted. I could tell, if we weren't all here, she'd be screaming. I finally had enough.

I got off the bed and circled around to where she was sitting and hugged her. "I'm so sorry. I'm so sorry you're going through all of this."

Mandi held me so tight it hurt.

"I love you, Nik," she said. "Please don't feel bad. I'm the one who did those things. I made those decisions, not you."

"What decisions?" Jaimes asked. "It's been so long. Are you really still in trouble?"

"Some of the charges have expired. Not all of them," the man said. "To be honest, I think the state was being unkind, but they wanted to ensure her cooperation. So, that's the avenue they pursued."

"The avenue they pursued?" Jaimes scoffed.

"The case became larger," Ava explained. "Mandi and I realized this when we were talking about the incident with Nik. My father was a friend and business partner of the man who owned the boat. He wasn't on the radar of law enforcement before. But my mother filed for divorce seven years ago..."

"Stop talking," Jaimes said, interrupting her. "Nik said he wanted to forget all about it, so shut the fuck up about the goddamn boat. Why don't you all leave?"

"This is a waste of time. Let's go," the man said, standing up.

Ava also got up to leave.

Mandi started to remove herself from my arms.

"Stay," I told Mandi.

"I told you. I can't go anywhere without the suit right now."

"But we had coffee together," I said, confused.

"We weren't alone. He was there," Mandi explained. "He was sitting at a different table. He shadows me everywhere."

"But you were going to come over? Weren't you?" I asked.

"I was going to let you know about Ava and the suit over coffee. Things didn't go the way I was hoping."

"I'm sorry." I didn't know what else to say.

"Do you really want us to leave?" Mandi asked.

"Yes."

"Okay," she said, her voice broke.

What was I putting her through?

"I need time," I explained. "You gave me a choice. I need time to think. Please, give me time to decide."

"How about you two go downstairs and give them a damn minute?" Jaimes said to Ava and the man.

So, they gave us a minute. The three of them went downstairs.

I could hear Ava petting Cosplay. She was calling my dog by a different name, a name that Shawn had chosen. I wondered if Ava was there when Shawn adopted her.

I often wondered if it was cruel for me to keep Cosplay. Shawn probably wasn't doing very well. Or maybe he was? Maybe everyone else was right. Maybe Shawn was fine. Maybe he found someone else to obsess over and control. Maybe I was nothing to him. Maybe I was just a toy for him to play with and to eventually throw away once I was too broken to be fun anymore.

"I'm sorry again that I got so angry at the coffee shop," I said, "but I still don't understand why you didn't tell us."

"Shawn told us that if we, in his words, 'needlessly upset you' that all deals were off," Mandi explained. "When Ava found out what her brother did, that he hired that boy, she contacted me. She said that involving the police would be a bad idea, considering what her family was like. You and Jaimes were in no condition to be involved.

"So, we confronted Shawn ourselves. We thought we'd threaten to tell his mother, but you were all he cared about. He didn't want you to know. He agreed to quit stalking you, destroy all the video files, and stop trying to hurt Jaimes. He had already convinced Ava to take the fall for stalking you. So, all we needed to do was not tell you, so you would continue to think he wasn't involved."

"That makes sense."

"Does it?" Mandi asked. "How could he not realize that we would tell you the moment he broke the deal?"

"He thought that once he took possession of me again, that I would stay even if I knew," I explained.

"What?"

"And he was almost right. It took everything in me to leave him."

The only person I talked to, really talked to, about Shawn and me was Lars. Mandi had no idea. I knew she didn't quite believe me. She didn't want to.

"It wasn't until we got back together again that I understood," I continued. "I wish I never understood how completely pathetic I could be."

"Don't say that."

"Mandi, I'm not saying that to put myself down. I'm not fishing for compliments or comfort. I'm serious. That's what upsets me the most. When I was with Shawn, I only cared about him. I only cared about not making him upset. I never said no to him, even when I was screaming it in my head. I gave him what he wanted, even if it felt terrible and wrong."

"Why?"

"I don't know why! When it comes to Shawn, I'm not rational. I get that now. He terrifies me, but not because of what he might do, but because of who I am when I'm with him. It's like..." I didn't have the words at first. "It's like he hollows me out, and he's the only one that can make me whole."

She was quiet for a while. I'd been found out again. I hated it.

"I feel like we all failed you," she finally said. "How did we not see it?"

"Stop it!" I said too loudly at first. "Stop it. Please. There's something wrong with me. Stop taking the blame. I'm a grown man. I should be able to take care of myself."

I said that and I meant it, but all I wanted to do was put my head in her lap and cry like a damn baby. So, I did.

"Are they all right up there?" I heard Ava ask.

I wondered what Jaimes was going to say to Ava. He didn't disappoint me.

"Shut up and eat your damn pizza rolls."

Wait

From Jaimes point of view.

Eventually, they all left. Nik was a wreck.

Always. Always, when things seemed to be getting a little bit better, the world would decide to fuck around with him again. It was obviously taking a toll. I used to encourage him to get angry, because I knew he needed to let it out. I'm not sure I was quite prepared for how angry and bitter, and frankly messed up, Nik really was. I was committed to helping him through it all, though. I loved him.

"You should eat something," I told Nik. "I made some snacks."

"Yeah, I heard," Nik laughed. "'Shut up and eat your damn pizza rolls.' That was beautiful."

"Do you know what you're going to do?"

"No. I told Mandi that I needed to sleep on it. I really have no idea if I want to know what's going on or not."

"Whatever you decide, I'll support you," I assured him.

I wasn't lying, but holy shit, how could he possibly leave it? My brain was trying to make sense of the bits and pieces of everything. Nik met Shawn's dad a long time ago and he doesn't remember. The guy that owned the boat and Shawn's dad were friends. Shawn's mom filed for divorce, around the same time, seven years ago. How the hell could those things be coincidences?

Mandi literally told Nik that she'd been lying to him about something, and he isn't curious? He needed to have a choice though, didn't he? If he was done with it all, then he was done with it all.

"You really will support me, won't you?" Nik smiled. "You really will."

"I wouldn't say it if I didn't mean it. Now, shut up and eat your damn pizza rolls."

Nik started laughing. "Yes, sir."

Did this boy have any idea what he did to me? There were times that I missed Lars. Lars and I understood each other. If I were with Lars, he'd know how I was feeling right now. And then there's Nik, who was currently stuffing his face with pizza rolls, completely oblivious. Sometimes I worried that we'd never understand each other.

"We're out of soda," Nik said.

"Do you want me to go get some?" I asked as I wiped the kitchen counter.

"Nah. I'll get some tomorrow. Water is better for you anyway, right?"

"It is."

"Do you want any?" Nik asked, offering me a pizza roll.

"No, I already ate some. The rest are for you," I said. I might as well ask him now. "Hey, Nik."

"Yeah."

"Did you and Shawn...?" I didn't want to finish the sentence.

"Yes. Twice. Why do you want to talk about this?"

Taking no shit from me, huh, Nik?

"Because I never want us to be like that. Obviously, you didn't want to. You were on those meds, right?"

"It was awful. It felt awful. I didn't want to do it. I did it anyway. When I didn't respond the way that he wanted me to, he got mad. He threw away my meds," Nik said casually and then ate another pizza roll.

It was so strange. When he talked to me about terrible things, a lot of the time he would tell me straight up. It was like he was talking about someone else or giving me some summary of a television show. It was information.

"That sounds horrible," I said.

"You overheard me talking to Mandi."

"I tried not to listen, but the house is small."

"Understandable."

He put down the food he was about to put in his mouth and stared at me. He looked disturbingly serious.

"You and I will never be like Shawn and me. Never. Never in a million years. But it makes sense that you'd be worried. I keep telling you not to put all the blame on Shawn."

"This isn't about blame. I just..." Damn it. I stepped in it, didn't I? "Nik. I need to tell you that I never, ever want you to do something with me that you don't actually want to do."

He looked hurt. Jesus, how could that possibly be upsetting? Sometimes he made no sense. He got up from the table and came over to me.

"Jaimes. I know," Nik said, still looking at me intently. "How could I possibly not know that? You've been so patient with me. It would've been easier for you to give up on us, but you didn't. You could've pushed me or given me ultimatums, but you haven't."

He got very close to me.

"You know that I can't read minds like you can," he continued, "but do you really think I don't notice?"

He got in front of me and put his hand up to the side of my face.

"Do you really think I don't notice the way you look at me?" He rubbed my cheek with his thumb. "You want me, but you don't want to own me. You care about me. Do you think I don't notice?"

Simply feeling his hand against my skin made me warm. I took his hand and kissed him on the wrist. Was this torture? Was this depriving myself?

Ever since we started dating, I hadn't been with anyone else. It was unusual for me to be with only one person. It was bizarre for my sex life to consist of cuddling and kissing.

Nik straight up told me that he didn't expect us to be exclusive but getting my rocks off with some random person wasn't worth it anymore. Being kept wanting was strange and oddly wonderful.

Since when did someone's hand against my face feel like this?

Nik lifted his head, and I thought he was going to kiss me. Instead, he whispered in my ear. "Go upstairs and wait for me."

Then, he stood in front of me for a moment, looking up at me shyly, before disappearing into the bathroom.

It took me a second. He was a wreck a little bit ago and now...? What exactly was he suggesting? If he were anyone else, I would know. I mean, wasn't it obvious? With Nik, for all I knew he wanted me to wait upstairs for a neck massage or for him to unveil one of Cosplay's new outfits.

Regardless, I found myself waiting upstairs, in bed, in my boxers, staring at the ceiling. I could hear Nik in the bathroom. I heard the toilet flush. I heard the shower turn on. None of this was unusual. I stayed the night many times before.

Part of me was aching with anticipation and the other part of me thought I was being ridiculous. Tonight could not possibly be the night. It was such a long day. It was such an upsetting, long, weird day. It couldn't be today. Maybe it shouldn't be today.

As I laid there, contemplating my situation, I came to the startling conclusion that it might be me. I might be the one who wasn't ready. My god, what had I become? Who the hell was I?

I heard Nik climbing the ladder. I looked over, waiting for him to appear. Jesus Christ. I was afraid. No, not afraid. I was nervous. I was really nervous. I saw his hand first. He was holding his clothes. He threw them toward the hamper, and they landed on the floor.

"Sorry. I wanted to take a quick shower," Nik said. His hair was slightly wet. He was naked. He was smiling. "I'm cold." He quickly crawled under the covers and pressed his body against me. "You're so warm."

"Am I?"

"I don't want to think about anything too serious right now. I want to be happy that you're moving in. Tomorrow, tomorrow I'll try to make sense of everything, but not tonight," Nik said, putting his arm over my chest and nuzzling me. "I'm sorry I was in a bad mood. I feel better now. I got a lot off my chest. You were really great, by the way."

"Was I?"

"Are you okay?" Nik asked.

"I'm fine."

"You're all tense."

"Am I?"

"You are. Is something wrong?" he asked.

"No."

"Please, tell me if there's something wrong."

What should I say? This was so embarrassing. "You seemed to be hinting at something."

"Hinting at something?" he asked, acting coy.

He crawled on top of me, holding the covers over his back like a cape and sitting on my hips.

"Hinting at what?" He smiled.

He was getting a kick out of me being shy. He was such a cute little jerk.

"I'm afraid I might hurt you," I admitted, maybe being a little too serious.

"You won't," he assured me.

"What if I do something wrong and you get upset or blank out? What if I don't notice right away? What if it's awful for you?"

I was the nervous one, wasn't I?

He lowered his body so that he was in my face. "Stop being silly," he demanded with an intensity in his eyes that was unmistakable. "Do you want me?"

"Yes. Yes. More than anything. Yes."

Morning

From Nik's point of view.

Jaimes was quiet. His eyes were closed. He was breathing slowly and deeply. I wanted him to say something, but he didn't.

"I'll be right back." I climbed down the ladder and went into the bathroom. I showered myself quickly and then prepared a warm wet washcloth for Jaimes.

When I got back, he hadn't moved at all. He was still lying on his back, on top of the covers. His chest was still heaving. He was sweaty. Everything about him was beautiful, even his scars, especially his scars. I was beyond feeling guilty and settled on feeling honored. He's the man that took two bullets for me. He's the man who took me as I was. I really wanted him to say something.

I crawled onto the bed and started wiping his body, starting with his chest and abdomen and working my way down.

"What are you doing?" he asked with a smile. "I could just take a shower."

"I want to do it."

"You're sweet and that was unexpected."

I stopped washing him in order to look at his face. I desperately needed him to reassure me that everything was okay.

"Unexpected? Is that good or bad?" I asked. "I mean, I was um...that was..."

I learned a lot about Jaimes' sex life from when I was his roommate. He wasn't remotely discreet. He was usually the dominant one, the one in control. He was sometimes even aggressive, if that's what the person he was with wanted. With me that's not what happened.

"I didn't know you had it in you," Jaimes said, sitting up. "I'm surprised."

"Was it a good surprise or a bad surprise?" I asked, letting my desperation show.

He looked at me like I was completely batshit insane.

"Do you think I would have reacted the way I did if it was a bad surprise? Holy shit, Nik. Is screaming 'Yes', 'Oh my god', and 'Jesus Christ' too subtle?"

"It's just that, I got a little carried away. I'm almost as surprised as you are. I thought I should take the lead because you seemed worried, so I did and then I, um...you know...and then..."

"I was there. I remember. If you need me to say it, I'll say it over and over again. You're amazing. I love you. I also owe Lars ten dollars now."

"You made a bet with Lars?"

He had better be joking.

"Sandwich plans have also changed," Jaimes said, laughing his ass off.

"You!" I threw the washcloth in the hamper, grabbed a pillow, and started pummeling him.

"Stop!" he called out laughing. I kept hitting him with the pillow until he grabbed it away from me and threw it down on the bed.

"Hold me until I fall asleep," I said.

"You don't have a job, and you stay up until 3 a.m. all the time."

"Don't worry. I'm kind of tired for some reason."

"Come here," Jaimes said and gave me a kiss. "I'll hold you for as long as you like."

Morning came quickly. I looked over and Jaimes wasn't there. I wasn't surprised. He had a routine of getting up early, taking a quick run, having a shower, and then making breakfast. I smiled when I heard a pancake hit the griddle. Such perfect timing. I got up and put on boxers and a tank top. I threw some dirty clothes that were on the floor into the hamper.

"I have to walk Cosplay quick, but then I'll be back in for breakfast. Save some for me, okay?" I called out.

"Okay."

I must have been hearing things because that didn't sound like Jaimes' voice. I hurried down the ladder and looked into the kitchen to reassure myself.

I froze.

"Expecting someone else?" Shawn asked.

Please be dreaming. Please be dreaming. Please be dreaming. This couldn't be real.

"How? How are you here?" I asked, shaking. "Where's Jaimes? Where's Jaimes? Tell me!"

"Somewhere else," Shawn said. "I already walked Kali, so don't worry about that."

I forced myself to walk forward toward Shawn. Cosplay was happily sitting by his feet, panting, and wagging her tail.

"Shawn, where's Jaimes?" I asked again as calmly as I possibly could.

Crap! Where was my phone? I needed to get to my phone. I looked by my desk. It wasn't there. I ran over to my hoodie hanging by the door. It wasn't in my pocket.

"I got rid of your phone," Shawn said. "Do you think I'm stupid?"

"Of course not." What the fuck was wrong with me? I was still stroking this psycho's ego. "Shawn, where's Jaimes?"

"Somewhere else. I told you. Did you not hear me?"

"Did you hurt him?"

"What do you take me for? I'm over it. He doesn't mean anything to me anymore. Neither do you," he said dryly. "C'mon have some pancakes."

I didn't believe him for a moment. "You didn't answer my question. Did you hurt him?"

"Why would I do that?" Shawn asked sarcastically. "Oh wait. I know why I would hurt him. If you don't do everything that I tell you to do. That would be the reason. Pancakes?"

Why was he here when Mandi and Ava were in town? What was happening? I had to keep my head on straight. I had to.

He put a plate of pancakes on the table and gestured that I should sit down. I did.

"Does your sister know you're here?" I asked.

"That traitor? No, she is completely unaware." He started making up his own plate. "She thinks she's so smart. I tapped her phone. What a stupid bitch, opening an attachment from her dear little brother. Now I know how she really feels. Cunt."

He kicked a cabinet door that was by his foot, paused, then kicked it harder, over and over again until it broke.

"Everyone betrays me. My father. My mother. My sister. You. Most of all, you."

"Why are you doing this? What do you want?"

"The truth."

"The truth about what? I'll tell you anything. I'll be honest about anything."

"Honest? You? The one who never says no, even when he's screaming it in his head. The one who thinks I'm poison. You?"

"You heard that?"

"I heard everything! How you hate yourself when you're with me. How you're terrified of me."

"Maybe you would be happier if you didn't spy on people."

"What do you expect me to do? How else can I know what's real? Huh?"

"What do you want to know? I told you that I'll tell you anything. Just don't hurt Jaimes."

"Jaimes. What a joke. If only that kid was a better shot, your slut roommate wouldn't have gotten in the way. He wouldn't have corrupted you and we'd be together. We'd be happy. We'd be living together." He poked at the breakfast he made us. "But it's too late now, isn't it? You hate me."

"Please tell me what I have to do. I'll do anything."

"Anything, huh? Tempting. Eat dog shit. Fuck yourself. Strangle your mother and leave her in a ditch," he laughed. "No? How about you tell me where the letter is?"

"What letter?"

"The one Mandi gave you."

"If I give it to you, will you tell me where Jaimes is?"

"Stop talking about Jaimes and eat the breakfast I made you."

"Eat my pancakes," I said, as if I was giving myself a command.

I cut off a corner and slowly brought it up to my mouth.

That's when I finally lost it. I couldn't imagine how I would have felt if I wasn't medicated. I started shaking uncontrollably and hyperventilating. I dropped the fork and it fell on the floor. Cosplay started licking it.

Shawn started yelling at me, but I couldn't understand what he was saying. Wait. The letter. Give him the letter. Where was the letter? Where did I put the letter?

"Top drawer," I muttered, somehow, and suddenly the room was quiet. "Top drawer."

Closet

From Jaimes' point of view.

"The guy who hired you is a painfully pale ginger teenager, right? His name is Shawn. He's a man-child with no real income," I said loudly enough so that they could hear me through the door of the closet. "I don't know what he's paying you, but he lives off his mom."

"Please don't make us duct tape your mouth."

"I'm serious. If you want to make real money, you should call his mom and tell her what's going on. She's fucking loaded. Like, she owns several businesses. You know, the insurance company with the mascot who's a pit bull in a superhero costume? That's her."

I heard them whispering to one another. Maybe I was making headway?

"I bet you he's living off whatever he was able to get from the ATM before she cut off his credit cards. He's also insane. Whatever he promised you is a lie. He only wanted you to kidnap me because he has the hots for my boyfriend."

"Your boyfriend? You're gay?"

Seriously, this was what they focused on? There were at least three of them. I heard three distinct voices. They must have drugged me somehow. I remembered going on my morning jog and then I was here.

Waking up in complete darkness was really fucked up, but otherwise I remained calm. How? I had no idea.

I couldn't see them, but I imagined that they were hanging out on their phones. They seemed pretty chill. Holy shit. Were they professionals? Like, professional kidnappers? They told me that they weren't going to hurt me and that I should sit tight. Maybe I was calm because they were calm?

"Yes, I'm gay. You have a gay man in your closet. That's good for a laugh, right?" I joked, trying to be my charming self. "I have his mom's phone number if you want to work with a sane person who actually has money."

I reassured myself that if Shawn still wanted me killed, I would be dead. Yes, that was reassuring. Maybe it wasn't even Shawn? That would be awkward. Who else could it be? Caleb's asshole cousin? Shawn's dad? My dad?

"We're not giving you your phone, but good try."

"He is smarter than the last one."

"True."

Yes, three of them. Three of them who apparently do this sort of thing all the time.

"His mom doesn't want him around my boyfriend," I explained. "She's not going to be happy about this at all. I bet she'd be really appreciative if someone told her what was going on. I'll tell you the code to my phone. You can look up her personal number in my contacts and let her know."

"Nice story, bro. Now tell me, why would you have some rich lady's phone number, who is the mother of some crazy teenager who likes your boyfriend?"

"I'm doing some graphics work for one of her businesses."

"Not buying it. Why would you have the personal phone number of the owner of the company?"

"Okay. You got me. It's because she's paying us off to stay quiet about something that I'm not going to tell you about because she's paying us off."

If I wanted to be believed, I had to be honest.

"I'll buy that."

Another started laughing. "The plot thickens."

"In fact," I continued. "He's not supposed to be in the country at all. She shipped him off because he's an embarrassment and messed up. And to be honest, guys, I'm really worried about my boyfriend."

"You're locked in a closet, and you're worried about your boyfriend?"

"This whole situation is terrifying and all, but Shawn is absolutely obsessed. I'm worried about what his crazy ass might do," I said with all sincerity. "Seriously. Please call Shawn's mom. I'm worried about Nik."

"That's true love."

"Amazing."

"Brings a tear to my eye."

"Guys? Please. My PIN is 4739. Her number is under 'Money Mom,'" I begged. "I mean, it was Shawn that hired you, right? He's a bad guy. He's a really bad guy. Unreliable, penniless, batshit, bad guy."

They were quiet for a while.

"You seem like businessmen, right? Nobody gets hurt and you get paid? I'm really worried about my boyfriend. 4739. Money Mom. Please. Call her. Tell her to get her son. She'll pay you. I know it."

They were quiet for a while longer. What were they doing? Were they ignoring me or looking through my phone?

"Oh, shit boys. We're in trouble."

"You didn't press the red button, did you?" I asked. "Did you?"

Letter

From Nik's point of view.

I was only vaguely aware that I was riding in the passenger seat of a car. I was acutely aware of the intermittent sun in my eyes as we passed by larger buildings. My head was resting on the window.

"When did you become such a basket case?" Shawn asked. "I hope you hate yourself so much after this that you jump off a bridge."

"You don't have to be so awful," I mumbled. "You don't have to put on a show."

"What did you say? Speak up."

"I said that you don't have to pretend. You're not some hardened terrible person. You're just in pain."

"Pretend? Do you think I'm pretending? I'll crash us into a family of four and kill us all. How about that?"

I wouldn't put anything past him, but this wasn't who he was. This was him trying desperately to pretend not to care because he couldn't handle how he was feeling. It was easier for him to think of himself as a hardened evil person than a hurt little boy.

I understood.

"I wish you could be happy. I wish you stayed away. I wish you actually didn't care about me."

"What? Watch your mouth and do as I say."

"Yes. Of course. I'm sorry."

"This is all your fault."

"I'm sorry."

Even after everything that happened, I still had to stop myself from telling him that I loved him. I was so programmed to say and do certain things. There was still a part of me that had the urge to do everything I could for him.

"No, you aren't. You're not sorry. Telling me not to put on a show? Hypocrite. Fake."

"Sorry."

"Stop saying that."

"But I am. I'm sorry that I let it get to this point. I'm sorry I didn't end this a long time ago. I'm sorry I gave you what you wanted instead of telling you, no. I'm sorry I ignored how awful we were together just to feel wanted and loved for one more day. I'm sorry I was so lonely that I continued an incredibly unhealthy relationship. I'm sorry that I hurt you."

"Truth comes out. You never loved me. You were thinking with your dick. You were using me."

"That's not what I said."

"You don't need to pretend anymore. Tell me you never loved me."

"What? No. I'm not going to lie to you."

"I'll kill us. I'll run a red light."

"Screw you."

He was quiet for a long time and then strangely laughed it off. "You're ridiculous."

"Where are we going?"

"To the bank. You need to come with me to access the account."

"This can't be about money."

"It's not."

Eventually we arrived. He parked the car in the ramp. I followed him into the building, trying to maintain my composure.

"I have to go to the bathroom," I told him, and darted in the moment I found it.

I did my business and then stood in front of the mirror for a moment. I looked terrible. Anyone would guess that I'd been crying. I washed my hands and splashed water on my face. I had no choice but to play along. I was his. As long as he could threaten Jaimes, he owned me.

I took a couple deep breaths. I ran the water again. I looked down at my hands and for a moment I was in the bathroom at the con. My hands were covered with Jaimes' blood.

Shawn walked in. "C'mon, let's go. Hurry up."

I looked over at Shawn, momentarily confused that he didn't seem to notice the blood.

"If you hurt him again, I'll kill you. I'll cut you perfectly, and you'll bleed out in seconds."

I was washing my hands for the third time. Shawn wasn't there. I was talking into a mirror. I was losing my damn mind.

"Nik! Stop stalling," Shawn yelled from outside the bathroom.

I dried my hands and followed him.

We sat in the waiting area, drinking complimentary coffee. I filled mine with creamer packets. I periodically looked over at Shawn, trying to keep myself grounded and aware of what was actually happening.

He was wearing ripped jeans and a T-shirt that said, "Save the Pandas." You wouldn't know his family was rich, except that his watch was probably as expensive as the tiny house his mom bought him, his tennis shoes were designer, and his grooming was, strangely but obviously, the product of money. He literally stank of money.

"Hello, I'm Karen, your banker. Thank you for waiting," a woman in a smart pinstriped suit told us. She extended a hand to Shawn, who got up immediately.

"Hello, I'm Shawn. I'm here with my friend, Nikola, to help him access his account."

"I can help you with that," she said, extending her hand to me. I shook her hand, but I knew I was acting weird. I didn't want to look up. I kept my arms crossed over my body most of the time. I wondered if she would pick up on something being off.

"He's shy. He doesn't mean to be rude," Shawn said.

"Oh, okay," she said, as if she understood. I suspected that she thought I had some sort of disability that affected my social function – which was true, I guess. Shawn had just subtly explained to her why I was acting strangely and why I had a friend helping me access my account. Manipulation was second nature for Shawn. The best lies are the lies that are also true.

We followed her into an office with glass walls and doors. Shawn took out the piece of paper with the numbers. She started typing on her computer.

"Oh!" she exclaimed spontaneously and then acted a bit embarrassed. "I see. We're going to need two forms of identification, such as: Drivers' License. State Issued ID card. Passport. Social Security Card. Birth Certificate. Utility Bill..."

"Two forms?" Shawn asked.

I took out my drivers' license and my health insurance card.

"That should work," she said as she picked up the phone and started pressing buttons. "There is also a security question attached to this account. If you can wait for a moment, I have to call someone in."

I could tell that Shawn was becoming slightly agitated, but he was acting as if he was simply a bit bored. Eventually, an older stout man came in. He looked carefully at my drivers' license and stared at my face.

"Please bear with us," he said. He gave me a piece of paper and a pen. "Please produce your signature." I did. He looked at the back of my drivers' license and examined the signature. Then, he examined my health insurance card. "We're good."

"Great," Karen said. "So, concerning the security question..."

"Purple and Blue Brigade, forever," I said before she could ask the question.

"Very good," the man said, looking over Karen's shoulder at the screen. "You may allow this gentleman to access his account."

"Thank you," Shawn said.

"If you want to access your safety deposit box today, Karen will be happy to assist you," he said to me and then left.

It all seemed over-the-top for simply accessing an account. Bringing in a second witness to check my identity? Mandi left me something in a box as well. That must have been what Shawn was really after.

"Would you like to set up online access?" she asked.

"No," Shawn said, almost too quickly. I suspected he didn't want the awkwardness of me not having my phone. "You wanted a card sent to your address, right?" Shawn asked me as if we had talked about it beforehand.

"Yes."

"Perfect," the banker said. "Now let me update the information on your account to include your current address. Is your current address the same address as what is listed on your driver's license?"

"Yes."

She typed on the computer some more. "There we go. It should be out to you within two weeks. If you want to set up online access in the future, simply come to any one of our branches and they will assist you. However, we also offer wealth management services in person if that's what you prefer."

"Thanks," I said.

What the heck were wealth management services? How much money was in the account? Good god, Mandi, what did you do?

"I would like to see what's in the box," I told Karen.

"Excellent, follow me."

"Then, I want to go visit my friend. I really want to go visit my friend," I said, glaring at Shawn.

As the whole ordeal was drawing out, I felt myself becoming angrier and angrier. My fear was turning to rage, and I didn't know what to do with it.

My mind started to flip through various ways to hurt Shawn. I imagined his head going through the glass door. I imagined hitting him over the head with a vase and taking one of the broken shards and stabbing him until he was dead.

I was scaring myself. Even in extreme circumstances, I never thought I was capable of doing such things. If it came down to it, could I? Could I really do something like that?

"Here we are," Karen said as we reached a small room with a table and a few chairs. "Wait here, please."

She disappeared into another room.

"Do you know what it is?" I asked Shawn.

"You don't?"

"No."

"Did Mandi seriously not tell you? Oh yeah, you told her not to explain it to you, didn't you? You wanted to run away. The mighty Flying Horse Warrior crying like a little girl about lying to you and being terrified of my dad. I remember that now. Such a coward. I used to admire her because of what she did, before I knew what she was really like. Why do you think I got into hacking in the first place?"

"What? What are you talking about?" I asked. Did he know about the ransomware thing?

Before Shawn could answer, the banker came back with the unlocked box. It wasn't very large, maybe the size of a loaf of bread, but a little wider. She placed it on the table.

"Should I give you some time?" she asked.

"We'll be taking the contents with us," Shawn said.

She looked to me for confirmation. I nodded.

"Would you like to continue to rent the safety deposit box and sign for the keys?" she asked.

"No. I don't need it anymore," I answered.

"Very good. Would you like a canvas bag?"

"Sure," I replied. "Thanks."

Shawn opened up the box while the banker was getting the bag for us. There were two things inside. An envelope and a hard drive. I picked up the envelope and opened it. There was a handwritten letter inside.

"Whatever you do, don't access the drive. You could get into serious trouble. Extremely serious trouble. This is everything. Uncensored. The boat crew know you have it. It's the last resort if anyone tries to hurt you. Mutually assured destruction. Keep the peace," I read silently.

"Mandi says that we shouldn't look at it," I told Shawn. "She said we could get in serious trouble."

When Karen came back, Shawn grabbed the bag from her and put the hard drive in it.

"That bitch doesn't want you to know what really happened," Shawn fumed, breaking the cool demeanor he was trying to keep in front of the bank employees. He stormed out.

Karen and I were standing in the room alone together. I folded up the letter and put it in my back pocket. She was stunned. She realized that the way I was acting wasn't right. I wasn't shy. It wasn't social anxiety. I was terrified. She probably thought Shawn was someone trying to steal my money. She didn't know what she should do about it. I could see it all over her face.

"Whatever happens," I said very quietly, "if you see something on the news, it wasn't your fault. This has nothing to do with you. Don't get involved. Please."

She blinked a couple times and nodded.

"Good luck," she said weakly.

I awkwardly smiled and then ran after Shawn.

Light

From Jaimes' point of view.

"Oh shit."

"It's her."

"Are you sure."

"I'm sure."

"You didn't press the red button, did you?" I asked again.

"No."

"What happens if you press the red button?"

"The cavalry shows up." I might as well tell them. It's not like they were going to be stupid enough to give me my phone back.

"Who is the cavalry?"

"You wouldn't believe me if I told you," I said.

"Tell us or we won't believe you," one of the guys joked.

These businessmen were having way too much fun while I was locked in a closet. At least they were looking through my phone. That was progress.

"If you press the red button, it alerts Flying Horse Warrior by opening up a link to her phone. It also gives her the phone's location and records everything onto a remote server."

"Her? Wait, Flying Horse Warrior is a girl?"

"He's full of shit."

They knew about Flying Horse Warrior? Maybe they knew about boat guy getting hacked?

"If you think I'm full of shit, press the red button and see what happens," I joked.

"Very funny."

"We still have to clear this up."

"Contact her. Tell her what happened."

"We can't let her know that we know who she is."

"We could let him go. He hasn't seen us."

"I have an idea."

They were quiet for a long time. They were quiet for a very long time.

"Guys? Guys! Are you there?" I called out.

Holy shit. Did they leave? I hadn't heard another soul besides those three guys since I woke up. For all I knew I was out in the middle of nowhere. I mean, I wasn't going to die. I'm sure I could get through the drywall before I starved to death. Still, I had to work hard not to panic.

"Hey! If anyone is out there, I'm stuck in a closet! Help!"

Fuck it. I stood up and threw my good shoulder into the door.

My shoulder made a huge dent in the wood. It was an ordinary hollow door. Yes! I did it again and the dent became larger – and I think I dented the other side a bit. I kept at it until I made a hole.

My eyes must have adjusted to the darkness in the closet, because the light through the hole was blinding.

Eventually, I got out. I was in a small cabin. I looked out the window. Damn, I was in the middle of nowhere.

My phone! I ran over and grabbed it off the table.

Oh shit! They pressed the red button. My kidnappers were so considerate.

"Mandi! I was kidnapped. I think the guys were hired by Shawn or somebody. Nik? Are you okay? I'm fine. The kidnappers got spooked and left. I'm not sure why, but they are gone.

"Oh wow! They left my wallet. Damn. Nicest fucking kidnappers ever. I also broke the closet door of the cabin because they locked me in there.

"I think they drugged me or something. I went for my morning run and woke up in a closet. I have a bit of a headache, but otherwise, I think I'm good. I'm thirsty. I'm really thirsty. Maybe I'm not feeling great."

Suddenly and unexpectedly, the panic set in. My muscles stopped working, and I fell to the ground.

"Someone, come help me. I'm all alone. I guess the adrenaline is wearing off or something. I don't feel so good. Someone, come help me. Mandi. Nik. Please, come help me. I was kidnapped, and now I'm all alone."

I pulled myself back up. I shook my legs out and tried to regain my balance and looked around.

"Wait, I think I know where I am. There's a list of rules on the door for the park. I'm at the state park. These places usually have an office or something, right? I'm going to go outside and try to find someone. Don't worry. I won't get lost."

I put my phone and my wallet in the pockets of my hoodie and slowly walked outside. The brightness of the outdoors was disorienting. I lowered myself down onto the front steps of the cabin and tried to calm down and get my bearings.

Why did they leave like that? I rubbed my eyes and tried to think. I ran through some of the things they said. Something about it being "her," and she couldn't find out that they know who she is?

What? Do they mean Mandi? No, that can't be it. Shawn's mom! They must have been talking about Shawn's mom.

My gears kept turning until something clicked. How would Shawn know professionals? I started laughing. He hired his mom's people, didn't he? That's so funny. She probably hired them anonymously somehow and when they recognized the phone number, they bailed. Maybe?

Who knows? Regardless, they were gone.

I had to get out of there. I waited until my eyes adjusted to the outside and stood up. There was a path that connected the cabins, but they were pretty far away from one another. I was hoping for a sign with an arrow that told me where the office was. I could use my phone, but that would mean ending the emergency link. I wasn't sure if that was a good idea.

"I'm feeling a little better. I'm outside the cabin. Nik, I'm really worried about you. I hope you're okay. We'll find you. Everything will be all right. We'll get through this. We always do. I love you."

Hurt

From Nik's point of view.

"So, what you do remember?" Shawn asked once we got into the car.

"About what?"

"The boat. Don't play stupid."

"Why are you asking me about that? What does it have to do with you?"

This was torture. I wanted to run or attack him or something, anything. My whole body buzzed like I had been hit in the face. I was worried about Jaimes, so I endured it.

"Answer the question," he insisted, starting the car after throwing the hard drive in the backseat.

"I told you about this before, many times."

"Were you honest?"

"Yes."

"Bullshit."

"Why would I lie about something like that? Huh? But fine, whatever. I met these college guys who invited me to a party on a boat. I was 17 and stupid, and I went with them thinking it was a normal party, maybe with drinking and people making out.

"When I got there, I found out it was basically an orgy with these older rich guys passing around teenagers who looked high and drunk. I wanted to leave, but we were on a boat, so I was trapped. I tried to hide, but the people I thought were my friends held me down and forced me to take some pills. The rest is bits and pieces.

"I woke up in the morning on the street. My clothes were ripped. I was sore all over. I found 200 dollars in my pocket and a small packet of meth. I threw away the drugs and gave the money to a homeless guy who helped me out. Are you happy now?"

"Bits and pieces?" He chuckled like it was a joke.

"Yes. A few words. A few sentences. The sounds of people laughing. I vaguely remember staring up at the ceiling. I remember being dragged by my feet. I think I was locked in a room at some point because I was banging on a door and shouting for someone to let me out. I don't want to talk about it. Please. Why are you doing this to me?"

"What sentences? What words?" he demanded as he drove too fast.

"I don't want to talk about it!"

"But you told that old guy you fucked, though, right? Pervert. You could tell some stranger, but you don't want to talk to me about it?"

"I could tell him because I didn't know him. I thought I'd never see him again. I don't want to talk about it!"

"I've never told anyone...blah blah blah...all your complicated feelings. You realize I listened to all of it? You were spilling your guts before you fucked that old man. It was repulsive. You told him things you never told me."

He paused as if he had just realized something. "Well – sort of." Then, started laughing, really laughing. "Things you never told me!" he repeated, as if it was hilarious.

"I don't understand. Was your dad on the boat? Is that what this is about?" I asked. "Is that why your parents got divorced?"

"My parents didn't get divorced over some sex thing. They ended their business relationship because my dad became a financial liability."

"Blackmail?"

"Yes, Nik, blackmail. What do you think that is?" He pointed to the backseat where the hard drive was sitting.

"Insurance. It's insurance," I explained. "Mandi called it, mutual assured destruction."

"She did? Hilarious." Shawn had another laugh and then got really quiet. "Say it."

"Say what?"

"I said, say it. You know what I mean." He clenched the steering wheel so tightly that his knuckles turned bone white. "Say it."

It wasn't like I had a choice. I did what he told me to do.

"You're so young," I said, as if I was reciting a pledge or a poem. "You're beautiful. Your skin is so soft. They told me you're a virgin. Are you scared? Just do what I tell you to. You're just a kid. Don't ruin it. I want you. Don't you dare run away. We're going to have some fun."

I heard a weird noise, and I looked over at Shawn. He was wiping tears away from his face. What the hell was going through his head?

It finally dawned on me what could be on the hard drive. I remembered what the owner of the boat was charged with. It wasn't only embezzlement. It was for illegal images. Images of me? The party? Maybe that was why Mandi didn't want me to access the drive. I was 17. I didn't know how old the other boys were.

"Shawn, you said you knew what was on the hard drive. We could be in big trouble. If someone took video or pictures of that party, it's illegal. I was 17. We should destroy it."

"Not yet."

What was he going to do? Make me watch? It didn't matter. I would get through it, somehow. All that mattered was Jaimes being all right. I needed to find Jaimes.

Eventually, Shawn's mom would show up and take him away again. Maybe this time, he would finally leave us alone. My desire to hurt Shawn was oddly subsiding. I wanted this all to be over with. I wanted him to go away.

"When you leave, do you want to take Cosplay? I mean, Kali?" I asked. "She remembers you. I know you took good care of her."

"What? Don't you want her anymore?" he said accusingly.

"That's not it. Look, I don't care about revenge or anything like that. I want you to be happy, somewhere else, away from me. If having your dog back helps you, then you should have your dog back."

We were getting close to the house now. I was worried he was going to take us out to the middle of nowhere, but he didn't. He was driving me back home.

"You are going back overseas, right?" I asked. "I'm sure your mom set you up somewhere nice where you could do some volunteer work or something."

"She did."

Shawn parked the car. He grabbed the bag from the backseat and got out. He got a satchel from out of the trunk. We both walked toward the house. Once we got close, I thought I could hear someone's voice.

I ran to the door, opened it, and looked around trying to find the source of the voice.

"I found the office," the voice said. "The office guy here is being really nice. He got me something to eat, and I drank a lot of water. I'm feeling a lot better now. Go find Nik first, okay? I'm fine. Make sure Nik is all right. Don't worry about me. I'll call a cab with the office phone."

It was Jaimes. The voice must be coming from my phone. I tried to follow the sound to the source. Shawn must have hidden my phone somewhere.

Just when I thought I had found it, Shawn got in front of me, opened a compartment under a chair-cushion, took out my phone and smashed it against the nearest table.

It didn't matter. Jaimes was fine. I could run. I could attack Shawn. I could do whatever I wanted. I realized this, but that's not what I did.

"Mandi, your sister, and some guy in a suit, they'll be coming for me," I said. "Please, let's destroy the hard drive and you can get out of here with Kali. You can go to your new home, and we can forget this ever happened."

"Forget it happened? You're so full of jokes. Forget it happened? You're a laugh riot!"

Shawn opened the case he had taken out of the trunk. It contained a laptop. He somehow plugged the hard drive into it.

"I want them to come," he explained. "I want my sister to be here. Then she'll know I'm not crazy."

I couldn't believe what I was doing. My curiosity took over. Was I really going to stay to find out what this was all about?

Cosplay was scratching at the door.

"I'm going to take Cos... Kali out," I said.

"Fine but come back or I'll send a copy of the video of you fucking that old man to your family. As if they'd care."

By the time I came back from walking Cosplay, Shawn had found whatever he was looking for. He was staring at the screen.

"Ready for some truth?" Shawn asked. His voice was somber and clear. He wasn't acting. He was himself. "You deserve the truth, don't you?"

Despite myself, I sat right beside him and looked at the screen.

"What am I looking at? Shawn, what is this?"

"The person who owned the boat invited all his rich business partners to parties. He secretly recorded them and used the footage for blackmail," Shawn calmly explained. "So, all the rooms had cameras."

"That's me." I pointed at a figure in jeans and a black T-shirt who was standing next to the door of the room. "And that's…oh my god…that's…"

"Surprise," Shawn said, his voice shaking.

"Is that you? Is that really you?" I pointed at a boy sitting on the bed. He was pale with curly red hair. This was seven years ago, but it was undeniable. It was Shawn. The possibilities of what may have happened flipped through my head. I wanted to vomit.

"This is when we first met." Shawn pressed the space bar and the video started to play.

"Let me out," my younger self said on the video, beating on the door. My words were slurred as if I were drunk. "What? Do I smell or something? I came here to have fun. Why did you put me in here? Jerks! Is this your idea of a joke?"

"I told them to bring you here," Shawn said getting up from his bed. "I picked you. You're my birthday present. You're for me."

"What the hell? Where did you come from, kid? You shouldn't be here. Birthday? What, are you 12?"

"I'm 13."

"13!" I kept beating on the door. "This isn't funny. Why the hell is there some kid here?"

"I told you why! You're mine. Now, do as I say. Don't you dare run away. Don't ruin it. What? Are you scared?"

"I'm not scared." I turned around to face Shawn. "You're just a kid. You're so young. You shouldn't be around this stuff. You shouldn't be here."

"You're a kid, too, so it makes it okay."

"Makes what okay?"

Shawn put his hand up to my face like he was inspecting a horse. "I want you."

"What? Like, want-me want me? No way! Stay away from me. Don't touch me!"

"Do you know who I am? Huh?" Shawn shouted. "I choose you. You're mine. I decided. You're going to be my first."

"Your first? Kid, are you serious?"

"I'm not a kid anymore."

"Yes, you are. This isn't right. You're too young. You should wait. When you're older, find someone who cares about you. It should be special. Not anything like this. Why are you even here?"

"Why do you get to have fun and I don't?" Shawn trapped me between him and the door. "It would be your first time, too, right? They told me you were a virgin."

"That's not the point. I'm older, okay? What drugs did they give me? I don't want to feel like this. This is so wrong. Please, kid, please, please stay away from me."

"Am I ugly?"

"You're not ugly. You're beautiful. You're a beautiful child. You need to stay away from me," I pushed Shawn away hard enough that he fell into the bed.

"How dare you?"

"I can't get out of here!" I yelled, bashing on the door some more.

"We're just going to have some fun. Why are you mad?"

"What am I going to do? What the hell am I going to do? Sleep. Sleep is escape." I started looking through the drawers and cabinets. I found some pills and a large bottle of clear liquor.

"What are you doing?" Shawn yelled angrily. "You're ruining everything."

"I'm going to take a nap," I said.

"I don't get it. Isn't this why you came? Am I not good enough for you? You want someone else?"

"This...whatever this is...is not why I came to the party. I wanted to hang out with people I thought were my friends. I didn't know it was going to be like this. And no, I've never been with another boy. And if this were your 19th birthday and we liked each other and we were friends, that would be different. This! This is messed up. There are all these older guys here acting like they own us and throwing their money around. I don't like it. I don't want to be here."

I threw a bunch of pills in my mouth and started drinking the liquor.

"Stop it!"

"I might act a little weird before I pass out. Don't worry. I probably won't die."

"What? Stop it! I thought you'd be happy! You'd rather die! What's wrong with me? Why don't you want me?"

"This is wrong, kid. I'm not going to let them do this to us." I sat down on the floor beside the bed. "It isn't because I don't want you. I don't want to hurt you. I'd rather..."

"Don't you understand. I'm here all alone. Please." Shawn grabbed my arm and put my hand on his face. "Why don't you like me? There's nothing wrong with me!"

"No. No, there is...nothing is wrong with you. You're...you're perfect." I became less and less coherent.

"Your skin is...so soft," I continued to babble, and I rubbed his face with my hand. "You're a...a...beautiful boy. I would rather die than hurt you...you're just a boy...Don't be like them out there. Don't be like them...don't...okay?"

"You ruined it. You jerk. You're my present. It was my birthday last week. You'll see. I'll get what I want."

"Shh. No. Find someone you love...really love. Both of us...both of us...okay." My words were barely understandable at this point. "We'll fall in love one day. You'll see. Promise." I said before I finally fell to the floor and was motionless.

"Wake up!" Shawn jumped on top of me and started shaking me. "Wake up! You worthless..." Shawn got back onto his bed when I failed to wake up. "I should piss on you. I should cut you up. I should cut you up and then piss on you. How dare you leave me all alone? I'm so bored."

He took out a handheld video game and started to play.

Shawn fast-forwarded the video. This whole time, our eyes had been affixed to the screen. I couldn't believe what I was seeing. It wasn't like I was watching myself at all. It was like watching TV. This wasn't something I recognized as having happened to me. I looked over at Shawn. He looked shocked. I suspected that he didn't remember it like this either.

Shawn continued to fast-forward the video while his younger self played video games. It had been more than an hour of real time. This was probably about the time that the pills I had taken actually started to take effect. I had no idea what I was doing back then, did I? I was already drunk and high. I could have easily died. I had no idea this happened at all.

I was lying there, unconscious, while Shawn played a video game for well over an hour. Then, I started to seize.

Shawn panicked. "Dad! Dad! Somebody! Something's wrong! Help!"

He kept screaming, but it took a while for anyone to respond. An older man entered the room and started to yell at him. "What the hell is going on? I told you not to leave the room and to be quiet."

"The boy. The boy is shaking!"

At this point, I had been seizing for almost three full minutes.

"Why is he in here? Did he do anything to you? Did he touch you?"

"I wanted someone to play with. Then he took some pills and drank a lot."

"You wanted someone to play with?" The man slapped Shawn across the face. "Do what I tell you. I told you not to leave your room and to be quiet."

"I didn't leave. I told them to bring him to me. I'm not a kid. Why do you get to have all the fun?"

"Don't talk back. Play your video games, be quiet, and don't tell your mom."

"Do something! He's still shaking. Why is he shaking?"

"Did he touch you? Because if he touched you, I'm going to throw him overboard. Do you hear me?"

"You're going to save him. You're going to save him or I'm going to tell mom everything. If you hurt him, I'll slit your throat in your sleep. I'd throw you overboard but you're too fat."

The man grabbed Shawn's throat and pressed him into the bed. "If you dare threaten me again, it will be the last thing you do."

Shawn started coughing when the man let him go. "I hate you. I hate you! I hope Mom leaves you poor."

The man grabbed my legs and started to drag me out of the room. I stopped seizing. I had seized for over four minutes.

Shawn sat on the bed, drew his knees to his chest, and started crying. Now that the door was open, the party outside was audible.

"Someone passed out, huh?"

"What should we do with him?"

"Do whatever you want," the man said.

"Seriously?"

"I have an idea."

They started laughing. They all started laughing.

"Please stop the video," I told Shawn. "Please stop it."
Shawn didn't move.
"Stop it!" I screamed. I grabbed the laptop and threw it across the room. Cosplay got really concerned and started barking.
"Now you know," Shawn said. "I thought you were dead, so I told my mom everything. My father denied it, of course. My sister and my mom thought I was making up a story about you. They thought that the boy on the boat was an imaginary friend I made up to help me cope.

"When the owner of the boat was hacked and arrested, my mom divorced my dad. Then, seven years later, I found you. I didn't even know your name, but I found you. I didn't tell anyone that it was you, not even you. You didn't remember me, but I knew it was you."

"I had no idea. I didn't remember you at all."

"I remembered you."

"You know they're coming. All of them. You might be arrested. You should go. You should take Kali and go."

"What do you care what happens to me?"

"I can't help it. Please. I need you to stay away from me. Stay away from me and stay away from my friends. Please."

"If you still care about me, why can't we be together? We can take all that money and do whatever we want. We can live wherever we want. You want to run away? We'll run away."

"You literally make me crazy. Do you understand? You ruined my career. You tried to kill one of my friends. After all that, I still want to make you happy. It's sick. It's wrong. It's not love. I don't know what to call it. Please go and never come back. Try to live a normal life. Please, be happy without me."

"You know, I thought you lied to me. On the boat, I thought you told me you were a virgin. So, when I saw you with your ex-girlfriend from high school, I thought you lied to me. There were a lot of things I didn't remember right, but that's the way I remembered them.

"You told me that you would rather die than hurt me when I was a kid. That's what you said. Nobody cares about me the way you do. Nobody cares about you the way I do. We are meant to be together. I wanted you so much, for years I wanted you. I dreamed about you. Then, I finally had you. You were mine, and Jaimes screwed it up."

"Keep his name out of your mouth. You need to go. You need to go now. I don't want to hurt you."

"You? Hurt me? More jokes."

"I'm not well, Shawn. I haven't been well for a very long time. You aren't safe right now. You don't want to know what's going through my head. I need you to leave. I need to never see you again."

"You think it's that easy to say no to me? Didn't I teach you better?"

Liar

From Jaimes' point of view.

"Can't you drive faster?" I insisted. "I told you to check on Nik first."

"We were almost there by the time you told us that," Mandi said. "You sounded like you were dying."

"I was dehydrated. Jesus. Don't you have a siren or something?"

"I'm not a beat cop," the man said, annoyed.

"Maybe I should try to call Shawn," Ava said.

"Why don't you call your mom and see if she knows where he is?" I suggested.

"Good idea," Ava said, taking out her phone.

"I keep trying to call Nik," Mandi said. "His phone doesn't seem to be on. Oh wait, his signal is gone completely. I can't track his phone anymore. Shit."

"What? What does that mean? Did he leave the house?" I asked, panicked.

"No, the phone was in his house this entire time. It means something happened to his phone."

"Please hurry. Please." I started to panic.

"I'm driving as fast as I can. If we all die in a car accident, we won't be of much help, will we?"

"Mom? Mom, do you know where Shawn is? Something's happened. Jaimes was kidnapped, and we can't find Nik." Ava paused. "I know. I know. I know how time zones work, but this is an emergency." She paused. "Yes, I'm still with Mandi and the fed. What do you want me to do? Get a cell next to dad? Yes, I'm cooperating." She paused. "Not get caught. Very funny, Mom. Could you check on Shawn, please?" She paused. "Mom! I am well aware that Mandi cannot impregnate me. Also, I'm not gay. Shawn is gay. I am not gay." She paused again. "I'll get right on that. Hey, straight-boy, my mom wants grandkids. That's what she's talking about right now. That's her top priority apparently. Could you impregnate me so that she can maybe focus on something else?"

"Not while I'm driving."

"Sorry, the only straight man in the car is busy right now, Mom." She paused. "I love you, too, Mom."

"What did she say?" I asked.

"What do you think she said? She's not very happy with me right now. I'm her last hope for the family line and I'm hanging out with my brother's ex-boyfriend's lesbian best friend and a federal agent. I'm supposed to be finding a rich husband."

"About Shawn. Fucking Christ."

"Nothing. She's going to check with his handlers. I'm going to try to call Shawn directly. For all we know he's on a beach somewhere, pretending to dig a well or build a school or whatever."

"Well, call him already," I said.

Ava put her phone up to her ear. "Straight to voicemail."

"Can you track his phone?" I asked Ava.

"No, I don't know how to do any of that stuff. That was all Shawn," Ava said. "Here."

She gave her phone to Mandi, who immediately started going to work.

"What? But at Lars' apartment..."

"I was taking the fall for Shawn. How many times do I have to explain?" Ava protested.

"Shouldn't we call the regular cops?" I asked.

"We'll arrive before they would at this point," the man in the suit said. "And we don't even know if Nik is at home or if Shawn is even involved."

"I woke up locked in a closet, so obviously something is going on."

"They just left?" the man asked me.

"They left after I gave them Money Mom's phone number."

"My mom has a name. Her name is Janice, not Money Mom."

"You know, I have a name, too. Nobody seems to care," the man said.

"Well, I think my kidnappers knew Janice somehow and thought they'd get in trouble with her."

"For kidnapping you?" Ava asked.

"No, for knowing who she is."

"Let me guess, she's living in the Caymans right now," the man said.

"No, she's in Malta," Ava said.

The federal agent burst out laughing.

"Why is that funny? We've had a condo there for years."

He kept laughing.

"Can we focus on finding Nik? Please," I said. "I'm worried."

"Shawn is making it look like his phone is in the middle of the Atlantic. Amusing," Mandi said. "And I'm still not getting a signal from Nik's phone."

I couldn't hold it together anymore. I put my hands over my face and began shaking.

"We'll be there soon," Mandi assured me. "For all we know, Nik accidentally dropped his phone in the toilet or something. Try to calm down."

"I'll try. It's just...if anything happens to him, I'll never forgive myself."

"None of this is your fault, Jaimes. There is a lot of blame to go around, and none of it's on you," Mandi said as she rubbed my back.

"When we get there, let me clear the building first, okay?" the man said.

"Huh?"

"He means, that he'll go in first and check it out before we go in," Mandi explained.

"Makes sense."

When we finally got there, we all piled out of the car and walked toward the house. The plan was that I was going to unlock the door and the man in the suit was going to go in quickly and look around. We weren't supposed to go in until he told us to. He had his weapon drawn.

I went up to the door to unlock it, but I heard voices inside.

"You think I'm joking?" Nik yelled. "I'll fucking kill you. I'll rip off your pretty face with my bare hands and stuff it down your throat."

Screw the plan. I ran into the house. "Nik!" I looked around frantically until I saw Nik and Shawn in the kitchen.

Shawn was lying on the floor. Nik was sitting on top of him. Nik's legs were holding down Shawn's arms. One of Nik's hands was pushing down on Shawn's face and his other hand was holding up a kitchen knife.

The agent came in behind me and pointed his weapon at Nik.

Holy fucking shit.

I could barely breathe, but I had to do something.

"Nik, it's me, Jaimes. Calm down. We're here. I'm okay. Everything is going to be all right. You need to calm down. Jesus Christ. Nik, calm down."

"We're never going to be safe until he's dead. I used to be a phlebotomist. I worked in a hospital. I used to have a life. He'll bleed out in seconds if I cut him right. He won't feel a thing."

"Shawn!" Ava called out once she got into the house. "Nik! No! Don't hurt my brother. Please. Stop!"

"Everyone be quiet," the agent said slowly and sternly. "Nik do not move. Do you understand?"

"He's not going to stop. You don't understand. He's not going to stop."

"Nik, I'm going to walk over to you slowly, and I'm going to take the knife out of your hand. Then, we're going to talk about this. Okay? Do you understand?"

"He killed Jaimes."

"I'm right here. I'm alive. My heart is beating. My chest is moving. My lips are red." I recited the things he needed to hear to remember that he saved my life. "I'm alive. You saved me."

"Ava!" Shawn cried. "Ava, he's the boy on the boat. It's him. He's the one who cared about me so much he was willing to die for me. He said that when we were older, that we'd fall in love. He would never hurt me. Never."

"Holy shit," Mandi said under her breath. She ran over to a laptop that was on the floor, all busted up. She picked up something off the floor and put it into her jacket pocket.

The agent kept slowly making his way toward Nik.

"The boy on the boat?" Ava asked, her voice quivering. "You think Nik is the boy on the boat? I know that he was there, but that's not what happened..."

"It is. It's exactly what happened. He's not a liar," Nik cried. "Shawn's telling the truth. That's why he's not going to stop. He's not going to stay away."

The agent took the knife out of Nik's hand and threw it into the kitchen sink. Nik didn't resist. The agent holstered his weapon.

"Coward," Shawn said. "It would have been a beautiful ending if we died together. Now you ruined it."

The agent tried to lift Nik off of Shawn, but Nik fought him.

"I'm so sorry. I'm sorry I lied," Nik yelled as he attempted to slip out of the man's holds. "I learned my lesson. You're so beautiful. Your skin is so soft.

You're perfect. I'm for you. I'm yours. I love you. Wait for me, and we'll be together forever."

What was Nik saying? Why was he saying those things?

"You're a liar," Shawn said. "You've always been a liar."

What was going on? How could Nik say those things?

The man in the suit lifted Nik off of Shawn.

"Jaimes?" Nik seemed disoriented, like he hadn't realized that we were all there. He ran over to me, crying. "Shawn's dead. Shawn's dead."

"No, he's not," I said. "The fed guy stopped you. You were threatening him, but we stopped you. You aren't in your right mind. Nik, please, be okay. Please be okay." I grabbed him and held him close to me. "Please be okay."

"You're wrong. I killed him. He's dead. He cut himself. He thought that I would save him like I saved you, but I let him bleed out. He died. We're free. We're safe."

That's when Ava started screaming.

Prison

From Nik's point of view.

"Can you tell me what happened between you and Shawn on the day that Jaimes was kidnapped?" She asked this question a lot. My answer was always the same. I was unsure why she was asking me today. It happened months ago.

"You know I can't remember," I answered. "Well, that's not entirely true. I do remember, but I'm wrong."

"You're wrong?"

"Shawn didn't hurt himself. I hurt him. It had to be me. I think my mind wouldn't accept what I had done and changed my memory."

"Manufactured memory is usually not that simple."

"It was an extreme situation, don't you think? I also seized for 4 minutes when I was a teenager. I knew there was something wrong with me."

"A seizure, even a seizure of that duration, doesn't necessarily..."

"Don't you think I know that? But something broke me. Isn't that obvious? I suppose, it's not unusual for someone to disassociate while murdering someone."

"It's not unusual for someone not to remember extreme events or for their memory to be unreliable. We've talked about this, but I'm asking you to..."

"I think it's interesting that I can admit to murder, and it's privileged information."

"How certain are you that you murdered Shawn?"

"All the scenarios that have gone through my head point to me being responsible. Even if he cut himself, which I highly doubt, I stood up. The moment I stood up, the pressure on his arms was lifted and he died. Either way, I'm the reason he's dead."

"Have you considered that you might find the idea of his death comforting, and that's why you believe that you killed him?"

"Yes. Does that make me a bad person?"

"That's not for me to decide."

"There wasn't any other way. I did what I had to do to protect Jaimes. Shawn didn't feel any pain. He wanted to die. His life was so miserable. He tried to be a good person. He would latch onto causes. You know, he was going to save the orangutans or whatever.

"For the longest time, I thought that something I did made him the way he was. Then, I found out that he had been that way since he was a kid. Jaimes keeps telling me, if it wasn't me, it would have been someone else. Shawn chose me, because he liked the way I looked or something. Who knows why?

"He chose me, and he wouldn't let me go. What was I supposed to do? Even if I gave myself to him, even if I gave up being a person, even if I gave up and let him own me and hurt me, he wouldn't stop."

"How do you feel about what happened?"

"Relief. Guilt, but not regret. I don't understand why I'm not in prison. I thought that circumstances might reduce my sentence, but I was certain I would be arrested. I should pay for what I did. I'm surprised his mom didn't put a hit out on me or something.

"I'm unsure why Ava doesn't hate me. She's taking care of Kali. She sends me pictures sometimes. Nobody seems to believe me. I think that since they don't want me to go to prison or get murdered that they are lying. I guess, I'm supposed to go along with it. It's so confusing."

"Have you considered that they are telling the truth?"

"No. What? He's living on some tropical island somewhere. That's the type of lie you tell children when their dog dies. That can't be true. I wanted him dead. I killed him. He can't hurt me anymore. He can't hurt Jaimes anymore. He's dead. I cut him correctly. I know what I'm doing. There's no return from that. I mean, he cut himself and I didn't help him, or he tried to...tried to...and I...could we please stop talking about this?"

"It's necessary because of recent events. I know it's difficult, but the reason we're talking about this today is because something has happened that may be shocking to you. Your partner asked me to help you process this information."

"What? What happened? Just tell me. Are Mandi and Ava okay? Are Lars and Caleb okay? Is Traci okay?"

"Yes. They're fine. Your friends are fine."

"Something shocking? Come out with it. Just tell me."

"Shawn has been arrested."

"What? No. You're supposed to be the one person who tells me the truth no matter what. You're taking this too far. Our conversations are privileged. You don't have to lie to me. Shawn is dead."

"Your friends were not lying to you. Shawn cut himself, but you saved him. He claims..."

"He claims! Shawn! Shawn claims! Shawn lies. Shawn's a liar. He's a sociopath. You study this stuff. How could you believe a word he says?"

"He claims that you took the knife away from him and tackled him in order to save him."

"He is lying. He wants to believe that I saved him. He's wrong! He's delusional. He wants to think that I'm so weak that I would do anything for him. He wants to think I'm so pathetic that I'd never hurt him even to save myself and my friends! He's a liar!"

"His sister noticed he was bleeding. A man that was with your group gave him first aid. He was taken to the emergency room, and he survived. His sister took him and his dog back to their mother. His mother arranged for Shawn to live at a secure residential facility, and Kali became his service dog. However, recently..."

Nothing she said after that made sense. It was all noise.

"Jaimes! I want Jaimes."

"I can ask your partner to come in, but I think it would be helpful for you to sit with this information for a while. What you are experiencing right now is called cognitive dissonance. It can be a very unpleasant experience when new information conflicts with strongly held beliefs. You'll need to prepare yourself. The case will likely get media attention."

"It's going to be on the news. It's going to be on the news that Shawn is alive. That's why you are telling me now, so I'm prepared to see it on the news?"

"If it helps you to know, it is likely that Shawn will be in prison for the rest of his life."

"What did he do?"

"After escaping from the facility, he murdered his father and several of his father's old business associates."

"He did what? He's alive and he did what?"

"He murdered his father and several of his father's old business associates," she repeated.

I started laughing. A strange, powerful euphoria overwhelmed me. It was frightening. Pieces of my life that didn't quite fit for months now simply magically snapped into place.

Someone just told me about a mass murder, and I started laughing. Was I a monster? I tried, but I couldn't stop laughing. I was also trembling.

Jaimes kept telling me that I was wrong about what happened, but I didn't believe him. Why didn't I trust him? I didn't believe it until right at that moment. It was also the moment I realized that the boy on the boat survived, and all the drunk laughing men drown in their own blood.

I was disturbed by how I was feeling but I remembered what Lars told me a long time ago. "We can't control how we feel. We can just control how we act." I had to forgive myself, somehow.

"Did he hire someone, or did he do it himself?"

"He personally killed them."

"Did he slit their throats in their sleep?"

"Yes. How did you know?"

"He promised that he would."

"Did he tell you about his plans?"

"Yes. A very long time ago, when he was a kid, a week after his 13th birthday, he tried to protect me. He made a promise, and he kept it. Am I a bad person? Am I a bad person for finding joy in people dying?"

"It's not my place to judge."

Peace

Nik walked out of his psychologist's office. Jaimes was nervously waiting for him. Nik was smiling.

"You look much happier than I thought you would," Jaimes said. "She did tell you, right?"

"Yeah. She told me that Shawn was alive, and I believed her this time. I'm sorry I didn't trust you."

"So, you don't think that you...you realize you didn't..." Jaimes said excitedly.

Nik nodded. "A bit of a breakthrough. I mean, if he's alive, I can't be responsible for his death, can I? Why didn't you show me a picture of him with a newspaper or something?"

"That's the first thing we did. You claimed that we photoshopped it."

"Oh, I remember that now. I really lost it, didn't I?"

"Yes," Jaimes said, giving him a hug. "You sure did."

"I don't know if my mind is still making stuff up, but I think, maybe he called my bluff. I warned him that I would hurt him, and he laughed at me. I know that. I remember that. He would have tried to test me, to mock me, and to prove that I was incapable of hurting him. I know that's what he would do, but I can't remember anything after that...not really...I just can't. I'm never going to know the truth, for sure, am I?"

"We're going to have to make peace with not knowing. Don't push yourself anymore."

"Is it really over? Shawn's dad is dead. Shawn is going to prison."

"Yes. You can thank Mandi for letting us know before it all hit the news. I guess Shawn was really angry at his dad."

"He was. He must have uploaded the video files from the hard drive that Mandi left in the safety deposit box. Shawn would have been able to find out exactly who they were."

"Hard drive? You think he found his targets from information on the hard drive? Do you know why he killed those men?"

"They took something that didn't belong to them. They took something that Shawn felt was his."

It didn't take Jaimes very long to realize what Nik meant.

"You?"

"Yes. Me. He killed them because they...because..."

"You don't have to say it. If it doesn't help you, you don't have to say it. You don't have to say another damn thing if you don't want to. Jesus Christ. This must be a lot for you. Let's go home. Let's take the day off. Let's order take-out. Let's watch silly movies or binge a TV show."

"That's exactly what I want."

"Then that's what we'll do," Jaimes said.

"What's going to happen to Cosplay?"

"Maybe they'll let Shawn have a dog in prison."

"That's not a thing."

"She's a certified therapy dog now."

"That works at the airport, not prison," Nik said. "Geez. I'm still getting used to the idea that he's not dead."

"I'll find out about Cosplay," Jaimes said. "I'll ask Ava, you know, after things have settled down."

"Gosh, I wonder how Ava and Mandi are doing."

"Probably feeling guilty about being relieved," Jaimes said. "Mandi was terrified of Shawn's dad and now he's just gone. Even if he was a bad guy, he was still Ava's dad and Shawn is her brother. She's probably not doing very well right now."

"That's how I'm feeling. Guilty. Relieved. Strange."

"Hey, if we get Cosplay back, at least we have a big yard for her to play in now."

"She'll dig up the garden," Nik said.

"She better not, that's where I buried the bodies."

"That's not funny."

"It's hilarious."

"You always take the joke too far."

"We should totally invite Lars and Caleb over for double-decker sandwiches."

"I hate you."

"No, you don't. I'm the love of your life."

"Shameless."

The End

Acknowledgements

Special thanks to Michael Rodriguez, Vas Littlecrow Wojtanowicz, Rev., and Gail Kern for your thoughtful input, to my editor Jenel Stelton-Holtmeier, and to my proofreader Olivia Penelope Lisbet Zimianitis.

About the Author

M. A. Melby grew up on a farm in Minnesota, writing poetry and stories, playing flute and bassoon, singing in church, and hanging out in the closet.

Once she left home, she jumped headfirst into the geek and queer communities. Eventually she earned master's degrees in physics and music, and taught science in college.

Recently, she sat down to write a short story and accidentally wrote a novel. Then, she wrote another one, and another, and hasn't stopped yet.

Epilogue

Life

From Shawn's point of view

He was shaking already, before he even sat down. That made me smile. I picked up the phone and stared at him through the plexiglass. I imagined him beneath me, when we were together for the first time. I felt warm.

He didn't say anything. He couldn't even talk.

"Did you really think I was dead?"

He nodded.

"Did that mind of yours finally break?"

He nodded.

"Why?"

His face got ugly, like he was going to cry. I hated that.

"You know, if you ask them, they'll put us in a room together."

He shook his head.

"Speak."

He whimpered. He cowered.

Hilarious. "What did you say? I couldn't hear you."

"No!"

"Good boy. Now, tell me why you're here."

"I need to know what happened."

"What?" This was genuinely amusing. "Is something wrong with your memory? Take too many drugs?"

"Please. Please tell me."

"Ask them. Ask them and they will put us in a room together."

"I said, no."

"You want to know what happened? You told me that you learned your lesson. You told me I was beautiful and perfect and that you loved me. You told me to wait for you, and that we'd be together forever."

"Why did I say those things?"

"Ask them to give us a room and I'll tell you everything."

"No."

"Fine. Come back to me when you're ready. Come back when you realize that you're making him miserable. Come back when he throws you away. I'll forgive you."

"I'm not coming back."

"Yes, you are. You promised me."

He always said so many things he didn't mean, but I could always read him. He was an open book. The more I called him a liar, the more he told the truth.

"Please, before I go, tell me you're okay," he pleaded with me. "I hear stories. Why are you even here? Couldn't your mother get you a place in a prison hospital or...something? Are you being hurt? Nobody deserves that."

"You can't help but love me." I bet he didn't even eat Greek yogurt anymore. "I told you so."

"Tell me you aren't being hurt."

"That doesn't matter. I'm here for a reason, Nik. My Nikola. I'm here for you. I'm here to talk to someone about a boat."

"What? A boat...the owner of the boat?"

"I keep my promises. Remember that."

I hung up the phone and walked away. Out of the corner of my eye, I could see him pounding on the plexiglass. I could hear muffled screaming. As I left the room, the guards were escorting him out.

He wanted me. He loved me.

He was such a liar.

I knew he would come back.

He had to come back.

We were meant to be together.

Stairs

From Traci's point of view

Of course, she warned me she was coming. I told her when practice was over. We were going to meet at the bottom of the stairs and go for coffee. That was the plan.

I had rehearsed so many words. I tried to prepare myself. I knew it wasn't going to be easy.

When I left the opera house, I looked around but didn't see her. Instead, I saw a huge bouquet of white flowers.

That bitch.

Despite myself, I started running down the stairs. Those famous stairs, that I climbed nearly every day, had eventually lost their appeal. I had learned, as many others did, to change into sensible shoes. One of the violinists was very keen on descending the stairs quicker than everyone else, but today, I was even faster than him.

I thought, when I got to her, I would tell her that a grand gesture was inappropriate. That she was out of line. That we agreed to something low-key. We would have coffee. We would talk. I would show her a few of Sydney's tourist spots. Then, after a couple days, we would say our goodbyes. That's what we agreed to.

I was angry.

But when I reached her, and she lowered the bouquet, she was crying like a child and the first thing she said was, "I'm sorry."

The bouquet was huge. It was amazing. It was full of white roses and lilies and baby's breath. She could barely hold it up, it was so heavy.

"I'm sorry. Nik bought it. He...um...I told him not to, but he had it delivered to me, anyway. I tried to tell him we weren't together anymore. He wouldn't accept it. I'm sorry. I tried to tell him...he's...he's making things more difficult...but he wouldn't listen."

"They're beautiful."

"Yeah, they are. It's not the flowers' fault. They smell nice, too."

I was worried that when I saw her, I would lose my resolve, that I would forget all the words I rehearsed and all the reasons we were no longer together.

I was right.

"I missed you, Mandi."

"Please stop, you're breaking my heart. It's bad enough that..." she said, looking at the flowers.

I put down my case and took the flowers out of her hands. I set them down carefully on the concrete.

The moment I opened my arms, she ran into me. I held her tightly because there was nothing in this world that would stop me from holding her when she was crying.

"I missed you. I missed you every day," I confessed. "Is it okay, Mandi, if I don't let you go? Can I do that? Can I?"

She pushed herself away and stared at me, like she was scared. "Traci, what are you saying? This was goodbye! I tried to make peace with that. I did everything I could to...be good...to respect that...to..."

"So did I."

"We're failures."

"Yes. Complete failures," I agreed. "But we tried."

"Let's get coffee."

"Yes. I think we have a lot to talk about."

"What's the coffee like down here?"

"I warned them about you, so they could make it super sweet."

Mandi wiped her tears and picked up the bouquet. She held it in front of herself and smiled at me. "Thanks. You're the best."

That's when I knew she was going to be my wife.

Banana

From Lars point of view

That boy. What will I ever do with him?

I read the text again. "Let's get banana pancakes."

What was Jaimes agonizing over this time? I wondered if it was even healthy for him to see me. We were all friends now, but the way he looked at me sometimes, I wondered if it was for the best.

"I'm free tonight. Will Nik be joining us?" I texted back.

"No."

Oh dear.

Made in the USA
Monee, IL
09 August 2023

40653170R00177